I0732789

THE HORRIBLE HUSBAND

A MURDER IN MARIN MYSTERY – BOOK 5

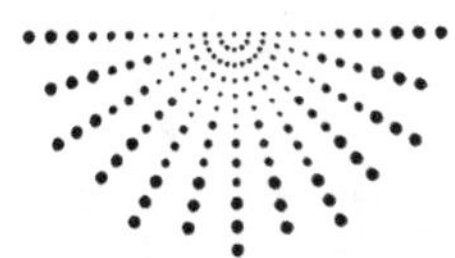

MARTIN BROWN

A BOOK BY

SIGNAL
PRESS

NOVELS IN THE MURDER IN MARIN SERIES

The Gossiping Gourmet

(Book 1)

The Wicked Wife

(Book 2)

The Phantom Photographer

(Book 3)

The Terrible Teacher

(Book 4)

The Horrible Husband

(Book 5)

The Malicious Mayor

(Book 6)

CHAPTER ONE

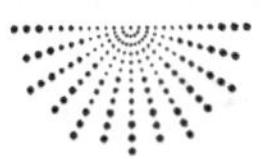

Sharon Austin, Karin Timmons, Holly Cross, and their longtime friend, Beverly Bent, agreed that The Cheesecake Factory at The Village shopping center in Corte Madera, California, was the perfect place to celebrate each of their birthdays.

On this bright, mild, Sunday afternoon in early September, Beverly was the honoree. All four of the women had grown up in Marin County, Karin and Holly in Sausalito, Sharon and Beverly in Tiburon.

Living just blocks from each other in Sausalito, Holly, Sharon, and Karin rode in one car and arrived ten minutes early.

"I love coming here," Holly announced as the three of them slid into an oversized booth, spacious for four people, but possibly snug for six. "I know we come here four times a year for birthday celebrations, but I never tire of this place."

"Agreed!" Sharon and Karin said in unison, then looked at each other and laughed.

"That 'SkinnyLicious' menu is perfect for eating something that watches your calories before you take the inevitable plunge into a slice of birthday cake," Holly explained with a laugh.

Karin and Sharon nodded in agreement.

"I know we're a little early," Holly added. "I'm hoping Beverly gets here on time. I promised Scott that I'd meet him at two-thirty at the Tam Junction Starbucks so we can go for a hike out to the beach along the Tennessee Valley Trail."

"That sounds like fun," Karin said. "What's going on with you and your millionaire math teacher?"

"What Karin really means," Sharon said, "is when is he going to pop the question? I know that's what she's been thinking because I'm wondering as well."

"Is that all you two do—speculate on my leaving the ranks of singletons?" Holly asked with a smile.

Karin and Sharon looked at each other and shrugged.

"I wouldn't say it's the only thing we do." Sharon winked. "But it's certainly high on the list."

"Scott seems like a great catch," Karin added. "And the fact that he's set for life financially doesn't hurt. You know, when Rob and I sit down to figure out how we're going to pay all our monthly bills, it's really not as much fun as you might think."

"It's not every girl who gets the chance to marry a sweet guy who also happens to be heir to a big estate," Sharon declared.

"Trust me, I know the difference between gold and gold-plated," Holly insisted. "But I don't want to be the extra baggage that Scott has to carry around for the rest of his life. I love my job, and I love working with Rob. But let's face it, making real money in the newspaper business is not now, and likely never will be, in the cards."

Karin laughed. "I don't think Rob would argue your point."

"When a guy loves you the way Scott does, he's happy because you're happy," Sharon added. "Take some advice from a couple of longtime married women. A guy, one who truly loves you, wants to be your knight in shining armor. From what I've seen of Scott, he's not looking for his financial equal. He's looking for a woman to love and adore. A woman he'd be happy to grow old with."

"And take care of you like a princess," Karin piped in.

"There's no doubt that I've been blessed to find such a sweet guy. I wish I could say the same for Beverly." In anticipation of their friend's arrival, Holly spoke just above a whisper. "I nearly broke the old wire antenna off my dilapidated Chevy yesterday morning while listening to her husband's radio show on KBUD San Francisco. I was heading over to Tiburon to meet Sylvia Stokes about a story she's been working on. Has either of you listened to the all-male blather on that station? Bill Bent, in particular, is a knuckle-dragging Neanderthal!"

Karin sighed. "Why in the world would I be listening to that nonsense?" She, too, looked around to make sure Beverly Bent wasn't within earshot. "It's so obvious the guy is a complete jerk!"

"Jerk is one word for him, I can think of plenty of others," Sharon arched an eyebrow. "I was listening to him while making breakfast for Eddie and Aaron yesterday morning. Please don't ask me why! He makes me so angry! Just a few minutes of his ranting, and I'm fully awake—and ready to hit someone! And I don't mean my husband. I'll say one thing for the guy, he makes me appreciate Eddie all the more!"

Karin puffed out her chest. Then, in a fake deep male

voice, she muttered, "This is Bill Bent on KBUD. Radio for the modern man."

"Modern man, my behind," Holly said with a laugh. "The guy looks and sounds nothing like what I think of when I hear the words, 'modern man.' I think of Eddie, Rob, or Scott. None of them would ever demean a woman the way that caveman does every weekday morning."

"Now, Holly, don't you think that's being a little unfair to poor Fred Flintstone?" Sharon asked. "As I recall, that caveman was a pretty good provider to Wilma. Whenever that quitting time whistle blew, he'd collect his pay and go straight home to his loving wife and that adorable little Pebbles."

"Maybe it's all an act," Karin countered. "A lot of these radio personalities do that, you know."

"I hope you're right, at least for Beverly's sake," Holly retorted. "If not, I have no idea how she, or anyone for that matter, could put up with Bill Bent for more than thirty minutes!"

"Have you heard him when he goes into one of his rants about 'his bride?'" Karin asked, using air quotes.

"You mean, 'Battling Bev?'" Holly asked.

"That's it!" Karin said louder than she had intended.

"I'm sure she hates that name!" Sharon shuddered. "He's lucky his 'Battling Bev' doesn't take an iron skillet and crack it over his thick skull!" She chuckled over the thought.

"You've been hanging around that detective husband of yours too long," Karin said. "Not every woman is going to want to kill their guy, regardless of how obnoxious he might be."

"That's true," Holly conceded. "But if it was me, I'd happily send him off to that great radio station in the sky!"

Karin and Sharon found Holly's wide smile uncomfortably convincing.

"Really, Holly?" Karin said. "Don't you think killing the guy for being a jerk, on or off the air, is a bit extreme?"

"Yeah, maybe," Holly replied with apparent reluctance. "But if he was my guy, I wouldn't let him get away with that nonsense!"

"Maybe Beverly just ignores him and his show," Sharon suggested. "And, maybe, it's just playacting. We rarely see him, so it's hard to say what he's really like. Off the air, he might be a nice guy. In fact, if it wasn't for these birthday lunches, none of us would see much of Bev, I suppose. I can tell you this: when the two of us were kids in Tiburon, playing the 'Who I would marry' game, Beverly never described anyone like Bill. To me, that's pretty sad."

"I can see why," Holly replied. "He sounds to me like the furthest thing from any woman's dream."

"Hopefully, there's a chance we're wrong about the guy. This may be wishful thinking on my part, but maybe it really is just a shtick he does to get high ratings," Karin suggested. "Bill just can't be as mean and arrogant as he acts on air!"

"Okay, maybe it's all an act," Holly replied. "But do you really think he can just turn it off and on—all those rants he spouts when he walks back through the front door of their home?"

"Now is not the time to figure all this out," Sharon said in a hush. "Beverly just walked in, and the hostess is showing her to our table. It's time we put on our happy faces, behave ourselves—and dare I say, mind our own business?"

"Why do you always look at me when you say, 'mind our own business?'" Holly asked.

"Just a habit, dear, nothing more. Really!" Sharon replied with a smile.

All four enjoyed SkinnyLicious lunch entrees and claimed that they were full afterward. Still, in keeping with their ritual, they ordered a super-sized slice of chocolate cake with four forks. Karin reached into her purse and brought out a sandwich-sized Ziploc bag that held four birthday candles.

"We can always depend on you for candles," Holly said.

"With two small children in the house, I'm always finding extra birthday candles in one draw or another." Karin used a disposable lighter to quickly light the wicks. Then, in low voices, Karin, Holly, and Sharon sang a quick rendition of the Happy Birthday song.

"This is nice! I love you, ladies! You're always so much fun to be with," Beverly exclaimed.

"What's Bill doing for your birthday?" Holly asked, more out of concern than curiosity.

"Working late, I suppose," Beverly replied in a soft but clearly discouraged tone. "He comes and goes at all hours. It's not easy, but that's the life of someone with a successful radio show."

"But he's on in the morning, why does he need to work late?" Holly asked.

She winced when Sharon gently kicked her under the table.

"Bill's job can involve a lot more than just his morning show," Beverly replied. "He's always doing promotional appearances. Some are arranged by the station for advertisers. Others are set up by his agent as paid appearances. He makes a third of his yearly income from work done outside his morning show!"

"I guess he's in demand. That must be difficult for you," Holly said.

Once again, Sharon kicked her—but this time, with a little more force.

"You might say that." Beverly shrugged resignedly. "But it's part of being the wife of a local celebrity."

"I don't imagine there are a lot of women's groups that ask him to speak." Holly looked across the booth at Sharon with a stare that said, *I dare you to kick me a third time.*

"That's true," Beverly conceded. "He's not in great demand with women's clubs, or mixed groups of men and women. But a men's group like Mountain Men of Marin loves having him at their annual fish fry. Motor Sports Club of Novato, too. Its members think he hung the moon."

"Really?" Holly asked. "I never heard of either of these groups."

"I'm not surprised. Not too many women in Marin have. You probably haven't heard of the Beer, Booze, and Broads Men's Group up in Fairfax either, I'm guessing," Beverly replied.

"The what?" Karin asked, astounded to learn such a club existed in politically sensitive, if not always correct, Marin County.

"Oh, they're out there, ladies!" Beverly frowned. "Thanks to Bill, I know more about misogynistic men than probably any other woman in Marin would ever care to know."

"Certainly more than the three of us know," Sharon murmured.

"Doesn't it get a little overwhelming?" Holly asked.

Having opened the conversation, she wasn't ready to let it drop.

"Overwhelming? How?" Beverly asked innocently.

Holly rolled her eyes. "You know—the whole, 'Me Tarzan, you Jane' routine. I mean, when I hear Bill on KBUD, I feel like I've gone back in time three decades or more."

"I get your point. But really, Holly, it doesn't bother me that much."

More than ready to change the subject, Karin announced, "Let's do gifts!"

"Yes. Presents!" Sharon exclaimed. She gave Holly her best wide-eyed let it drop look.

On the short drive between Corte Madera and Tam Junction, Holly wasted little time before asking Karin and Sharon, "What did you think of Beverly's answers? Frankly, I think she's covering up."

"Covering up for what?" Karin asked.

"Hard to say," Holly replied. "I don't think she's too crazy about Bill."

"Ya think?" Sharon gave a short laugh. "I can't imagine why any woman would be. It's one thing to wake up one morning and realize your husband is a misogynist. It's something else to turn on the radio every morning and listen as he announces that fact to the world. But I'm still not sure how much of his blather is real and how much is an act."

"So, you're wondering if Bent is a misogynist, or he only plays one on radio between seven and ten in the morning?" Holly asked.

"Exactly!" Sharon declared.

"For Beverly's sake, I hope it's all an act," Karin said. "It would be relatively easy to live with it, I suppose, if he was simply playing an obnoxious character."

"As opposed to being one twenty-four seven?" Holly asked in a pointed tone.

"I would like to think Bill is just playing a character," Sharon said.

"Real or fake, I don't suppose there's much we can do about any of this," Karin replied. "Other than feeling bad for Bev, it's her choice to stay or go. I honestly don't think there's anything the three of us can do about that."

"No, there isn't," Sharon responded. "Fortunately, they don't have kids. As complicated as separations and divorces can be, when kids are involved, everything gets much more complicated."

"If that jerk was my husband, they'd find him one morning floating face down in Corte Madera Creek," Holly announced.

"Lucky for Wild Bill, he isn't your husband. And doubly lucky for you, Scott is a much better catch," Sharon concluded.

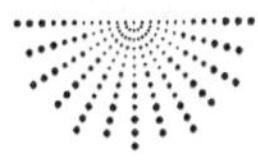

CHAPTER TWO

By the time Beverly Bent got into her aging Ford Explorer and turned the ignition key, the smile she had worn throughout her birthday gathering had vanished. She thought for a moment of turning off the engine and walking into the recently remodeled Nordstrom, located steps away from the entrance to The Cheesecake Factory.

Whether buying or browsing, shopping always lifted her spirits. But instead of turning off her car and pushing the door open, Beverly sat and thought for a brief time about the conversation she just had with her three girlfriends.

Holly had been her usual nosy and pushy self. Still, it's hard not to admire and appreciate a friend so determined to raise the self-evident truths that she was continually hoping to avoid.

Beverly laughed over the thought of Bill coming home and her sharing that he was topic number one at her birthday lunch. Undoubtedly, he'd shrug and say something cruel. "Don't your friends have anything better to do than sit around and criticize a man who works long hours to keep a roof over his wife's head? Do any of these women work, or are they stay-at-home wives like you?"

Beverly could point out that two of them were mothers raising young children. And Holly works long hours five days a week as the associate editor of a group of community newspapers. But why waste her energy? Bill was uninterested in details. He never welcomed any attempt by Beverly to enlighten him on any subject.

Bill inevitably would retort with something dismissive and mean-spirited. "Sounds to me like a bunch of busybodies! If your lady friends weren't spending so much time minding everyone else's business, they'd get more accomplished. Perhaps, turn themselves into something more than gossiping know-it-alls."

Beverly would again try to respond, but Bill would dismiss her with the same disregard he used on the air with countless callers. Few could deny that Bent was ready at a moment's notice to verbally crush those who offered views in conflict with his. Tongue-lashings were his specialty. Neither his callers, nor his wife, were safe when his temper was fully engaged.

A short time later, when Beverly pulled into the driveway of her home on Corte Madera's Summit Drive, she was displeased to see Bill's car there. Sundays were usually his day for golf, fishing, or simply hanging out with his pals at the Silver Peso Bar in nearby

Larkspur. To her disappointment, Bill had decided to spend the afternoon at home.

Often she wished that he had an evening slot on KBUD. He would be home when she woke up in the morning: not great, but at least he'd be gone from midafternoon and probably not home until late at night. Frequently, despite his early show, he'd come home after Beverly had fallen asleep holding onto a good book. She gave up asking where he had been convinced there was very little chance that he'd answer honestly.

KBUD marketed itself as Bro Radio for the Bay Area. Among a twenty-four-hour lineup of obnoxious male hosts, Bent was without question the station's superstar. He was best known for his five-minute segments at seven and eight each morning, called "Get Bent." Here he would tear into a Bay Area or nationally recognized woman for her "Feminista attitudes." Frequently he asked his listeners: "When do any of us get our 'Me Too' moment? Guys, we need to stand up to this Feminista Generation before they destroy all we hold precious!"

Beverly made it a point not to listen to Bill's show. On occasion he would ask something like, "Did you hear how I destroyed that woman caller this morning? The one who suggested that men should take on more responsibility in the home: parenting, cooking, cleaning house! You know, the usual nonsense these women spout. I let her have it. I mean, I really let her have it!" he laughed.

To all such inquiries, Beverly would respond with robotic repetitiveness: "Yes, dear, I did. You certainly set her straight."

Never did her husband quiz her on any of the specific content of these on-air confrontations. Beverly often wondered if he knew, or at least suspected, that she was not one of his daily listeners. If he suspected such a betrayal, he was reluctant to push for details. "Hubby," as Beverly often called him, was pleased when his wife made his favorite dish: roast beef, mashed potatoes, and glazed honey carrots. Next to his wife preparing a satisfying home-cooked meal, other issues in his marriage paled in comparison.

CHAPTER THREE

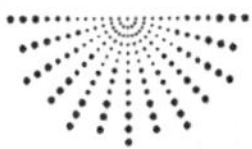

Holly was surprised when she looked down at her cell phone's display screen to see Beverly Bent was calling.

Why in the world would she be calling me on a Monday morning? Holly tapped, "Accept," then asked, "Hi Bev, everything okay?"

"Yes—and no! We've got to talk! Can you and I do lunch one day this week?"

"Sure, if we make it one o'clock or later on Friday afternoon. That's the only time of the week Rob and I can come up for air. All editions for the week are finished, and we're just planning articles and page layouts for the following week. What's up?"

"It's better if I wait to tell you in person."

From her tone, Holly could tell Beverly was sorely tempted to give details. After hesitating for just a moment, Holly declared, "Okay. Where do you want to meet?"

"Can we do Flores at Town Center?"

"Sure. Great Mexican food! I love that place."

"Good, I'll see you at Flores this Friday at one," Beverly said and clicked off before Holly had a chance to ask any more questions.

I wonder what she's up to? Holly thought.

Ten minutes later, Rob came into the office. Holly wasted no time asking about leaving for an extended lunch hour on Friday.

"I have a college friend in town for the weekend, and the only day she can see me is Friday," Holly announced. "I'll be gone between one and two-thirty. Can we make that work, Rob?"

"Sure, let's just get started a little earlier than usual—say eight on Friday."

"Done, boss man," Holly said, extending her hand to seal the deal.

"Unless we hear otherwise, we've got Eddie at five on Friday at Smitty's. But you'll be back well before that. Correct?" Rob asked with a raised eyebrow.

"Absolutely! Besides, I wouldn't miss my end-of-week martini."

"You mean two martinis," Rob said with a smile.

"I didn't know you kept count."

"I'm a journalist. Careful observation is a habit of mine."

As happens in a job as hectic as Rob's and Holly's, the workweek passed in an endless blur of deadlines. While it required both her and Rob to stay focused through each workday, every evening Holly found her mind wandering to Beverly's request that they meet on Friday.

It was a level of distraction that even seemed apparent to Scott.

The two met Thursday night for supper at Sushi Ran, one of the Bay Area's best sushi restaurants. By a stroke of good fortune, it happened to be located one block from Holly's apartment on Caledonia Street.

It was busy, as it is every night. Still, the owner, Yoshi Tome—a longtime advertiser in every edition of *The Standard*—always found a table for Holly.

Since learning the shocking truth regarding his birth mother and his newfound fortune, Scott slowly became accustomed to wealth rarely experienced by those from working-class families. In spite of his surprise inheritance, he remained in his position as the lead teacher in Marin Academy's math department.

As Holly told Rob, Eddie, Karin, and Sharon, "Scott is equal parts prep school, math teacher nerd, and shy, sweet, affectionate guy." He was a good deal taller than Holly, something she found awkward at first. In time, Holly grew accustomed to standing on her toes and pulling Scott down for a kiss.

"When he gives me a hug, I'm pressed up against his chest with the top of my head nestled below his chin, but it doesn't bother me. I'd rather be with a gentle giant than some thoughtless Neanderthal, like Beverly's blabbermouth husband."

Yoshi greeted Holly and Scott with a wide grin that never failed to make others smile. After seating them, he sent over hot sake and a plate of edamame.

While they pondered that night's menu, Scott glanced

over at Holly and chuckled. "I know that look, Holly. Something's up."

"What look?" she asked innocently.

"That faraway, something-is-on-your-mind look."

"It's nothing, really."

"Nope. Not buying that," Scott shook his head.

"Why not?"

"For starters, those wheels in your head are constantly turning! I'd probably be just another high school math teacher looking on the Internet for discount grocery coupons if it wasn't for that ever-curious mind of yours."

"I have no idea what you're talking about," Holly murmured innocently.

"Really? You've already forgotten that you were the one who unraveled the mystery of my birth mother?"

She shrugged. "Well...I..."

"Play innocent if you want, but we both know the story by heart. Now come clean. What's going on in that ever-curious mind of yours?"

"Oh no, you don't! You're just going to think I'm having trouble minding my own business."

"Undoubtedly! But helping seventeen-year-olds as they struggle through trigonometry isn't half as much fun as knowing what you've got going on."

"Geez, are you this persistent with your students?"

"Yep. If those kids want to get into a top college, or at least, their parents want them to, you have to be persistent."

"Okay, I hear you." Holly hesitated. "But all I've got at this point are my suspicions; I might be totally wrong."

"Your suspicions changed my life, so if anyone respects your intuition, it would be me."

"Thanks. It's hard for me to distinguish between my intuition and my being nosy."

"I agree the incurious aren't troubled with the occasional desire to stick their nose in where it arguably does not belong. But you're in the news business. Being a snoop comes with the territory. If all you and Rob did was reprint everything people in government and industry told you, that wouldn't be reporting news. That, as the expression goes, is 'serving as a conveyor belt for garbage.' It can make people uneasy and make you unpopular at times, but that's part of your job."

"Okay, I give! But don't tell me I should mind my own business when I finish telling you."

"If I'm about to tell you that, I'll bite my tongue. And if I don't, you have permission to do so or at least nibble on my ear." Scott said as he reached across the table and took her hand. "You know how I love that."

Holly relented and filled Scott in on Beverly's birthday lunch four days earlier.

"So, you think Beverly wants to meet you for lunch tomorrow to ask for your advice about her husband."

"Yes, or something like that. I can't imagine she just wants to chat—particularly given the fact that we see each other four times a year—whenever one of us has a birthday."

"Do you now regret bringing up the topic of her husband's radio show?"

"I couldn't help myself! Bent is so unbelievably obnoxious. Have you listened to his show?"

"Nope. I can listen to an hour of radio jabber and learn absolutely nothing. It feels like I'm putting my mind on ice. These guys rant about the same stuff repeatedly," Scott sighed. "I'm too much of a nerd. I'd rather listen to a Ted Talk podcast. I'm always looking to learn something new. In truth, guys like Bent have nothing to offer."

"My God, he's just such a bully! And yet, a lot of people— tune in to hear his show every weekday morning on KBUD!" Holly shuddered. "Even the station's call letters are obnoxious."

"From what you've shared, I think this guy Bent really gets under your skin."

"He certainly does! I don't know how Beverly keeps herself from picking up a vase and banging him over the head."

"Let's hope she doesn't do that. I know all about taking a bad bang to the noggin." Scott frowned, thinking of the attempt made on his life a year earlier. Something that would have never happened if he hadn't stumbled into an inheritance he never imagined receiving. "And Bent, probably won't be wearing a bike helmet if a skillet comes flying towards his head."

"Oh, sweetie, I'm so glad you're still around and that you got to keep all your marbles." Holly lifted Scott's hand and kissed it.

"That makes two of us," Scott said as he leaned in to give Holly a kiss.

"You look too lovey-dovey to want something to eat, but we're trying to run a business here," Kenzo, their regular waiter, exclaimed jokingly.

Scott and Holly both laughed. Quickly they put in their orders.

After dinner, they went up to Scott's place: the old home of Henrietta Hammer, Holly's fifth-grade teacher. Scott had long thought Henrietta to be his aunt. It took Holly the longest time to adjust to the idea that she was in love with the son of a teacher who made her and every other student wish they could have skipped the fifth grade.

But, as Sharon told her one afternoon when they shared a walk along Sausalito's waterfront, "Love often comes when we least expect it. Accept it as a wonderful gift and leave it at that."

CHAPTER FOUR

In spite of her conversation with Scott the previous evening, Holly was still uneasy when she entered Flores the following afternoon. She found Beverly looking at a menu while waiting near the host station.

After they were seated, Beverly wasted no time getting to why she suggested the two of them meet.

Over dishes of Huevos Poblanos and Carne Asada, Beverly, tearfully at times, shared the reality of daily life with her overbearing husband.

"Holly, you have no idea what he is like."

"If it's anything like he is on air, I can only imagine."

"It's actually worse."

"So, it's not an act, he really is as hostile to women in private as he is on the air?"

"Absolutely."

"Beverly, why did you want to share this with me? Don't get me wrong, I'm glad you have. I'm just wondering, why not Sharon? You two have been friends far longer."

"I'm embarrassed to admit this, but I have to be honest. I

like for Sharon to think that Bill's radio persona is simply an act. I don't need her feeling sorry for me. I'm not the only woman to live with a man who, to put it kindly, is difficult."

"Difficult is an understatement."

"Agreed! With his on-air work and the celebrity he has become, it's like there's no escape. My life has devolved into bro talk radio seven days a week. When I'm not sitting with him hearing his program's rebroadcast, Monday through Friday nights between eight and eleven, I'm hearing him spout his views on female inferiority."

"You poor dear. If it was me, I would have killed him a long time ago."

"Don't think the thought hasn't crossed my mind. I get nervous when I'm cleaning the carving knife while doing the dishes, and Bill walks past..."

"Is it really that bad?"

Beverly answered with a nod, followed by a muffled sob. "Holly, I knew when you talked about Bill on Sunday, you were hoping that I would hear you. Everything you asked, and I'm sure there was more you wanted to know, are questions I have thought about for a long time. After I left the three of you, I sat in my car and wondered if I should call it quits with Bill. Usually, I would have pushed my concerns aside, walked into Nordy's, and shopped my worries away. It was my birthday, and Bill got me nothing, not even a card.

"So, I thought of doing what I've done in recent years, buy myself a gift to make up for the one that I would not be getting from Bill. This past Sunday, I couldn't do that. At some point, I have to stop avoiding this issue and confront it honestly."

They both sat silently for a time. Holly wondered what she could do to help, realizing the future direction of her friend's life would depend on choices that only Beverly could make.

"Holly, thank you for making me think about all this. It's something I have to do more of, and if I don't, I might just go mad."

"Are you thinking of walking out?"

"Possibly. Or just killing the jerk and burying him in the backyard."

"Don't go down that road kiddo. No matter how tempting."

"Truth is, Holly, I get faint at the sight of blood, so my bludgeoning Bill is not too likely."

Holly was tempted to ask if Beverly had considered poison as an alternative but sensed this was no time for humor. Instead, she asked, "Is there any chance you can get Bill to go with you to see a marriage counselor?"

Beverly burst out laughing. After she caught her breath, she took Holly's hand, squeezed it, and said, "I'm not laughing at you!"

"Huh?"

"Holly, you have no idea how many times I've thought of doing just that. Asking Bill if we can meet with a counselor. Each time I back away, laugh at myself and think, that's never going to happen!"

"Are you sure of that, Bev?"

"If I suggested anything like couples counseling, I'd just be feeding Bill another laugh line for his bro talk radio listeners. Don't tell me you can't imagine him riffing on that subject for days?"

"Really?"

"Absolutely. I can hear him now." Beverly puffed out her chest, lowered her voice, and said, "So the little lady thinks we need counseling. The truth is, I don't have time for psychobabble. So, I tell her you wouldn't have the time either if you worked the hours I worked and had the responsibilities I have!"

"But didn't you say he was against your taking a job?"

"Of course, but you can't call Bill out for going two ways on a one-way street. He's the cop on the beat, the judge and the jury of everything that goes on in his world. He reminds me regularly that everything we own, house, cars, furnishings, and particularly every stitch of clothing on my back, is bought and paid for by his work."

"Wow he really is a Twentieth Century man. And I'm not talking late century, more like mid-century at best."

"Now you're getting the picture," Beverly said with a smile and another squeeze of Holly's hand. "So, what would you do if you were me?"

"Bev, you don't want to know."

"Why? You're going to suggest I pick up that iron skillet and bang him over the head?"

"Well, I, ah…"

"I'm not a violent person, Holly. There are nights I have fantasies of plunging a carving knife into Bill's back, but I'd never do that."

"Well, Bev, I wouldn't either, but you have to admit, Bill has a talent for bringing out the worst in people."

"I can't argue with you about that."

"Good God!" Holly announced. "It's already past two, I better hustle back to the office before Karin's husband has a meltdown of his own."

"Is Rob a good guy to work for?" Beverly asked wistfully.

"He is! He can be a jerk at times, but…"

"I suppose most men can be now and then. My husband, unfortunately, a good deal more than others."

"I won't argue with that."

"Holly, can we talk again?"

"Absolutely," Holly said, but the knot in her stomach told her that she might be getting herself in deeper than she should.

T raffic was light heading southbound into Sausalito. Holly felt good about the time she spent with Beverly but bad that she could not be of more help. There are all sorts of men in this world, Holly reasoned. Rob, Eddie, and Scott were proof of that. Perhaps when they met for their traditional end-of-week cocktails, she could ask them both about Beverly's predicament. It was rare for her to solicit Rob and Eddie's advice on relationships. Still, when it came to Bill Bent, they might be able to give her some insight into the mind of a man she could not imagine waking up next to every morning.

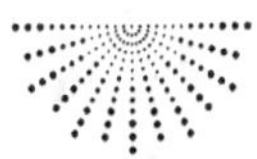

CHAPTER FIVE

Rob was less than thrilled that Holly was more than twenty minutes late getting back to the office. When she announced, "I've got something I need to talk to you and Eddie about when we sit down at Smitty's," she caught his interest.

"Want to give me a clue?"

"Nah, we're too busy, and I was too late getting back. Let's just say I need a couple of men-of-the-world types."

"Holly, I never knew you thought of us like that."

"I don't really, but among the few men I'm close to, you're probably my best bet."

"Thanks, I guess," Rob said with a half-smile as he jumped back into the balance of his workday.

The tradition of Holly, Rob, and Eddie having cocktails at Smitty's on Friday afternoons at five dated back several years.

In a town where people don't just recognize each other, but likely know your marital status, whether you're a parent or not, and how you earn your living, Smitty's offered a needed degree of privacy. Whether it was Eddie discussing a case, or Rob and Holly sharing a story they were working on, the quiet they found here made the lackluster surroundings an acceptable trade-off.

In spite of its well-worn appearance, the place was still vibrant every night from eight until closing. This was particularly true on Friday and Saturday nights when the music pulsing from the ancient sound system could be heard blocks away. But between five and seven any afternoon of the week, the three of them could discuss nearly any topic without drawing unwelcome attention.

Smitty's had one other key advantage. In celebrating a birthday, or only a good week at work, all three lived two to four blocks from Smitty's front door. Walking home was always an available alternative.

"There are nicer bars in Sausalito," Rob reminded Holly, "but none so quiet, private, and convenient."

"And none with the happy hour prices they have," Holly added with a wink and a smile.

Eddie walked in just moments after Holly and Rob sat down in ancient captain's chairs that surrounded an equally aged, clear laminate, dark wood table.

"What's up, kids?" Eddie chirped.

"You sound awfully chipper," Rob responded.

"Nothing special. It's just great to have the weekend ahead

of us. By Friday, like the two of you, I'm more than ready for a break."

"Tough week?" Holly asked.

"Not really. It's been pretty quiet of late. There was a stick-up at a twenty-four-hour convenience store in Novato earlier in the week. We nabbed a suspect the following day. He's on the store's security cam, so this one was a no-brainer. Nothing made it into the county newspaper, or onto radio or television, so the boss is happy. And when the boss is happy, I'm happy."

Most weeks, Eddie enjoyed his position as the county's lead investigator. But his boss, Sheriff Jack Canning, recently elected to a record-setting fifth term, grew nervous whenever one or more crimes were topic number one, either with local residents, elected officials or, worst of all, the media.

"What about you two? How goes the world of community newspapers?"

"It was a pretty slow week," Rob said as Gail, their usual waitress, placed tall Guinness drafts in front of him and Eddie. Then she gave Holly her usual dry Vodka martini with three large olives speared on a long cocktail toothpick.

"Holly had lunch today with the wife of a local celebrity," Rob said. "She came back twenty minutes late, but being the great guy that I am, I made only a small stink about it."

"You're a prince among men," Eddie said as he raised his glass and tipped it in a toast to Rob. "Don't you agree, Holly?"

"Oh, he's special alright," Holly said as she took a long and much-needed sip from her favorite cocktail. "Speaking of a prince among men, or in this instance, I should say a dark prince, I have something I need to pick both your brains about."

"Pick away, Holly," Eddie said with a smile.

"The brain trust is open for business," Rob added as all three pulled their chairs into a tighter circle.

"Well, I'm happy to hear that, because I really need some advice."

Holly proceeded to tell them first about the birthday lunch for Beverly on Sunday, followed by the lunch she had with her hours earlier.

"And why did she call you and not Karin or Sharon?" Eddie asked. "Not that I doubt the wisdom of her choice."

"Well...I kind of got the conversation rolling last Sunday by asking if Bill at home was at all like the guy weekday mornings on KBUD."

"And..." Rob said, prompting her to continue.

"She said she appreciated my honesty. You know not everyone does."

"We know," Rob and Eddie said in unison.

"So, what did she want to discuss?" Eddie asked.

"She wants out of her marriage. If she could, I think she'd pack up and get out tomorrow. Actually, Beverly would have done that by now if she had someplace to go."

"You don't think he's abusing her physically?" Eddie asked.

"I honestly don't know. I suppose that's a possibility. But at a minimum, he's driving her nuts. I guess you could call that emotional abuse."

"Well, I've listened to the guy a few times in the morning driving up to headquarters," Eddie said. "More out of curiosity than anything else. For my two cents, he comes across as a loudmouth jerk. I asked Sharon one night what she thought of Beverly being married to a guy whose claim to fame is putting women down."

"What did she say?" Holly asked.

"Sharon said that Beverly insisted it was an act, and at home, he's nothing like the guy we hear on KBUD."

"I've also heard him a few times," Rob added. "Like Eddie, I'm not into talk radio, give me classic rock if I have to drive somewhere. Springsteen, The Doors, Billy Joel and so many others. They're all better than wasting my time listening to Bent."

"I'll second that," Eddie said quickly. "So is Beverly really thinking of leaving him?"

"I think she thinks about it a lot."

"But?" Eddie asked.

"I think she's trying to work up the nerve. Kind of like the kitchen sink's garbage disposal. You know it's switched off, but you're still uncomfortable about putting your hand down there."

"That's a helluvan analogy," Rob said.

"Sounds to me like she's scared of the guy," Eddie said with a scowl.

"I think Eddie's spot-on. Beverly feels intimidated and probably nervous about how he might go after her on his show if she files for divorce. Who would want to be on the receiving end of that?" Rob asked.

"Exactly!" Holly responded. "It's pretty sad, but I'm guessing she feels trapped. And she knows that for the ten years of their marriage, during which she has played house frau, she's let her career slip away."

"What did she do before she married Bill?" Eddie asked.

"She was an account manager with a technology company in San Francisco."

"Maybe she can go back there," Rob offered.

"Unlikely. She kind of did the, 'take this job and shove it' routine with her boss," Holly explained.

"Ouch!" Eddie said with a wince. "Probably wouldn't matter anyway. Ten years out of a job in tech is a lifetime. Not to mention in today's job market, mid to late thirties is the new fifty plus."

"Really?" Rob asked.

"Trust me, pal, the three of us are lucky we've got steady jobs."

"Beverly's clearly uncertain about going back into the job market. Particularly with a resume that shows how many years she's been out of the workplace. I'd like to encourage her to break free of Bent, but if she does and falls flat on her face, I'm not sure I want to be there to help pick up the pieces."

"Maybe you should stay out of it," Rob suggested, waving Gail over and suggesting a second round for himself, Eddie, and Holly. "This round is on me. I was kind of grumpy with Holly this afternoon when she got back late to the office. Now I'm feeling regretful about that. You were trying to help a friend in need."

"Wow, Rob," Holly said with a mischievous grin. "I should tell you about unhappy women more often. I think it brings out your nurturing side."

"Well, I sure hope that my little Alice never marries a jerk like Wild Bill. And Karin and I are going to do our best to see that Micah respects women and never acts like a bully."

"Agreed. Sharon and I are going raise Aaron to treat everyone respectfully. That said, I would enjoy giving Bent a punch in the nose. That's off the record, of course."

"He's definitely the kind of guy that gives our gender a bad name," Rob added.

"Neither of you knows the half of it," Holly offered as Gail brought them a second round. "Bent's show is repeated at night on weekdays between eight and eleven. Something he sits and listens to with her most nights."

"Yikes! That's got to be torture for her. I know it would be for me," Eddie said, as Rob grimaced.

"You are two of the better specimens of your gender. Bent must have a lot of listeners who like him enough for KBUD to rerun the entire show Monday through Friday nights."

"We'll run out of fresh drinking water," Eddie said, shaking his head, "before we run out of people who say and do dumb things. Spend a week doing my job, and you'll see what I mean."

"I don't doubt it, pal. So, Holly, what have you learned from Beverly about Bent's on-air nonsense?"

"It's pretty ridiculous stuff. He riffs about how wives and girlfriends will complain about their husbands and boyfriends but never make an honest effort to understand them. The 'walk a mile in my moccasins' routine. The rest is stuff like if women, wives specifically, worked a little more and complained a little less, fewer marriages and relationships would fail."

"If I went home and started spouting that stuff, Sharon would probably come after me with one of those old iron skillets she inherited from her grandmother."

"Not my Karin," Rob said confidently. "She's not the bang him over the head type. She's more of the here's a pillow and a blanket go sleep on the old couch type."

"Trust me guys, Bill goes from bad to worse. You should listen to his show for a couple of nights."

"Not me, I'm just not into all that chatter," Rob said. "To me, it sounds like massive amounts of sound and fury, all signifying nothing."

"That's quite a statement coming from a guy who buys

ink by the barrel," Eddie said, lightly punching Rob on the arm. "You know, maybe what Beverly needs to do is fight fire with fire."

"How is she going to do that, Eddie?" Holly asked.

"A few days ago, Sharon mentioned to me that she came across a new Bay Area radio station. We didn't talk about it much, but it's as much for women as KBUD is for guys."

"Do you remember its call letters?" Holly asked.

"Let me think," Eddie replied, looking up at the paint peeling from the ceiling of the old barroom.

"You didn't write it down in that little pad you carry around with you all day?"

"No, I didn't, Holly. That's for crime investigations only."

"Well, excuse me, detective."

"Wait a minute, I do remember. KLIB! Kind of catchy, don't you think? They call it 'Talk Radio for the Liberated Woman.'"

"Really?" Rob said with a half-smile.

"Yeah, man, really. Sharon told me it was a hoot. They were having this discussion about ten things men always get wrong in relationships."

"Holly, are you thinking what I'm thinking?" Rob asked, putting his hand on Holly's shoulder and giving it a squeeze.

"I think I am, Mr. Timmons."

"What are you two talking about?"

"Eddie," Rob said, "what would you say if Holly approached Beverly about going after a job at KLIB?"

"I'd say it sounds like you two are stirring up trouble again."

"Eddie, don't you think Beverly would be welcome to work in any capacity at KLIB when they know she's Mrs. Bill Bent?" Holly asked, clearly excited.

"I suppose she would. But that might be closer to the fire than Beverly is comfortable getting."

"Beverly is looking for, among other things, a financial lifeline, and KLIB might be happy to give it to her. What are the lyrics to that great Garth Brooks song?" Holly asked while starting to hum a few bars. "Oh yeah, I remember: 'Life is not tried it is merely survived if you're standing outside the fire.'"

"Sounds like risky business to me," Eddie said with a doubtful expression. "I hope she doesn't get too badly burned."

"Nothing ventured, nothing gained," Holly said, already excited by the idea. "Beverly would have an easier time walking away from her marriage if she felt more secure about having a successful life after Bill Bent."

"You're right about that," Eddie nodded.

"Holly should ask her to consider going for something at KLIB," Rob suggested. "Remember our favorite expression, 'The answer to every question never asked is....'"

"NO!" The three friends said together. They finished their drinks and went off to their separate lives, hoping Beverly could summon the courage to begin building a life of her own.

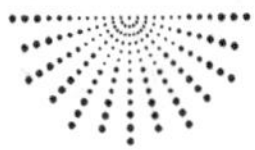

CHAPTER SIX

Holly waited until mid-morning on Saturday before calling Beverly.

"I've got an idea you might like."

"What's that?" Beverly asked, surprised to hear from Holly less than twenty-four hours after their Friday lunch.

"It's too good to share over the phone. Can you meet me? We can do a walk and talk."

"Bill just left for a promotion KBUD is doing for a GMC truck dealer up in Petaluma. Big advertiser. He won't be back until four or later. So sure, I want to hear what you're thinking, and I could also use a good walk."

"Great. Meet me at Dolliver Park in Larkspur at noon. We can walk down Madrone to the Dawn Falls Trail and then follow it up King Mountain. I love that hike, and I haven't done it in a long time."

"That's a lot more ambitious than my usual walk, but I'd like to give it a try. Staying here at the house just makes me think about life with Bill, and your idea would be a lot more fun than that."

"Good. Meet you at the park!"

Holly was in high spirits on the quick drive from her apartment through Sausalito and up 101 to the Corte Madera exit. Traffic on Tamalpais Avenue and Magnolia Drive, the main roads connecting Larkspur and Corte Madera, was very light. Modern-day Corte Madera, Spanish for cut wood, began in 1834 as a land grant by a Mexican governor to rancher John Reed. The town which, like its neighbor Larkspur, was home to massive redwood groves, contributed much of the lumber that built homes throughout the region, beginning with the gold rush of 1849. Massive piles of timber were transported on flatboats along Corte Madera Creek and out across the bay to the booming city of San Francisco.

Dolliver Park, just across Corte Madera's town line into Larkspur, is bordered by Magnolia and Madrone Avenues, which still have rows of massive redwoods. On several streets, in both towns, passing vehicles have to maneuver around several of these giant trees.

The walk from the park to the Dawn Falls Trailhead is one mile. Beverly, who lived within walking distance of the park, was waiting for Holly on one of the park's benches.

Holly walked up while Beverly was watching four children playing on a wood climbing structure that sat in the center of the small park.

"Those kids have endless amounts of energy," Holly said, sitting down next to Beverly.

"I was so lost in thought watching the children play, I didn't hear you walking up."

"You and Bill ever talk about starting a family?"

"The first year we were married, we talked about it a lot. Actually, it would be more truthful to say I talked, and depending on his mood, Bill listened or simply tuned me out."

"Were you disappointed?"

"I was, but more at first than I am now."

"Why is that?"

"The longer we've been together, the more I've thought it wouldn't be fair to bring one or more children into an unhappy home. Bill's home when he was a kid was a pretty unhappy place, and as you know, he didn't turn out so great."

"Bill have any siblings?"

"Two. An older brother and a younger brother."

"I'll bet his mother had her hands full with three boys."

"I can only imagine. Bill's mother died five years ago. Bad heart, at least that's what my father-in-law gave as the reason. She was a quiet, sweet woman. But she was skittish as a cat whenever Bill's father would raise his voice. Something that happened often. At least during the handful of times I was with them."

"You know they say when it comes to boys, a lot of their behavior towards women is shaped by the way their dads treated their moms."

"That certainly seems to be the case with Bill and his brothers. Neither of them has their own radio show, but that doesn't stop them from complaining endlessly about the women in their lives."

"Sounds like one hell of a family."

"Trust me, Holly, you don't know the half of it."

"I don't doubt it. Should we get going?"

"Sure," Beverly said, standing up and doing her best to sound upbeat.

They walked at a steady pace and before long left paved roads and the occasional vehicle behind. They entered the heavily wooded Dawn Falls Trail, which follows Corte Madera Creek for a short time before climbing up one side of King Mountain.

"Ever see a rattlesnake along here?" Beverly asked.

"A couple of times."

"They don't make you nervous?"

"Nope. Rattlesnakes don't have any interest in attacking people. Keep your eyes open, don't step on one, and you'll be fine. That's why the coiled rattlesnake flag became a symbol of the American Revolution. It was the colonists' way of telling the British to stay on their side of the Atlantic, and we would get along just fine. Step on us, however, and we'll strike back."

"I never knew that."

"That's one thing about putting out a newspaper, you collect a thousand-odd facts for countless reasons. The history of the Don't Tread on Me Flag was something a reader asked about just before Independence Day. So, we did a little feature on it. Benjamin Franklin helped popularize the idea of using a rattlesnake. Britain had a custom of sending their criminals to the colonies. Franklin suggested we send them rattlesnakes in return. Speaking of the business of news, talk radio to be precise, I have an idea I want to discuss with you."

Having hiked above the tree line, Holly sat down on an outcropping of rocks that had a view looking north toward the Mt. Tamalpais Watershed and a seemingly endless stretch of green hills. Some were spotted with several houses, but most were preserved as open space. The midday sky was an endless blue, and the air was fresh and dry.

"Great time of year," Holly said, sounding as though she hadn't a care in the world.

"Holly, if you wanted to get me out of my funk, I think you've done it. I know it sounds selfish and silly, but I've been a seriously unhappy camper for a long time. If you've got an idea of something that might help change that, I'm all ears."

"Okay. This is out of left field, but it might work. I want you to think about it before you tell me I'm nuts."

"Telling people that they're nuts, and jumping down their throats, is my husband's idea of conversation, not mine. I know if I want to create a better life for myself, I need to be open to new possibilities. So, lay it on me, sister. What's your big idea?"

Holly pitched Beverly the idea of her meeting with the station manager of KLIB, "Talk Radio for the Liberated Woman," as they identified themselves in all their promotional advertising.

Beverly's first reaction was shock, followed by a growing sense of curiosity.

"Holly, don't you think KLIB, or any employer, will have a problem with someone in their mid-thirties who has been out of the workforce for ten years?"

"Normally, and it saddens me to say this, I think that's true. In today's workplace, you'd have a tough time landing the kind of job that would support you living apart from Bill, but I think you've got something they want."

"You're thinking of the possibility to embarrass Bill. Correct?"

"Bev, you need to give this some serious thought. KBUD

started its 'Bro Talk' format the year before hiring Bill. I did a little digging online last night and learned that Bill was brought in because their ratings were underperforming."

"You're right. I remember him talking to me about that."

"The station needed to shake things up. So, they went to a young DJ at a San Francisco rock station which was getting a real bump in their ratings because Bill was talking about 'the establishment's pro-women's lib dogma.'"

"That's also right."

"So suddenly this new guy at a station that had been struggling in the ratings started getting a lot of attention. When his contract was up, KBUD came along and offered to double his salary, and they gave him radio's most coveted slot, Monday through Friday's morning drive, seven to ten. It was a gamble, arguably a big one. Still, it paid off beyond what his new employer, and probably Bill himself, could have imagined."

"That's showbiz," Beverly said, shaking her head.

"Bev, you could be that chance for KLIB to do the same. Break out of the basement and become a top-ten rated station in one of the country's best radio markets."

"But Holly, the last time I was behind a microphone in a broadcast studio was the late shift at my college's radio station. Bill is an experienced on-air talent, who now has a track record that runs ten-plus years."

"I'm not suggesting that you go in there pitching the idea that you could be their top on-air personality. Just go in applying for a staff position. In fact, KLIB has a couple of current openings, I checked this morning and found them posted online. My guess is that they're going to like the idea of having Bill Bent's wife, the Bay Area's most infamous misogynist, as part of their team."

"But my real value to them would be as Bill's on-air competition."

"You know that, and I know that. But first, get your foot in the door and become friends with everyone there. How long do you think it will be before Bill starts jabbering about his 'ditzy wife' working for KLIB? One thing I've learned from Rob, the best way for people at the bottom of the ratings to get noticed is to have the people at the top of the ratings complain about them. I give it two to three months before KLIB's management starts talking to you about doing some on-air work, maybe less time than that. Trust me, they'll start small. Probably suggesting you do a few promotional spots for upcoming events. Walk for a cure or something like that. If all goes well, they'll soon hand you a bigger opportunity. They're not going to start by tossing you into the deep end of the pool, but as your confidence grows, along with their belief in you, they're going to be itching to get you more airtime."

"That makes sense," Beverly said as Holly could see her fear melting away and being replaced by a growing sense of confidence.

"Remember," Holly added quickly, "let it be management's idea. The more on-air time they give you, the more Bill will complain about how much he dislikes KLIB. Every time he opens that big yap of his, it will give KLIB a boost in the ratings. Once that happens, you'll be in the driver's seat."

"Sounds pretty far out there," Beverly said with a nervous laugh that hid her trepidation. "But I think you're right about how this could play out."

"Bev, if I'm right, it could all happen without much pushing on your part. You don't need to be perfect on your first attempt. Just be your bright, engaging self, and the pieces could fall into place. You certainly have a good voice for radio. I think you already know that."

"Lots of folks back in college told me that they liked listening to my show."

"Bev, it's like bowling a strike: drop it down the center of the lane and let the ball do the work."

"And if that ball goes into the gutter?"

"Throw another ball. As long as Bill's yakking about how awful KLIB is and their ratings are going up, the situation can only get better for you. Trust me, Bev, don't overthink this. Things will turn out fine if you let events unfold naturally."

"Maybe you're right, Holly. I have nothing to lose and possibly a great deal to gain. So, riddle me this, wise one: When do I get to the part where I can tell Bill I want out of what he thinks is a happy marriage?"

"You've hung in there for ten years, right?"

"Don't remind me," she responded with a laugh.

"I can't tell you what you need to decide about the future of your marriage. I can only tell you what I would do."

"...And that is?"

"Well, you have no financial independence right now. California is a no-fault fifty/fifty divorce state. Still, while that sounds simple, I've heard of men with deep pockets dragging divorce proceedings out for two or more years to work out a more advantageous settlement. I'd give it time. Let this KLIB thing develop naturally. I'm pretty sure Bill will start climbing the walls pretty quickly. Bullies don't like being on the losing end of any argument. Meanwhile, save your money. When you feel secure enough to commit to your own place, you two can separate and let the lawyers work out the final settlement."

"That makes sense, too."

"With money, or without, divorce and all that goes with it is not going to be a fun journey, but what's that great Chinese proverb?"

"The longest journey begins with the first step."

"Exactly! Getting yourself out from under Bill's thumb and into the workplace will do a lot for your self-esteem, and it's critical in taking that first step."

CHAPTER SEVEN

Beverly needed a day to catch her breath and consider all Holly had suggested. She knew that acting boldly had never been her strong suit, but if she wanted to start a life free of Bill's incessant bullying, there might never be a better time than now.

To take that all-important first step, Beverly arranged an interview with the general manager of KLIB, who, to her surprise, was looking for a general staff assistant.

Tom Joseph agreed to have her come in on Wednesday at eleven for an interview. After getting off the phone with Beverly, he asked one of his on-air personalities, Betsy Baker, if she had a minute for a question.

"Sure, Tom. What's up?"

"You know Bill Bent, that morning drive time Neanderthal at KBUD?"

"Absolutely! What about him?"

"Isn't he always joking about his wife, do you remember her name?"

"Beverly. Why?"

"Nothing, probably just a coincidence. I don't want to keep you. Go get ready for your show."

Back in his office, Tom tapped his iPad and brought up information on Bill Bent. In seconds he located Bill and Beverly Bent of Corte Madera. He recalled Beverly saying, "I'm coming from Corte Madera. That time of day, it should take me no more than twenty minutes." Either he was about to interview Bill Bent's wife for a position at KLIB, or this was one hell of a coincidence.

everly arrived five minutes early for her interview at KLIB. There were enough photos of Beverly online that when Tom Joseph saw her, he felt confident that this was indeed Bill Bent's wife.

The interview went much the way countless other interviews had gone for Tom since taking over the station's operations three years ago.

A review of job responsibilities, a long glance at Beverly's surprisingly short resume, followed by an exchange of pleasantries. Finally, Tom arrived at the question he had been waiting to ask since he reached out to shake her hand.

"I just have to ask. Is your husband Bill Bent, the morning guy on KBUD?"

"Why, yes, he is. I hope that won't be a problem," Beverly said with an innocent smile and a slight blush.

"No, no problem at all. I'm just a little surprised."

"How so?"

"Have you considered that KLIB's programming is the ideological opposite of KBUD's? I mean, your husband is all about what he calls 'natural male dominance.' Our programming celebrates the value women bring to every aspect of our society. We want to see women overcome centuries of subservience in male-dominated societies. Your husband is an outspoken representative for continuing the unequal roles and opportunities women have traditionally confronted."

Beverly paused for a beat and thought carefully about her response. "I've been a regular KLIB listener for quite some time, and I think your message has great value. It's vital for women to hear and I'd be proud to be part of your team."

"That's fantastic," Tom said with a smile and perhaps, he thought, a little too much enthusiasm. He lifted Beverly's one-page resume off his desk and stared thoughtfully at what it said. In truth, he was buying a few precious moments before moving forward. Quickly he considered the possibilities. The job for which Beverly was applying was loosely described as a general assistant to the station manager, with specific clerical tasks such as reviewing programming logbooks, broadcast and advertiser compliance regulations, and such.

The upside was obvious. But so was the downside. She could screw up, and Bill Bent might have some fun on the air, suggesting his wife couldn't cut it at KLIB.

On the upside, her joining the staff could provide an unexpected lift to his station's ratings, which had been struggling since the inception of the station's new, female-centric format.

Bent, who Joseph told others, "was an obnoxious jerk with a huge megaphone," might find his wife's new job at KLIB to be highly embarrassing. Hopefully, he'll make a stink about that while on the air. After overcoming the hesitation he felt every time he needed to make a decision that could lead to a very good or very bad outcome, Tom decided to roll the dice on Beverly. Two more quarters with anemic ratings and the station might be up for its third format change in less than five years. Or worse, put up for sale by the station's owners, The Louis Broadcast Group, LBG. Tom Joseph thrust his hand forward and said, "Welcome aboard, Mrs. Bent."

"Wonderful!"

"When can you start?"

"I'm ready to start now, so you tell me."

"No time like the present. Tomorrow morning at nine?"

"Absolutely," Beverly said enthusiastically.

"Let me show you your desk, although your job will keep you moving through the day, so you won't spend much time there."

"I won't let you down, Mr. Joseph. I'm very grateful for the opportunity."

"Call me Tom. I'm going to need you to fill out some paperwork. All standard new team member stuff, and I'll send you home with a copy of our employee rules and regulations package. You'll have to review every page, initial each and sign on the last page. Our human resource department gets pickier about these things with each passing year. The Louis Group has its headquarters in Philadelphia. Totally, the company owns and operates nearly two dozen radio and television stations. We're a relatively small operation here in the Bay Area, but not in all markets. And like all corporately owned stations, we have to follow management's playbook."

"Well, I'm excited to be a part of the team."

"We're happy and excited to have you."

❧

Beverly's first call after leaving KLIB was to her new mentor, Holly.

"Oh my God! You were spot on. When I met the station manager, I knew he must have done an online search about me because the first thing he asked was whether I'm the wife of Bill Bent."

Beverly was so excited she spoke for nearly five minutes without pause, and when she did stop to take a breath, Holly said, "I couldn't be happier for you. When's your first day?"

"I start tomorrow morning at nine, if you can believe that!"

"Wow, that's great! When are you going to tell Bill?"

"Well, I hadn't given that any thought. To be completely honest, I never imagined I'd be offered a job."

"Don't sell yourself short, Bev. I'm up to my neck in work. Call me tomorrow night at home and let me know how your first day went. Okay?"

"I will. And thank you, Holly. You've lifted my spirits greatly. I think my life is going to get a lot better from this point on."

"You deserve a happy life."

When their workday ended, Holly turned to Rob and said, "I've got a little news for you about Beverly Bent."

"What's that?"

"She applied for a position with KLIB, and they hired her on the spot."

"That was fast. You're thinking her new employer wants to get some sparks flying between the Bents, correct?"

"We'll see. I think a hothead like Bill will almost certainly take the bait. I can almost hear their promos for 'The Battling Bents' playing now."

"That's certainly possible. Management might tell their loudmouth morning guy to knock it off. On the other hand, with as much male energy as they likely have, getting into a barking match with KLIB might be irresistible."

"That's my guess. Bill Bent, and his fellow bulls at KBUD, are likely to see this as a red cape being waved in front of them. My guess is they'll charge now and think later."

"You do like getting yourself into the middle of things, Holly. Not long ago, it was Scott and the secrets of his wayward birthmother, now your new rescue mission is Beverly Bent. I'm not sure anymore if you're a saint or a sinner."

"Maybe I'm a little bit of both, boss man," Holly said with a big smile. "I'm always happy to be of use for a good cause."

Certain spouses reliably show up after work at or near the same time. That was never the case with Bill. This day, as Beverly fretted as to how, when, or even if she would share the details of her new job, Bill left no word whether he would be home at two, four, six, eight, ten, or later. It was more irksome than usual for Bev as she considered and reconsidered her approach to breaking two shocking bits of news. First, that she had accepted a full-time job; second, she was now employed by KLIB.

It was more than enough to send Beverly to the door of

the refrigerator to pull out a chilled bottle of chardonnay. Having had a single glass poured from the same bottle from the previous night's dinner, she began to work her way through the rest. One glass calmed her nerves, the second glass gave her liquid courage, the third put her to sleep in an oversized brown leather recliner, which was positioned in front of a 70-inch flat-screen TV mounted to the wall.

When Bill had brought the television home, Beverly made a few feeble objections regarding its outlandish size. An argument Bill swiped aside, telling her, "Get over it. I'm a man, size matters!"

To Bill, this recliner, with a cup holder designed to keep his beer cold built into one arm and a space on the opposite arm for chips, peanuts, and his remote control, was the best part of coming home. Beverly suspected she was a distant third in importance to her husband's recliner and television. Bill's addiction to Giants' baseball, Warriors' basketball, Niners' football, and Sharks' hockey on the big screen turned their once-peaceful living room into a nightly, and all week-end, sports bar.

Sundays, particularly in football season, was a relentless assault on any desire Beverly had for a peaceful day. Viewing started early with national games broadcast from the east coast and concluded by nine or ten that night with late games on the west coast. In a home that lacked a downstairs family room, Bill converted the living room into what Beverly saw as a cross between a sports betting parlor and a Man Cave. When Beverly worked up the courage to express her displeasure, Bill batted her wishes aside. "This is my reward for busting my butt all week working, while you get to sit around and play the grand queen doing your cross-word puzzles, or whatever else it is you do."

On rare occasions, Beverly attempted a different tact by stressing all the things they could do together on a Saturday or Sunday.

Without missing a beat, Bill asked, "Such as?" His tone dared her to go further. When sufficiently frustrated, however, Beverly would summon the courage and press on: "There's a new show at the DeYoung Museum that's supposed to be wonderful."

"Museums are not my thing, Bev. I thought you knew that before we got married."

"Piano Power is going on this weekend at the San Francisco Botanical Garden. I hear it's wonderful with different pianists playing in various places throughout the grounds."

"You've got to be kidding. I go into the city to work Monday through Friday. I'm not going over the bridge to see a bunch of artsy types eating cheese, sipping wine, and applauding politely. Go with a friend. I'll be watching my games."

Beverly was accustomed to rejection. Bill's dismissive tone, however, gnawed at her. It was at times like these Beverly experienced the fleeting thought of plunging a knife into Bill's back. Perhaps someday while he sat hunched over the kitchen table devouring a deli sandwich while a mélange of various toppings and dressings splattered onto his plate. Better still, dropping a hammer on his head while she was several steps up on a ladder fixing one of the curtain rods as he strolled past wearing nothing more than a t-shirt and boxer shorts, holding his ever-present can of beer.

These thoughts came and went quickly. Perhaps the hammer was the best approach. Balanced on a ladder and having a hammer "accidentally" tumble from her hand just as he walked past seemed a plausible scenario. On the other hand, a knife lodged between her husband's shoulder blades was a tougher sell even if she maintained an air of innocent detachment. Bill backing into a knife was likely a laughable concept, and his running into her as she carelessly carried a pair of scissors was only a bit more credible.

Fantasies vanished quickly as reality took hold of her. In addition to a series of implausible accidents, there was the problematic reality that Beverly grew faint at the sight of blood.

If she ever summoned the courage to strike Bill Bent with the full force of ten-plus years of pent-up anger, there was still the stark, inhospitable environment of prison likely awaiting her. Beverly wondered if the relatively brief elation of striking back at her tormentor was worth the loss of her future.

In the deep shadows of late afternoon, Beverly awakened to find herself curled up in her husband's oversized recliner. Feeling the dry mouth and aching head of one too many glasses of chardonnay, Beverly rose and walked in a half-sleep state to her bedroom. She slipped off her dress and most of the rest of her clothing. Clad only in a pair of white cotton panties and a soft cotton nightshirt, she curled up on her side of their California King bed. With Bill's and Beverly's lean frames, it was a needlessly oversized bed, but as Bill suggested, "One night, perhaps, we can have a play date with one of your girlfriends." Like so many of Bill's lewd comments, Beverly was at a loss whether she should object, ignore his suggestion, or throw something at him.

As she usually did in reacting to an offensive comment,

Beverly acted as if she never heard what he said. Simply put, she was not listening, or so she wanted Bill to believe. She did not want to engage in a conversation about the merits, or lack thereof, of any of his oft-expressed fantasies.

On the station's repeat broadcast one night, Beverly listened while her husband told his sidekick, Barney Benson, "I asked Beverly about a three-way."

"Yikes! How did that go, Wild Bill?"

"Not good, Barney. But I figured it was worth a try."

"Nothing ventured, nothing gained, right pal?"

"Exactly, Barney."

Routines like this could go on for the better part of his show, particularly if Bill opened up the phone lines to his listeners.

After the rebroadcast ended, Beverly turned to Bill and said, "I wish you could avoid talking about our private lives."

"You mean the ménage comment I made to Barney?"

"Yes."

"That was pure comedy. Trust me, the listeners loved it. After the show, Barney told me we should do it again in a couple of weeks, and keep it as a running joke."

Beverly fumed silently, announced she had a headache and went off to bed.

Bill opened his third beer for the night and turned on ESPN's wrap-up of the day's games.

Beverly woke up when Bill slipped into bed beside her. She clicked her phone on the bed stand. It said one-thirty.

"Where have you been?" she asked while feeling a desperate need for some water.

"Out with the guys at one of my favorite dive bars in the city," he said contently. "You smell like you had a drink or two yourself."

"I had one wine too many."

"Want to make love?"

"Would you get me a glass of water? I'm so parched."

"Wine can leave you feeling like that. I'll be happy to get you some water if you agree to a little lovemaking. I'm feeling a little lonely tonight."

"Never mind, I'll get it myself."

By the time she returned to bed, Bill was already asleep. Beverly put her head down on one of the soft, oversized pillows. She put another pillow over her head, hoping to escape from the sound of Bill's snoring.

The next time Beverly was aware of her surroundings, it was eight in the morning. Bill was long gone by then, having to be at the station no later than six every weekday morning. How he managed to do his show on so little sleep never failed to amaze her.

Beverly sat up in bed, wondering, as she did most mornings, how she would fill her day when suddenly it hit her: I have to be at KLIB at nine! OH MY GOD!

Fortunately, the previous afternoon she had picked out a dress and shoes for her first day of work. She threw two pieces of bread in the toaster, gulped down a strawberry banana yogurt, a cup of tea, and rushed out the door.

A little past eight-thirty, she was backing down her driveway. Three traffic lights later, she was on 101 North doing sixty miles per hour while looking at the usually slow southbound commuters heading toward San Francisco. She was thankful that her new job took her in the opposite direction of traffic, going north in the morning and south in the afternoon.

What effects remained from her one too many glasses of wine the night before vanished by the time she pulled off the highway onto Rowland Boulevard. She parked in a lot reserved for KLIB staff and guests. Beverly took one last look at her hastily applied makeup in the visor's small light-up mirror, then said aloud, "Good enough," and rushed out of her car and into the building.

Her body vibrated with a mixture of excitement and trepidation. Would this day be the first step in coming out from under Bill's shadow, or would she prove unworthy of the expectations both Holly and Tom Joseph had of her?

Beverly knew this was the time to take a deep breath, center herself, and move forward.

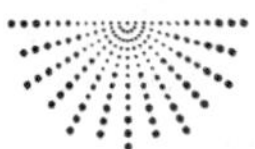

CHAPTER EIGHT

Moments before Beverly stepped into his office, Tom Joseph clicked off KBUD's top-rated show, Wake Up with Wild Bill. Her famous husband was in the middle of a segment in which he told listeners, mostly disgruntled husbands, boyfriends, and aggrieved ex's to, "Get real, get strong, and get moving! If you don't have an equal voice in your relationship, you're down for the count. You need to pull yourself together and stop whining."

Countless times Bent told his loyal fans to stop apologizing: "She's taking you for a ride, man! Who's calling the shots in this relationship? You can do a lot better than her. But you're not going to until you have a true sense of your own value!" Barney Benson, who served as a one-man Greek chorus, added his two cents. "Value what Wild Bill is telling you. Get up off the mat and take back what's rightfully yours!"

Throughout the time he listened to KBUD's morning show, Tom Joseph grew increasingly disappointed that Bent never complained about his wife joining the staff of KLIB. He wondered if Beverly had not shared with him the news of her new job. It was unlikely that a man who personified the proverbial bull in a china shop would not come charging at the red flag KLIB was waving by giving his wife a job.

Beverly was obviously pleasant and intelligent, but there were doubtless more qualified applicants, who likely required less on-the-job training. Joseph was well aware of the risk he was taking in bringing Beverly on board. In a perfect world, Bill Bent would already be blasting away at KLIB. Giving his station attention it desperately needed. He had no intention of forgetting his number one reason for hiring Beverly, who came into his office with a nearly blank resume, having spent the last ten years out of the workplace.

KLIB's director of operations, Joan Mason, took Beverly around, introduced her to the staff and explained her responsibilities as the station's new traffic coordinator and assistant to the station manager. "The term traffic in broadcasting regards how, when, and where different advertising and promotional mentions are spread throughout the day," Mason explained. "It's an essential function in the operation of any station. On-air talent and their program producers have to know when ads play and when promotions are mentioned. It may seem informal to the listener, but it's deadly serious to those paying for advertising and the broadcast companies that survive on the support of their sponsors."

Shortly before noon, with Beverly's pad full of notes and her mind attempting to absorb all this new information, Joan brought her into Tom Joseph's office.

"Beverly's a keeper," Joan boasted, as Tom extended his hand in greeting.

"I'm glad to hear that. We have a little tradition at the station. On the first day of work, the newest member of our team has lunch with the station manager. So, if you don't have any other plans, I was hoping you'd be able to join me today."

"That would be wonderful."

"Good, I have a couple of calls to return, and I'll come by your desk and pick you up in ten minutes."

As they slid into a booth at China Palace off Redwood Boulevard, Beverly tried to recall the last time Bill had taken her out to a restaurant. For the life of her, she could not remember.

Both of them ordered quickly and passed on the suggestion of a beer or wine, saying simultaneously that they needed to go back to work.

"So, how was your first morning?"

"It was a lot to take in, but Joan is great, and I took plenty of notes."

"Good! You'll get the hang of it, I'm sure. Programing traffic, on-air scheduling, and maintaining accurate logbooks are as important in the broadcast business as daily audits are in banking. A station that doesn't stay abreast of their advertising revenue is not going to be in business very long."

"I've already learned that. And I'm thankful you gave me a shot at the job, Mr. Joseph."

"Tom, please. We think of ourselves as a team. Every one of us has a different set of responsibilities. But we succeed or fail together. So, we're driven by a common goal. Make KLIB a success, whatever it takes. If we can do that, we all come out winners."

"Well, it's a great group of people from what I learned this morning. I'm looking forward to being a valued member of the team."

"I'm sure you will be."

After their food arrived, Tom moved onto the topic he wanted to discuss.

"By the way, how did your husband take the news that you've joined the staff of KLIB?" Tom asked with a mischievous smile, suggesting, perhaps, that Beverly's awkward position had a lighter side.

"Well," Beverly hesitated, "I haven't told him yet."

"Haven't told him? I'm surprised. If I were you, it would have been the first thing I mentioned. Are you concerned that he might be displeased with your choice of workplace?"

"I suspect he'll be unhappy to hear that I've taken a job, period. The fact that it's with KLIB will only add more fuel to the fire."

"Wow. Sounds like you're dealing with a Twentieth Century kind of guy."

"I've heard that assessment of Bill previously. Seems as good a description as any."

"So that misogynist routine of his is not just an act."

"I don't think it is, Tom, since the guy you hear on KBUD is the guy I've been listening to since the earliest days of our marriage. And in time, to be honest, he's only gotten worse."

"Your relationship with your husband is none of my business, but I've been told I'm a good listener."

"I don't want to trouble you with my home life."

"You're not troubling me in the least. And whatever you

tell me is just between us, the egg rolls, the egg drop soup, and some spicy green beans and chicken fried rice."

Tom's playful answer provided Beverly with an opportunity to relax and consider letting her guard down. She could not remember when, if ever, she had discussed the details of her marriage with any man. It might be enlightening to hear what another man had to say about life under the thumb of Wild Bill.

"Tom, I don't think you want to get me started on the topic of my husband."

"Try me. It's probably true that many men, perhaps a majority, are not good listeners, but my male role model, as is the case for most men, was my dad. He was a good listener. He and my mom had their share of arguments. Still, he always told me that a successful relationship depended on being able to hit the pause button and listen closely to what your partner is trying to say."

"Wow!" Beverly said as she sat back, drank a little water, and paused to consider what Tom shared.

"I don't have to be the world's most sensitive guy to realize that you're having a tough time with this topic, so maybe we should…"

Beverly briefly put her hand over Tom's and then quickly pulled it back. "Bill and I have been married for ten years. Let's just say it seems like a lot longer."

"I'm sorry to hear that. I had a six-year marriage. We were both in our mid-twenties when we met. Still at a stage of life that is often described as young and dumb. I've always had a passion for broadcasting. Hobby shops and cooking were Marsha's only two passions. She was charming, but how can I say this, she lacked any interest in having a career."

"Was she focused on starting a family?"

"No, not really. In the time we were together we never had a serious discussion about starting a family. I think she was a lot more focused on smoking pot and hanging out."

"What brought you together as a couple?"

"You'll laugh when I tell you this, but I wanted us to get married because I thought she was very nice, very pretty, and made the best apple and cherry pies I'd ever had."

"Oh gosh," Beverly said with a smile. "You guys really were young."

"I think you mean to say 'immature,' and that's okay. Truth be told, we were! I was unprepared to understand what I truly wanted in a life partner. We did a series of stories, a couple of months ago, about the high divorce rate in America."

"It's huge, isn't it?"

"It is, but most people don't know that if you remove the marriages of couples between the age of eighteen and twenty-nine, the national divorce rate drops by half."

"I guess that's why they call it young and dumb. Both Bill and I were in our twenties when we married."

"I'm starting to suspect that Bill Bent on the radio is not all that different from Bill Bent at home."

"That's pretty much the case."

"I'm sure that's not easy."

"It isn't. But let's talk about something more pleasant."

"Sure!"

"Being out of the house and working once again is wonderful. I promise you I'm going to do my best to make you happy about putting me on your team."

"I already am, Beverly. And I mean that."

CHAPTER NINE

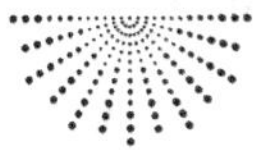

To Beverly's delight and surprise, in what felt like a short time, the first full month in her new job passed in a blur. So much of what bothered Beverly was lessened by the simple act of leaving home every day. Days, and entire weeks, passed far more quickly than they had previously. Time off from work spent with friends became more precious, and time to read, work out, or shop, gained far greater value.

Beverly's concern about discussing with Bill any details of her new life seemed less relevant with each passing day. Bill was gone every weekday morning by five-forty-five, and on those couple of occasions when he came home before her, Beverly provided a casual excuse suggesting she was doing volunteer work at the Bay Area Discovery Museum in Sausalito, or the Marin Animal Shelter up in San Rafael. Bill would give a shrug, or a grunt, and never asked for details. Beverly's long-held resentment over her husband's lack of interest in her daily life suddenly became an unanticipated blessing.

Meanwhile, Tom Joseph's concern over KLIB's sliding audience ratings continued to heighten. Beverly's first month marked the station's third consecutive slip in the ratings. Once again, he considered speaking to Beverly about doing some on-air work for the station. She could start with public service spots where there was no need for her to say her name. And, hopefully, expand her broadcast presence from there.

In the time since they lunched together, Tom had given Beverly a great deal of thought. He knew he was attracted to her but was cautious not to make that apparent.

Bill Bent had to be so self-absorbed, Tom reasoned, that he did not recognize what a wonderful woman he had married.

Tom also realized that any inappropriate male/female interaction in the workplace, particularly given the culture at KLIB, could quickly end what had been, until now, a promising future in radio.

Perhaps there would come a time when Beverly would come to her senses and walk away from her marriage. She might be more tempted to do so, Tom reasoned, if she felt she had a viable career. Equally important, a position that paid far better than her current one. Getting Beverly on the air could thereby serve a double purpose.

Still, nothing prevented Tom from fantasizing about Beverly when he sat alone at night, sipping an aged scotch and hoping to focus on a good book.

Early one morning, at the start of a new work week, Tom looked in the mirror as he tied a red necktie into a perfect Windsor knot, brushed a few specks of dust off his blue blazer, and said, "This is the day!"

Beverly entered Tom's office shortly before ten. He

flashed a bright smile. A thought quickly crossed Beverly's mind: When was the last time Bill appeared happy to see me? She felt bereft in knowing she could not recall.

Beverly pushed the thought aside. Her boss had called her into his office for only the second time since she started at KLIB. This was no time to think about her troubled marriage.

Tom quickly told her his idea. "I don't mean to embarrass you, but I think you should consider doing some work behind a microphone. You have the voice for the job, I'm certain of that. I'd like you to start by making some public service announcements."

"Sure," Beverly said excitedly. "That would be great."

"I'll get it set up and let you know when we're ready to go forward with a few test spots."

Hours later, driving home, Beverly could not resist calling Holly.

"Are you out of work yet?" Beverly asked.

"Just left, Bev. What's up?"

"I wanted to say you're a genius."

"What did I do that was so brilliant?"

"After I got the job at KLIB, you said it would take about a month before they asked me to do some on-air work."

"I remember..."

"Well, today they did. You were spot on. I just started my fifth week at the station, and the boss called me in today and asked if I'd make some public service announcements."

"Have you told Bill yet that you're working at KLIB?"

"Nope."

"Beverly, don't you think that's a little odd?"

"Holly, every aspect of my life with Bill is odd, I can just throw this into the mix."

"Your call, Bev."

"Any choice I make in Bill's estimation will be the wrong one. Other than those one or two occasions during the month when he suddenly finds me desirable, we are little more than roommates, so I'm not feeling motivated right now to tell him anything. I leave for work after he's gone for the day, and except for two times this past month I'm always home before him. In fact, it's not unusual for me to have gone to bed before he comes home. At least one weekend per month, Bill goes off fishing with his buddies. Something he'll announce just a day or two in advance."

"Doesn't that bother you, Bev?"

"The less I see of Bill Bent, the happier I am. So no, it doesn't bother me. He can disappear every weekend for all I care."

What a disaster of a marriage, Holly thought. And struggled, as she had previously, to hold herself back from sharing that opinion with Beverly.

"Well, if these spots lead to more on-air work, and I suspect they will, your secret about working at KLIB won't remain a secret much longer."

"That's fine. I'll deal with that when it happens. Holly, with each passing day, I'm less concerned with what my husband thinks, says, or does."

CHAPTER TEN

In the two weeks that followed, Tom, along with the entire staff, was impressed with Beverly's work behind the microphone. To everyone, it was clear that, as Tom said repeatedly, "She's a natural!"

The station's program manager, Ann Oliver, led a growing chorus of staff asking Tom, "When are you going to expand Beverly's on-air work?"

Having wanted to do that from the first time he listened to her behind a microphone, Tom was happy to go along with the growing consensus. The only remaining questions were the time slot and the format of her show.

Then, as if touched by the hand of fate, Tom's leading morning person walked into his office one morning and announced she had accepted an offer from a station in Chicago. Like most talent not rooted by strong family ties, any opportunity to move to a bigger market and a station with a larger audience was a smart choice.

Tom quickly called Oliver in and said, "Ann, I'd like to

give Beverly her own show, but I can't start her in morning drive, that would be throwing her into deep water."

Oliver thought for a minute and said, "Tom. I think I have a solution, slide Betsy Baker into the morning slot and make Beverly her sidekick."

Tom sat back in his chair for a few moments and stared up at the ceiling, while Ann waited silently for his response.

After a moment, Tom lowered his glance and said, "Baker and Bent in the Morning."

"That's fantastic, Tom." The two stood to shake hands on their newest program.

"What now?" Ann asked.

"Let's get Beverly in here. Both of us will pitch her the idea. She might be a bit shocked. But let's give it a try and see how she handles it."

Sunday at noon, Beverly was the first to arrive at The Cheesecake Factory. This time, Sharon's birthday was the cause for celebration.

A few minutes after she sat down, Sharon, Karin, and Holly entered and found their way over to Beverly's booth.

After hugs and kisses, everyone was seated, and Holly, who had brought Karin and Sharon up to speed on Beverly's work at KLIB, asked, "So how's it going at the radio station? We're all anxious to hear the latest."

"I think it's fantastic that you're working there," Sharon added enthusiastically as Karin nodded and smiled.

"I got big news on Friday, I wanted to wait until we were all together before telling any of you individually. I'm still trying to adjust to the idea myself."

"Oh my gosh," Holly said in a rush, "don't tell me you're getting a regular on-air slot."

Beverly nodded excitedly, "The morning drive talent announced Friday that she's taking a job with a station in Chicago. They're moving Betsy Baker up from the ten to one slot, to mornings from seven to ten, starting a week from Monday."

"They're giving you Baker's midday slot?" Holly asked in a rush.

"No, that would be totally crazy since I've never handled a program on my own. The station manager asked me to be a co-anchor with Betsy. They're calling it 'Baker and Bent in the Morning.'"

"Oh my gosh!" Sharon said, taking both of Beverly's hands as a huge smile flashed across her face. "You just gave me goosebumps!"

"Pretty amazing, huh?" Beverly asked.

All four of them sat back for a few moments and reflected on how much had changed in Beverly's life in the time since their last birthday gathering.

Beverly brought Karin and Sharon up to date on everything that had happened since she and Holly had their fateful lunch.

Holly knew that one question was sure to be asked. It was Karin who jumped in first. "What does Bill think of all this?"

"He doesn't know yet," Beverly replied sheepishly.

"You mean about your getting a show?" Karin asked, sounding surprised.

"Well, that, but more importantly, that I started working at KLIB."

"How could that be?" Sharon asked instantly.

Beverly explained as she had to Holly, "Bill leaves early and comes home after me, so I…"

"Gosh, that's going to be awkward," Sharon said with obvious concern.

"You're probably right," Beverly said, regretting the conversation went so quickly to a topic she had hoped to avoid.

"I just can't imagine, with how Bill carries on about a woman's place being in the home, that this is going to go well," Karin said, quickly regretting her candor.

The expression on Beverly's face became one of stoic resolve. After a few awkward moments of silence, Beverly spoke in a soft, deliberate tone.

"Bill's going to do what Bill's going to do," Beverly announced. "I have no doubt that will include blowing his stack at some point."

"By that, I hope you don't mean getting physical," Sharon said quickly. "I'm sure I could get Eddie to put a good scare into him if he were to dare lay a finger on you."

"Oh no, Sharon, not that," Beverly said as she patted Sharon's hand. "I don't know if this is good or bad, but Bill's specialty is verbal abuse. The why-should-I-give-a-damn variety. As far as physical violence, that has never happened, not once."

For a few awkward moments, the four women sat in silence. Sharon placed her hand resting atop Beverly's. She wanted to wish all the pain away that Beverly must have grown accustomed to over the past years. And she thought of the blessing of a loving relationship that she and Eddie were fortunate enough to share.

"You know, I'm not as foolish as I might appear. Over the

past weeks, I've not told Bill about my job because I saw no reason and no benefit. We live essentially separate lives. I often think he holds on to our marriage because it's good for his show. Why should I listen to his haranguing me about working at KLIB when there was no reason he ever needed to know? I left after he went to work, and on the couple of days when he's gotten home before me, I've told him that I was out doing charity work."

"But you do realize, within a day or two of your show starting, he's going to find out?" Holly asked.

"Absolutely. So what? He's not going to kill me! He's going to tell me I'm making a fool of myself, and more importantly, I'm embarrassing him. Worst case scenario, I should say best case, he leaves me and asks for a divorce. If any of the three of you had lived with Bill as long as I have, you wouldn't think his walking away was bad news."

For what seemed like an eternity, all four friends sat in silence. Beverly knew it was up to her to change the subject. "Am I the only one who wants to celebrate Sharon's birthday and forget about my husband, or do we have to keep talking about that loudmouth, obnoxious bully?"

The tension drained away quickly, and the four friends enjoyed the rest of the birthday celebration. Later, however, in Karin's minivan on the return trip to Sausalito, Holly said, "I hope this doesn't end badly for Beverly."

"Agreed," Sharon and Karin said as they nodded.

"Beverly's got an interesting week ahead of her," Holly said.

"As her oldest friend, I wish I could be there for her, but I know this is one storm she's going to have to ride out on her own."

"I'm afraid you're right about that," Karin said. "I have no idea how she's hung in there all this time."

"You know what I would have done?" Holly asked.

"Kill him!" Sharon and Karin answered in a flash.

"I guess you two know me too well."

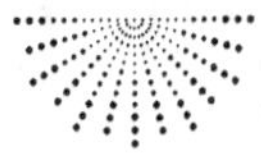

CHAPTER ELEVEN

Baker and Bent in the Morning started with a bang.
Sharon and Karin listened to as much as they could between the hours of seven and ten. Holly, since her job started at eight every morning and required her complete attention, planned on listening to the program's rebroadcast from eight to eleven that night.

Tom Joseph made sure that KLIB's broadcast and nightly rebroadcast times mirrored those of KBUD's Wild Bill morning show. *If he doesn't take this bait*, Tom thought, *he's never going to come after us.*

On her drive home that afternoon, Beverly wondered about the inevitable confrontation with Bill that was all but sure to come this afternoon or the following day.

During Sharon's birthday celebration, Beverly never explained to her friends how conflicted she was about sharing any details of her private life with a radio audience.

There was a time when Bill's disgruntled husband was simply a character he played five mornings a week. In recent years, he fully embraced the role. The aggrieved provider to an unappreciative, unhelpful wife. A woman who appeared to have no higher purpose than serving as an arm charm at dinners with sponsors, or a convenient foil for his commentaries, suddenly had a message of her own.

To Beverly's relief, a blessed peace held for the first two days of her new show. But halfway through Wednesday's show, Barney Benson said, "I think you've been keeping a big secret from us, Wild Bill?"

"Barney, you know I'm not the kind of guy to keep secrets. Especially not from you and our loyal listeners," Bill volleyed back teasingly.

"I hate to disagree pal, but not sharing with us that your bride, the beautiful Beverly Bent, is part of the new morning team on KLIB is keeping a pretty big secret."

"Barney, I know recreational marijuana is now legal in California, but I think you're one toke over the line, good buddy. Beverly isn't on KLIB, I don't think she could find that station on the dial."

"Well, I hate to be the one to burst your bubble, but your loving Bev most definitely is the newest voice on KLIB. I guess from now on we can call you two the 'Battling Bents.'"

To Barney's surprise, Bill was not taking well to his usual good-hearted ribbing. Does he really not know about Beverly's show? Barney wondered as Bill turned several shades of red.

"We've got to take a break for news and weather at the bottom of the hour," Bill barked into his microphone. "We'll be back with more of Get Bent in the Morning on the other side."

As the studio's on-air light blinked out, Bill pulled off his headset, looked at Barney, and said, "Have you lost your mind?"

"Bill, I'm guessing she never told you? Well, how was I supposed to know? She's co-anchor on KLIB with Betsy Baker, they're on every weekday morning from seven to ten."

"There's no way Beverly could be doing a morning radio show. That's impossible. It's got to be a gag."

Barney shrugged. "I don't know what to tell you, pal. KLIB's new show is all over their website."

"I've never even thought of looking at that station's webpage."

"Well, if you did, partner, you'd see the smiling faces of Beverly Bent and Betsy Baker looking back at you."

"Barney, this is completely nuts!"

"Seriously, Bill, I thought you were keeping it under your hat. I had no idea you were in the dark about this," Barney pushed down on the red button that allowed them to talk with their show's producer, Mike Adler. "Mike, could you give us a quick stream of KLIB's live broadcast, so Bill knows I'm not making this stuff up."

"Sure, Barney," Mike said as he pushed a switch on his control board and allowed a minute of KLIB to play into Barney and Bill's headsets.

"This is Betsy Baker, and this is Beverly Bent, with Baker and Bent in the Morning on KLIB. We've got news coming up, followed by Beverly's interview with California Congresswoman Jackie Speier on the growing role of women in both houses of Congress. So, stick around."

The color drained from Bill's face.

"You really didn't know?" Barney said, finally recognizing what moments before seemed unimaginable.

Both men slowly pulled off their headsets and stared at each other in silence.

Bill's mouth went dry. He drank half a glass of water in one gulp, "I just…"

"You look like you got hit in the back of the head with a rock. I thought you were keeping this to yourself. Bill, I would have never ambushed you like that if for one moment I thought you didn't know. I mean it's kind of a great idea. I know our audience share is at least double, perhaps four times the size of KLIB's, but still, it's a cute gimmick."

"What do you mean, a gimmick?"

"I thought maybe you had already discussed this with station management. Pushing an idea like the Battling Bents. That should have people talking east to Walnut Creek, south to San Jose, and north to Santa Rosa and all points in between. Wow, I guess I was wrong big time!"

While Barney sputtered, Bill muttered a string of obscenities to himself. His show was about to enter its second half. He needed to quickly regain his balance. After all, they had ninety minutes of airtime in front of them.

"Listen, Barney, let's drop this Battling Bents thing for now. I want to tell you that Beverly and I cooked this up, but we didn't. I've got to sit her down tonight and find out what in the hell she's thinking to pull a stunt like this without telling me. Right now, I'm not sure if she's brilliant, malicious, or completely insane. There'll be plenty of time tomorrow to see where we can go with this."

"You're going to ask her to quit?" Barney said with a surprised look.

"I don't know what I'm going to do. So, let's just drop it for now."

To Tom Joseph's disappointment, as he sat at his desk listening to Bill Bent's morning show, there were no more mentions of Baker and Bent during the second half of Bill Bent's show.

But Tom was convinced that this was just a starting point. Most likely, it would escalate into the on-air battle he hoped for from the moment Beverly Bent walked into his office.

Tom had meant to call Beverly into his office after she got off the air. But, as was often the case with his job, time got away from him. There was an advertiser who was upset that the station's promotion of his annual mattress blowout sale produced disappointing results. And there were the corporate bean counters at LBG, continuing to quiz him about the station's prospects for improved ratings in the coming quarter. And, if not, what staff cuts was he prepared to make in order to decrease the station's flow of red ink?

By the time Tom was done answering his daily set of questions from the owners, sponsors, and dealing with small interoffice problems, Beverly had already left for the day.

When Tom got home and started to prepare his usual dinner for one, he thought about Beverly and wondered how her evening was going. Not well, he assumed. Just as he was about to open a can of chili, his third in the last five nights, he closed the cupboard, turned off the stove's front burner, grabbed his car keys, and headed out for a drink.

Suspecting that Bill had finally learned the Bay Area's worst kept secret, Beverly was anxious to find a way to delay her arrival home. A detour into Nordstrom's should keep me busy for an hour or two, she reasoned. But it was not even five when she got bored with shopping and walked back to her car. Her phone's display showed two missed calls from Bill and one voice mail message. Beverly thought of listening but, convinced it would be one of Bill's venom-laced rants, she devised another way to delay her arrival home.

She hadn't checked out the happy hour at her favorite Mexican restaurant, Flores, just two minutes away on the opposite side of the Freeway's Corte Madera exit.

That should delay my getting home by another hour, perhaps more! By then, if I'm lucky, Bill will have stalked off to go have dinner by himself.

Further delaying her arrival home was better than running head-on into the huge argument that was surely awaiting her.

There were two empty seats at Flores' bar, the restaurant where Holly and Beverly had lunch six weeks earlier. Beverly took one, a few moments later, Tom Joseph grabbed the other.

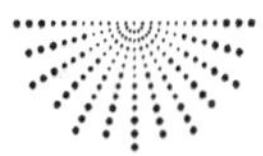

CHAPTER TWELVE

"My God, what are you doing here?" Beverly asked.

"I didn't want to spend another night at home with a can of chili, a bottle of beer, and the Giants baseball game. So, I got in my car and came down here," he responded candidly, instantly regretting his decision to do so. Looking around, Tom added, "Wow, it's true what they say, this is probably the nicest bar in Marin County."

"Better still, the food is great."

"Good to know, can I buy you dinner?"

"I shouldn't stay. Bill's already home, but…"

"He's not said anything about your new job at the station?"

"Well, let me order a margarita, and then I'll be ready to catch you up."

Over their first round, Tom shared the story he never got to tell her earlier in the day.

"Oh my God, then Bill does know. I thought he must have found out given the missed calls and the voice mail he left on my phone. I suppose it's hard to keep a secret that's broadcast throughout Northern California," Beverly replied, hoping to interject a bit of humor into a situation she considered anything but funny.

"I can't believe you've kept this a secret for so long."

Beverly gave a shrug and said, "Full disclosure, neither can I."

"How do you think he's going to react?"

"Not well," she said with a shrug.

"Barney Benson told him about Baker and Bent in the Morning just before they cut to news and weather at eight-thirty. When they returned neither of them said a word about you or KLIB."

"I would think that was Bill's doing."

"Well, it certainly sounded like he was caught off guard by Benson announcing your new show."

"Along with other unpleasant qualities," Beverly explained, "Bill's a control freak. From his perspective, I'm guessing the only thing more upsetting than my taking a job at KLIB is the fact that I did it without telling him. Perhaps it would be more accurate to say, I didn't go to him to ask his permission." Nearing the end of her margarita, it was clear that she was being helped along by the right amount of liquid courage.

"I guess it all depends on the guy. I've never been an on-air guy. I've always been on the management side of the business. Still, if I was married to a woman who managed another station in the same market, I'd say good for her. Given the cost of living in the Bay Area, the only thing better than one working spouse is two!"

"For Bill, my being a stay at home wife has more to do with his oversized ego than anything else."

"I know it's none of my business, so feel free to kick me..."

"I'd never kick my boss," Beverly said with a smile.

"Has Bill ever talked about starting a family?"

"In passing, but those occasions are rare. As for me, I've kept my mouth shut about the subject."

"Why is that? If you don't mind my asking."

"I'm a single child raised by an unhappy couple. I decided I didn't want to repeat that pattern. Bill never appeared to have any interest in starting a family, and I have a hard time imagining him finding the patience to be a loving parent."

"Oh," Tom said softly. "You know, as I started to tell you when we had lunch, my wife had no interest in starting a family. I'm so thankful now that we didn't. I'm sure I would have loved our child, but raising a split family in the unstable world of broadcasting can be a heavy load to carry."

Neither Tom nor Beverly appeared inclined to go home, so when they were asked about ordering another cocktail, they happily agreed. And when the bartender asked if they wanted to look at a menu, they nodded approvingly.

It was going on nine when they finished their meal and the last of their drinks. Beverly had noticed on her phone's display that there were now two more missed calls from Bill. The second call, at eight-ten, was followed by another voice message.

She was enjoying her time with Tom. The very thought of going home to her husband, particularly after three margaritas, seemed like a needless way to spoil a lovely evening.

"I wonder what a room at the Corte Madera Inn costs for the night?" Beverly suddenly asked.

"Don't feel up to going home?"

"Not particularly."

"Well, you're in luck. The station has a trade with those folks, let me see if I can get you a room on the station's account."

After a few minutes on the phone, Tom said, "All taken care of. Are you okay to drive over? It's less than a half-mile from here."

"I can make it that far. You know, Tom, I wouldn't mind if you wanted to come to the hotel so we can spend a little more time together. I wish Bill was as easy to talk as you."

"There's a part of me that would love to do that. But if there is one thing I've learned in the broadcast business, it's never, and I mean never, mix business with pleasure."

"Oh…" Beverly said with obvious disappointment.

"If you worked at any radio station in the country other than the one where I was manager, I'd be happy to keep you company until daybreak. But in this business, our having a personal relationship would be like throwing a match onto dry grass to see what might happen."

"You mean," Beverly said with an appreciative smile, "things could easily get out of control."

"With a woman as bright and as attractive as you? Absolutely!"

Thirty minutes later, Beverly slipped into bed and reluctantly took one more look at her phone's display. Same as last time, several missed calls and two voicemails.

Her finger hovered over the play button. Finally, she couldn't resist. Her curiosity overwhelmed her common sense.

In the first message, Bill said only two words: "CALL ME!"

The second message was a great deal longer. "Who the hell do you think you are?" it began. From there in went downhill.

As bad as Bill can be, Beverly thought, he's generally not that abusive. Her going to work for KLIB, and worse, becoming one of the station's on-air personalities was, as Bill suggested, "The final straw in a lousy marriage."

Beverly was tempted to hit delete and not listen to the end of the message, but curiosity got the better of her, so she played the rest.

"Our relationship was built on trust," Bill continued. "If I can't trust you, we're at the end of the road. That's sad because you probably just got some bad advice from one or more of your empty-headed girlfriends. And you, of course, incapable of thinking for yourself, didn't realize how great a life I have made for you. You know how to reach me if you ever want to talk. Maybe you care enough about our future to at least try."

Bev tapped off on her screen and tossed the phone to the bottom of the bed. She threw the cover over her head in the hope of quickly falling asleep. She had consumed enough alcohol to do so. Still, her annoyance at hearing Bill's admonishments was too great to simply set aside. For a time, she thought about calling Sharon, or Holly, but it was too late on a weeknight with work and school in the morning. She was too upset, and the fear of slurring her speech was too high. Through it all, she never shed a tear. Bill Bent was hardly worth the effort.

CHAPTER THIRTEEN

Beverly arrived early the following morning at KLIB, more than an hour before the start of her seven o'clock show. At this time of the morning, the only staff at the station were its overnight broadcast team, their on-air producer, and to her surprise, Tom Joseph.

Bev went straight into Tom's office and closed the door.

"Can we talk?"

"Sure," Tom said, hoping they would not delve into the events of the previous night.

"Bill is furious with me. Apparently, I'm another ditzy woman taking bad advice from other brainless women. He's essentially told me to shape up or ship out."

"Did he define what his order to shape up constituted?"

"Not exactly. I think Bill had several drinks in him. Most nights, he's a two-drink kind of guy. Last night he sounded like he had two doubles. For all I know, he downed half a bottle."

"Beverly, I have to confess, I'm partially to blame for all this."

"You're not. You knew sparks would fly if I got on the air and Bill and I started in on each other. But you were not aware of the real state of our marriage and how much Bill actually believes that babble he chatters five days a week. More than once, my gal pals have asked me if his rants about women are all an act. It's pretty embarrassing to admit that the guy you married is as bad as the character he plays on the radio."

"What can I do?"

"A couple of things. I'm committed to staying put. Right here at KLIB, working with Betsy and doing our show."

"Good. I mean, great! I think the two of you are off to a terrific start. Listener comments have been very encouraging."

"I don't want to fly directly into Bill's path. I'm not scared of him. I've just had heard enough of his rants and his abuse. All my friends were surprised that I never told him about working here. I didn't want to deal with the inevitable harassment I was certain would follow.

"To make a long story short, I want to move out. That means I might need some financial help in the form of an advance from the station. I can't give you a dollar figure, but I know I'll need something more than what I have now in savings to get free of Bill and start living in my own place."

"I think that can be arranged. Just keep doing a great show. As you and Betsy start bringing in a bigger audience share, I'm sure our corporate overlords will place a bet on your future in the form of a healthy bonus. I'll do everything I can to help that happen. In fact, I'll call my boss at corporate today and see if we can arrange a two-week pay advance to help meet your immediate needs."

"Thanks, Tom. I'm sorry that I got a little out of line last night. I think one, possibly two margaritas, is probably my limit. You were smart to send me off to my hotel room alone."

"It's because of us being able to have a discussion like the one we just had, that staying friends, and nothing more, is the best way for us to move forward. Right now, as you well know, your life is complicated enough."

It was shortly before seven the following morning when Beverly reached out to Holly.

"Forgive me for the early call, I'm on the air after the morning news and weather," Beverly said.

"I'm awake, or at least trying to be. My day starts early as well," Holly explained as she stood barefoot on her cold kitchen floor pouring water into her coffee maker. "What's up?"

"Bill found out about Baker and Bent in the Morning."

"There was no way to keep that cat in the bag for much longer. Did he blow his stack?"

"And then some. I stayed away from the house last night. I couldn't face dealing with Bill. Not right now, anyway. Would you consider letting me crash at your place for a few days?"

"Sure, kiddo. That's the least I can do considering how I helped to put you on a collision course with Bill. Anyway, I spend half of my nights up at Scott's place. I'm sure he wouldn't mind an extra snuggle tonight."

"Holly, you're the best."

"I'm no saint, Bev. But if you can't be there for your friends, you don't deserve to have any."

After she thanked Holly and promised to meet up with her later in Sausalito, Beverly arranged to have one of the station's engineers record the seven o'clock hour of Get Bent. She was determined to listen to the opening minutes of Bent's show when she and Betsy took their first news and weather break at eight o'clock.

Not to her surprise, Beverly learned later that Bill was in fine form from the opening moments of his show. "My wife thinks that the kitchen is for two things, it's the place from where you order takeout and where you reheat that takeout the following night. Now that she's doing her own show, she'll at least have some idea of just how demanding real work can be."

"Wild Bill, are you suggesting women, and more specifically wives, are lazy?" Benson asked in his usual light-hearted manner.

"Let's say there are a lot of women who don't know what their husbands go through every day of the year trying to be good providers. So, to that extent, I'm glad my bride is doing some honest work for a change. But, sadly, she couldn't share with her husband what she was doing. How about all you guys out there: have you ever been blindsided by your wife or girlfriend? We want to hear from you. Let's have an honest discussion during the first hour of today's show about shared responsibilities in creating happy relationships."

Beverly walked back into the studio just as Betsy was about to open the second hour of their show. Beverly declared: "One topic I'd like to add to this morning's show is how a woman can step out from behind the shadow of a controlling male."

Betsy shrugged and said, "Sounds great, let's give it a go."

When their red studio light came on, indicating they were

back on the air, Betsy reintroduced herself, her broadcast partner, and then added, "I know Beverly wanted to get us started for our second hour today, what have you got Bev?"

"Betsy, I just heard Bill Bent spouting off about his wife, that would be me, and wives in general. Apparently, we're lazy, dishonest, and untrustworthy. Let's say our bad qualities far exceed our good qualities. So, I thought that might be a good topic to discuss with our listeners. Bill Bent seems to think women are lazy, stupid, and essentially worthless. Women and men who, unlike my husband, are not stuck in the Dark Ages know better! Let's talk about why certain men have no interest in crossing that bridge into a new century."

With that, the first shots in the Battle of the Bents had been exchanged. No one could say where this would lead, but as Tom Joseph told his boss, Sam Slade, during a conference call that morning, "The battling Bents has the potential to be a ratings bonanza. I'm certain this will pull us out of the bottom third of the quarterly ratings book and get us the recognition we need and, I honestly believe, deserve!"

"I'm happy to hear that, Tom. You're going to need some impressive numbers if we're going to save KLIB, not to mention your job with LBG," Slade said in his typical master of the universe tone. "Keep up the good work," Slade barked and hung up.

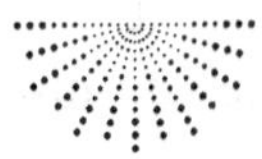

CHAPTER FOURTEEN

In less than four weeks, the "Battling Bents" were the talk of the Bay Area. KLIB went from being stuck near the bottom to being one of the five top-rated stations in a highly competitive market. Advertising rates zoomed upward. Management at both stations busied themselves, attempting to come up with additional ways to monetize the on-air couple, who now were separated and rumored to have filed for divorce.

KLIB and KBUD were not the only ones to benefit from the train wreck of Bill and Beverly's marriage. Other radio, television, print, and Internet outlets benefited as well from the bickering Bents. And everyone took notice. From devoted listeners to psychologists and relationship counselors, no one was without an opinion regarding the famous couple and the modern state of marriage.

Beverly's "couple of nights" as a guest in Holly's apartment was well into its second month when Scott asked Holly over burgers and sweet potato fries at Sausalito's Le Garage restaurant, "Do you think Beverly is going to make a move to get a place of her own?"

"You growing tired of me as a house guest?" Holly asked with a sly smile.

"No way, sweetie. You could move into my place tomorrow," Scott insisted. "God only knows my mother's old house certainly has enough space. If we ever argue, we can go to separate parts of the house and not run into each other for a week or longer."

"Beverly told me that she's looking at apartments up in Novato. She's finding better rates than down here so close to San Francisco, and she'll be just minutes from the radio station."

"I listened to some of Bill Bent's blather on the way up to Marin Academy this morning. Yikes, he has nothing good to say about Beverly or women in general. Personally, I like women."

"I'd prefer it if you kept the 'like' part of that to one woman in particular!"

"You know I only have eyes for you."

"I do, sweetie. But when you're worth millions, certain women see you as the perfect catch."

"Sounds like something Bill Bent would say."

"Agreed. But remember, both Bent and a broken clock can be right twice a day."

"I can't argue with that. In Bent's view, all women are deceptive gold diggers, cold-blooded schemers, and generally wrong far more often than right."

"Agreed, and not all husbands are, as Beverly has suggested, selfish, egotistical, unbending, unkind, and unfeeling. Just the really rotten ones."

Holly finished the last of her sweet potato fries, looked at

Scott, and said, "How did we ever manage to find each other?"

"Like most good things in life, God's grace, random chance, or a bit of both." Scott took Holly's hand and kissed it. "The odds are that at some point, all of us will meet a worthy soul mate. The hard part is recognizing your partner when they appear."

"Maybe the two of us should go into competition with Bill and Beverly and do a radio show called 'Happily Ever After.'"

"Not a bad idea if we weren't both all-in with the jobs we currently have."

"True, but it would be nice for there to be a couple that's the polar opposite of the Bents; instead of tearing each other down, building each other up."

"I think Beverly married the wrong guy and had a tough time accepting that truth. For most of us, getting into a relationship is a lot easier than getting out of one."

"True that!"

"I don't think this whole thing with the Battling Bents can go on indefinitely, do you?"

"One thing I've learned in the news business is whatever hot topic you've got going today, will vanish quicker than you would imagine. Some burn out in a day or two, some last longer, but in a world with countless distractions, people get bored pretty quickly and move on."

"What do you think will happen to Beverly when the audience eventually grows tired of the Battling Bents?"

"Not sure. Beverly's a natural at what she's now doing, so my guess is that she'll move on to topics not centered around the complete jerk she married. But regardless of what comes next, doing this radio show has changed Beverly's life forever. And I'm glad for her. She was under Bent's thumb for years, and now she's reinvented herself. When this all dies down, the Beverly that comes out of it will be a new person. She now has a career in radio, with a sample reel that would impress any producer or station manager. I have no idea if she'll stay at KLIB or end up doing a talk show in Seattle, Chicago, Tampa, or a hundred other places. When all this started Beverly thought her life was going in one direction, down! I'm glad she found out how much she can accomplish by setting aside her husband's low opinion of her."

"Getting out from under the thumb of a horrible husband can make all the difference. I promise you I'll never be that guy."

"I'm pretty certain that whatever dysfunctional environment created Bill Bent is the polar opposite of the forces that created you. Both your mother and aunt were guilty of loving you too much. I would guess that Bill Bent grew up in a home where he was loved too little. Perhaps the same is true of Beverly. Unhappy homes have a way of creating unhappy people."

Beverly's mother, Mary Ann, a widow who lived in the same Tudor-style home in Tiburon in which Beverly grew up, called to ask if she had "kissed and made up with Bill yet."

"No, Mother, and I seriously doubt that will ever happen."

"Really, Beverly? I know Bill can be difficult, but your father was disagreeable at times. Still, he and I never lived apart."

Before responding, Beverly thought of how she and Betsy handled calls from women who viewed their marriages as an obligation, not a loving partnership.

"Mom, we all have to make our own decisions. At this point, it's highly unlikely Bill and I will ever again be a couple."

"I know he's a bit of a curmudgeon," she said with a short laugh.

"Really, Mother, 'a curmudgeon?' That description might work for your bridge club, but I'll call Bill an obnoxious bully. And that's my being polite."

"I wish you would try to patch things up. He's always been a good provider."

"Women today expect more than a good provider. Haven't you been listening to my show on KLIB?"

"Oh, I'm so hooked on watching The View every morning that I keep forgetting to listen. I'll make more of an effort, I promise."

"Got to go, Mom, I've got another call coming in."

"Let me know if you and Bill patch things up. I'll keep my fingers crossed for both of you."

Beverly got off the phone, wondering the same thing she often did about her mother: Does she ever hear anything I say?

Beverly's salary more than tripled in two months as she successfully transformed herself from a clerical staff assistant into one of the Bay Area's best-known radio celebrities. Tom and the entire staff at KLIB began to breathe a good deal easier when the new ratings book showed their station's audience to be five times the size of what it had been before Baker and Bent premiered.

Tom and two other friends at the station helped Beverly move into her new apartment. Settled in that night, happily alone, Beverly felt a surge of confidence that her life was going to turn out better than she previously imagined.

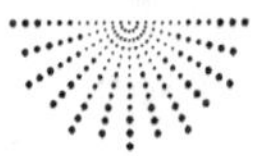

CHAPTER FIFTEEN

Happily settled into her new one-bedroom apartment just off Grant Avenue, the commercial hub of Novato's quaint historic district, Beverly came up with a new segment for her morning show, "I Married a Jerk," in which listeners were invited to share their stories of marital woe. At a program planning session with Tom Joseph, her idea was approved along with two other segments, "Dating Disasters" and "My Boyfriend is a Blockhead."

The team at KBUD countered with two new segments, "Deadbeat Wives" and "Is Your Wife a Cheat?" The nastier the rhetoric, the higher the ratings climbed for KLIB. To everyone's amazement, in twelve weeks, the once-failing station was pulling neck and neck with KBUD, a level of ratings success that neither Tom nor his bosses at LBG ever thought possible.

Then something happened that no one saw coming. It began early on a Tuesday when Tom, monitoring the seven o'clock hour of Get Bent on KBUD, heard only the voice of Barney Benson.

"Wild Bill has not arrived at the station yet, but we expect him any moment. In the meantime, let's take a listen to one of our favorites here at KBUD, the one and only Lyle Lovett, singing his classic hit, 'My Baby Don't Tolerate.'"

Tom checked back periodically through the second and third hours of Bent and Benson. Barney filled the show with a blend of music and segments typically used as filler on days when promotional work caused Bill to miss his morning show.

To Tom's surprise, on the following two days, KBUD started with rebroadcasts of Bill's earlier shows, interrupted only by live updates for news, traffic, and weather.

By Friday, when Bill continued to be AWOL, Tom asked Beverly if she had any idea why her husband had suddenly vanished.

"I heard he hasn't done his show since Monday. But I'm not all that surprised. He would do that now and then. Get too much bourbon in him and vanish for a few days. There's a reason why he earned the nickname, 'Wild Bill.'"

"The times when he vanished must have made management mad as hell," Tom said, obviously astonished by what he had just heard.

"They certainly were displeased, to put it politely. But with Bill's ratings, they did their best to look the other way. Now and then, someone in management would track me down and ask if I had any idea where their most valuable talent had gone. I'd explain he probably went fishing, most likely somewhere up around Mount Shasta or beyond. People forget that California has thousands of square miles of open space, particularly in the northeastern part of the state up around Modoc National Forest, for example. Anyway, Bill never liked to share the location of his favorite fishing spots with anyone, especially his wife."

"Didn't an answer like, 'I have no idea where my husband has gone,' surprise them?"

"Perhaps. But there was no reason it should. If they listened to Bill's show, they would have heard his usual rant about men being the kings of their castles. Let's just say Bill was not the reporting-in type."

"Wow! Bill was what my dad would have called a real piece of work! What did he have to say for himself when he showed back up?"

"Something hurtful."

"I'm curious: What would that be?"

"Let's see," Beverly said, looking up for a moment at the ceiling of Tom's office and then lowering her eyes to meet his. "I suppose my favorite was, 'Worried I'm going to disappear and leave you with a big house payment?' or something equally obnoxious and mean-spirited."

"Double wow!" Tom said with a smile and a shake of his head. "How did you manage to put up with him for as long as you did? I suppose that's really none of my business, but..."

"That's okay, Tom, believe me, I understand. If I was you, I'd be wondering the same thing," Beverly paused for a few moments. She wondered how to explain the inexplicable. "I learned from watching my mom. My father was lord of the manor, and when I got older, well into my mid-teens, I asked her why she never pushed back against my father's endless list of demands and expectations. She always gave a long sigh and told me, 'you'll understand when you're older.' Repeatedly she'd say, 'Your father works very hard, and we should be grateful that he does so much to provide for us.'"

"Sounds like she's not what we at KLIB would call a 'Twenty-First Century Woman.'"

"That's putting it politely, Tom. I hope my wayward husband reappears soon. The Battling Bents have less to discuss without Bill's daily dose of ridiculous observations."

"He'll reappear soon enough, I suspect. Once you've gotten to the point that your audience likes you for you, and not because of this back and forth with Bill, they'll keep listening. In fact, I think both of you are already at that point. The Battling Bents gave your show a big lift, there's no doubt about that. It's a level of awareness you can't buy. But now that you and Betsy are a team and a known quantity, I think you'll keep getting strong ratings with or without Bill's big mouth to give you a boost."

"You mean until the new, new thing comes along?" Beverly asked with a half-smile and a raised eyebrow.

"True, but that's show biz. Very few shows stay fresh beyond two or three years. But I feel pretty confident that you and Betsy will be one of them. You're bright, easy to listen to, and most importantly, you have something to say."

F riday afternoon at five, Rob and Holly were seated at their usual table at Smitty's, wondering how much longer it would be before Eddie arrived.

"What did you think of the week that was?" Rob asked. "Tougher than our usual grind, or more or less the same?"

"You know, with four editions to get out every week, we work at such a pace, that a lot of times the workday passes in a blur. Kind of like working on an assembly line, when you finish one piece, another one is coming your way."

"I know the feeling. But if you're like me, the only thing worse than busy days are days that drag on for hours."

"Agreed."

"There are lots of times that I think it's nowhere near noon, and I look at my watch and see that it's past one."

"Speaking of time, I'm giving Eddie just another couple of minutes before I order myself a martini. I certainly didn't come here to eat stale pretzels and soak up the atmosphere."

"I'll second that!" Rob nodded.

"Second what?" Eddie asked as he came up behind them.

"The idea that Smitty's is not a place you come to for the atmosphere," Holly said as she stood to give Eddie a kiss on the cheek.

"It's been a while since you've done that," Eddie said as he smiled.

"I'm just happy to know I can order my martini now."

"So, this little Friday afternoon gathering we have is more about the booze than spending time with friends?"

"I love you both, and I look forward to seeing you every Friday, Eddie. But at the end of one of our workweek marathons, I'm also looking forward to seeing that martini. Think of me as the mouse in a maze. Take away that little bit of cheese, and where's my reward?"

"What's new in the life of Marin County's top detective?" Rob asked.

"I do have some news that's going to surprise you both."

"Well, let's hear it, Copper," Holly said, hoping for a mystery. "I just finished a story about a middle school science fair that we're running as our lead in next week's Mill Valley edition. I'm definitely up for something a little more exciting than that."

"Well, we'll have to see how interesting it gets; right now, it's just a missing person case. Albeit a rather famous person, particularly in recent days."

"Wait, don't tell me," Holly said as she wrapped her hand around Eddie's forearm and gave it a squeeze. "Is it Beverly's dumbass hubby, Wild Bill Bent?"

"It is! Mister Get Bent himself," Eddie said as he saw their waitress, Gail, and waved her over to the table. "Our usual," the three friends said in unison.

"I didn't know Bent had gone missing," Rob announced.

"You were probably too busy covering the opening of San Anselmo's newly remodeled library to have heard anything about the disappearance of one half of the Bay Area's best-known broadcast couple," Holly said teasingly.

"Geez, you're right," Rob said. "I'm out of the loop. Did you know about his disappearance, Eddie?"

"Nope," Eddie said as he thanked Gail for handing him a tall Guinness. "I'm a crossword puzzle in the morning kind of guy. Between the puzzle and Sharon trying to rouse Aaron to get him dressed, fed, and off to school, that's enough entertainment for me for one morning. I didn't know a thing about Bent going missing until Jack Canning called me into his office shortly after I got to headquarters this morning."

"Canning?" Rob asked with evident surprise. "I thought he doesn't get antsy about things like a missing person unless the county's one and only daily newspaper, *The Independent*, starts asking questions."

"That's exactly what happened. Some reporter at *The Independent* called our illustrious sheriff a half-hour earlier and asked if the department had any comment on Bent's disappearance. He's apparently not been seen since his last show on Monday. The reporter was wondering if we suspected that his disappearance involved foul play. You know Canning, just a whiff of anyone in the media poking around about a story, small or large, and he breaks out in a sweat."

"Nothing we haven't seen before," Holly suggested with the hint of a sneer. She distrusted Canning and his endless scheming to stay close to the media to help assure he remained on the right side of the voters. One out of every four years, he happily cooperated with the press. The other three years of his term, he rarely returned their phone calls.

"So, have you started looking into what might have happened to Bent?" Holly asked.

"After I met with Canning, I arranged to see Beverly up at KLIB. I got there shortly after she finished her show at ten. She and Sharon have known each other forever, but the two of us never socialized with her and Bill. I'd see them at a party now and then, talk to her for a few minutes, but nothing more than pleasantries. Still, it seemed to me that her broadcast work has made a real change in her."

"How so?" Rob asked.

"She seems to have a lot more self-confidence than I remembered. The couple of times I talked to the two of them, Bill kept interrupting, and when he did, she'd go silent. Frankly, I never thought much about it, but the Beverly I spoke to today is not shy about expressing herself."

"I imagine co-anchoring a morning radio show five days a week has a lot to do with that," Rob said.

"No doubt."

"Did she give you anything useful?" Holly asked with that

edge of excitement in her voice, which appeared when a whiff of intrigue entered the conversation.

"I wouldn't call it useful, at least not at this point. But certainly interesting."

"How so?" Rob asked.

"Remember Clark Gable's last line in Gone with the Wind?"

"Sure," Holly responded. "'Frankly, my dear, I don't give a damn.'"

"That's the one," Eddie said as he smiled. "Her husband's been missing since Tuesday, and she's like, frankly, Eddie, I don't give a damn. Not her words but clearly her sentiment."

"Sad, isn't it?" Holly said. "I haven't spoken to her in a couple of weeks, you know she stayed in my apartment for over a month?"

"Yeah, Rob told me you invited her to use your place. That was really nice of you."

"While she was at my place, and I was staying up at Scott's, Beverly and I found the time to take a couple of weekend walks and share a few meals. I've got to tell you both I have never known someone so totally over a relationship as Beverly. That 'I don't give a damn' vibe you were getting from her is an outward expression of her true feelings. She is as over her guy as any gal I've ever known."

"From what I've learned from Karin," Rob added, "the last time you ladies had one of your birthday gatherings, it was more than obvious that Beverly had turned the page on her shared life with Bill. From what I can tell, I say good for her."

"Neither of you are thinking Beverly's behind Bill's vanishing act?" Eddie asked.

"Not me. It's just something of note," Rob said. "At least for me."

"If you're suggesting that she dumped him in the bay or buried him in the backyard, I'd find that easier to believe if she hadn't come into her own over the past few months. As Bent's browbeaten wife, I could see her killing him any day of the week. But not Beverly Bent, co-host of a popular radio show that might be going into syndication."

"What does that mean in radio?" Eddie asked.

"It means she does the same show she's doing now, but because it's syndicated, her compensation for doing that show can skyrocket," Rob explained.

"Most times, when you interview one spouse about the other, you can pick up on their feelings. That can range from indifferent to concerned to a complete state of panic. The 'I couldn't care less' reaction concerning a missing spouse is not one you see too often. She did offer up the idea that Bent might have just gone off fishing for several days. He knows how much he's worth to KBUD, and there would be few if any serious consequences if he pulled a relatively brief disappearing act. In fact, Beverly made a point of explaining that he's vanished before. She told some of her co-workers that as well."

"Are either of his parents still alive?" Rob asked. "Maybe he's been in touch with one of them."

"His mother is deceased, but his dad is still kicking. He lives in the same house that Bill grew up in."

"Where's that?" Rob asked.

"Kingman, Arizona."

"Kingman!" Holly exclaimed. "What was there to do growing up in Kingman?"

"I don't know, Holly. I suspect not a whole hell of a lot. Maybe go to the Route 66 museum?"

"Isn't that where Highways 93, 66, and Interstate 40 all meet up?" Rob asked.

"That's the place, pal," Eddie responded. "I've gone through there a couple of times on the way to Flagstaff or heading up to Vegas."

"Was the dad of any help?" Holly asked.

"Nope. The only thing that seemed odd was the old guy was about as concerned about his son's vanishing act as Beverly."

"Popular guy!" Rob said with a shake of his head.

"Real popular," Eddie nodded in agreement. "His most interesting comment was that Bill had pulled off a vanishing act after he finished high school. So, like Beverly said, his disappearance isn't particularly surprising to those who know him well. Apparently, he got his start in radio at KGMN in his hometown. It has a country music format."

"Strange isn't it, how people can be," Holly said. "You imagine you know them, but when you start digging, you discover how little you really do know."

"Well, I've barely scratched the surface on Bill Bent, and I already have the feeling this guy has a walk-in closet's worth of secrets."

"If anyone is going to pry those secrets loose, my money is on Eddie Austin," Rob said as he tapped his glass of Guinness into Eddie's.

"Thanks, pal."

"So, what's your next move?" Holly asked, perched on the edge of her chair.

"Interviews and more interviews. People he works with, whatever family or friends he has, who might know anything about him. Neighbors, who perhaps saw something odd, but opted to keep questions or concerns to themselves. The search for missing persons can be tricky business. Not a favorite area of investigation for most law enforcement officers."

"Why is that?" Holly asked.

"You can get lucky, but a lot of times, you come away with a basket full of suspicions. More questions about the missing individual than answers or leads to a handful of clues that turn into dead ends."

"Bent is pretty well known, you wouldn't think he could just vanish without a trace," Holly said.

"Jimmy Hoffa was pretty well known, no one has found him yet," Eddie replied. "Given the fact that if Hoffa was still alive, he'd be well past one hundred, it's fair to say no one has yet found his remains."

"You know, in the years we've been publishing *The Standard* I can't remember doing a missing person's story," Rob said. "You have your little kid who vanishes, and everyone goes into a panic. Then they find he fell asleep up in the neighbor's old treehouse they built years earlier when their children were young. But it's nothing nefarious."

"Marin County is not a high crime area. Particularly the towns that *The Standard* covers," Eddie said. "Neighbors occasionally hurl insults at each other, but that's about it. Robberies occur when owners are away on a cruise, not with a bang over the head while they're out walking their dog at night."

"You're right," Holly said. "I honestly can't recall our doing a story about a missing person. The couple of times I've heard anything about a missing person, it's resolved before we went to press. I don't even know what procedures the police follow when they have a missing person. Don't they wait like twenty-four or forty-eight hours before they begin a search?"

"That's a bit of an urban legend. Truth is, there's no uniform set of procedures involving a search for a missing person. Different departments and jurisdictions have their own set of standards. Mostly because the circumstances can be radically different from one case to another. Age, naturally, is an essential factor. A missing five-year-old is far more urgent than an angry seventeen-year-old hiding out from her parents. The mental health of the subject is critical for obvious reasons. Other health-related questions are equally important, with a wide range of physical and psychological issues playing a role. In the case of Bill Bent, age, mental health and physical capacity all have a limited role as possible factors. However, from what I have learned so far, Bent has a pretty bad temper. Plus, a likely drinking problem, and he's intensely disliked by his spouse. On the other hand, when it comes to Bent being disliked, that could be said about hundreds of other individuals within a twenty-mile radius of where we're sitting."

"That daily radio show of Bent's irritates a lot of people," Rob added to Eddie's thought.

"And God knows how many listeners of KLIB would be delighted to see Bill Bent tied to a rock and dropped in the bay," Holly added with a mischievous smile.

"Judging by that twinkle in your eye," Eddie observed, "I guess I should put you on my list of possible suspects."

"Eddie, I'm just teasing. I mean Bent deserves a bang over the head with an iron skillet, but I don't think I'd go so far as to drop him in the bay. Well, maybe just a quick cold dip to put a good scare into him."

"What about a robbery or some other violent act?" Rob

asked. "If the theory that Beverly has is correct and he went off fishing somewhere, he might have been a crime victim."

"Agreed. That's why I already checked usage on Bent's credit cards. Last time one of his cards was used was the evening before he vanished. It was at a bar that both of you know."

"Which one?" Holly asked.

"The Silver Peso, up in Larkspur. Nothing about that is unusual. Beverly tells me he's a regular up there."

"Wow, the good old Silver Peso," Rob said with a faraway look. "Larkspur's version of Smitty's. Eddie, you and I took a few dates there in our time, after a Saturday night movie at The Lark Theater."

"No posh spots for you two," Holly said, shaking her head.

"It's about the booze, and the poor lighting," Eddie suggested with a smile as he gave Rob a light punch to the arm.

"You learn anything else from his credit card, or should I say cards?" Rob asked.

"Nope. Just that there has been no use. Which in itself is concerning since it's not his normal pattern of behavior. I'm sure there were times he used cash, but he was certainly not shy about using his credit cards. Over the last couple of months, he used at least one of his two cards just about every day. So, either he's out of commission, or he's..."

"Dead?" Holly asked, nearly chocking on the last of her martini.

"That's one possibility, the other is that he knows cards leave a record of your whereabouts, so he might be using cash. And for lodging, he could be staying with a friend, or he paid in cash for a fishing cabin up in God knows where."

"But since his cards haven't been used the last several

days, he might be at the bottom of the bay," Holly suggested with the hint of a smile.

"Am I the only one who finds it disturbing when Holly appears excited by the possibility that someone has been murdered and their body dumped in the bay?" Eddie asked.

"Not at all," Rob responded. "It is unsettling, but she's the best associate editor any community weekly could hope to find."

"So, you're hoping that if this turns into a murder investigation, Holly is not the one who takes the rap?" Eddie asked.

"Exactly, pal."

"Hey, wait a minute. Isn't there a chance that he took too many pills, got into bed, and never woke back up?" Holly asked.

"You're suggesting that he's home alone, and his spirit has gone to that great radio station in the sky?" Eddie asked.

"Sure," Holly replied. "Why not?"

"It's not impossible, but unlikely. Next week I'm going to invite Beverly to go with me to her house. I could get a court order, but Bent has been missing a relatively short period and remember, as an adult of supposedly sound mind, you have a right to vanish without having the law bust into your house to see if you're lying dead in the living room. Even the British, with cameras on every street, have not suggested a camera be placed inside of every home."

"I suppose," Holly said grudgingly.

"Bill Bent would have to be eighty-something or have a known impairment, for people walking into his home to check up on him. He's not a fugitive from the law, Holly. People do have a right to vanish from their workplace, home, etcetera without being the subject of a manhunt."

"The question, of course," Rob said, "is did he choose to disappear? Or did someone make him disappear?"

"That's it in a nutshell. Right now, all I can do is snoop around and hopefully learn more about the man's life when he's off the air. And Holly, let me know if you hear anything from Beverly that you think I should check out."

"I'm on it, Copper."

"I'm not sure if that's reassuring or troubling."

"Trust me, Eddie," Rob said. "When it comes to Holly, it's a little bit of both."

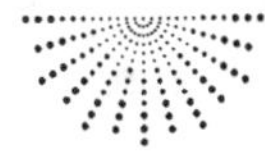

CHAPTER SIXTEEN

Eddie knew the disappearance of Bill Bent could resolve itself at any moment or remain an unsolved mystery for years to come.

As with any missing person, the chance of Bent vanishing and not being found increased with each passing day. Of the approximately 50,000 adults reported missing in America each year, only a fraction of one percent remained unfound after twelve months. Dead or alive, it was likely that Bent would reappear.

Eddie also knew to keep the ancient Chinese proverb in mind: "The longest journey begins with the first step." His immediate question was, what step to take first?

Beverly's only apparent concern was how Bill's disappearance might impact her ratings. There was little actionable information she provided beyond the notion that Bill might be hidden away in a cabin in an obscure location. If that were correct, he likely rented the cabin using an alias, taking with him little more than a tackle box, a fishing pole, a rifle, a few changes of underwear, and a case of whiskey.

What, if anything, was missing from the Bent home would have to remain a mystery until Beverly took Eddie into the house. A preferable route for Eddie to take at a time when a court-approved search of the premises, with no evidence of foul play, was premature.

Eddie hoped that Barney Benson, Bill's radio sidekick for the past seven years, might have something of value to contribute. Just one added piece to the puzzle could prove invaluable. Eddie arranged to meet him in San Francisco on Tuesday.

Benson greeted Eddie with a smile in the radio station's lobby, which was on the twenty-third floor of an office building located near San Francisco's Union Square.

Before Eddie began, Barney, a man who looked like he enjoyed three big meals a day, asked, "Would you mind if we ate while we talked? I had breakfast an hour before going on at seven, and by now, I'm starved."

"Sure," Eddie said. "I had an egg and a piece of toast around seven this morning, I'm pretty hungry too."

Barney, still holding onto Eddie's hand after shaking it, patted him on the arm and said, "Follow me, there's a good place nearby."

They headed out of the building and went just a block and a half up Post Street to the corner of Taylor, where they walked into the Honey, Honey Café. The waitress reminded Eddie a little bit of Gail back at Smitty's, with an equally warm smile and a relaxed, welcoming manner.

"Good morning darling," Barney said as he gave her a kiss

on the cheek and declared, "This is my pal, Eddie Austin. He's a cop, so be on your best behavior, Doris."

"I'm always on my best behavior, Barney," she said with a laugh, as she led them to a corner table where they sat opposite each other.

"Sweetheart, we're starved, so I'm going to have my usual." Eddie took a quick look at the menu, thought for just a moment, and then opted for the grilled chicken sandwich on sourdough bread.

"Black coffee," both men said simultaneously.

"Now, how can I help you, Detective Austin?"

"Eddie, please."

"And call me Barney."

"I spoke to Beverly Bent on Friday afternoon. She said this isn't the first time Bill has gone AWOL."

"Beverly's right. But this is longer than any of his previous disappearing acts."

"She told me that, as well. Why would Bent vanish in the first place? Even if it was only two or three days?"

"Good question! All I can tell you is Bill is a very talented guy. He's faster thinking on air than anyone I've ever worked with, and I've worked with a lot of talented folks. Remember, we're doing a show over a three-hour time slot, five days a week. Even when you take out time for news, weather, and advertising, that's still a lot of banter. And when it comes to the gift of gab, I'd put Bill up against anyone. On the downside, Bill can be a real pain in the neck. But in the radio business, great people with rotten ratings aren't nearly as appreciated as difficult but talented people with great ratings."

"So, it's all about audience size?" Eddie asked, suspecting he already knew the answer.

"Ratings and advertising revenues are in lockstep. If advertising dollars are rolling in, station managers will suppress a lot of frustration and put up with a great deal of nonsense. Few guys I've known during my three decades in broadcasting can stir up more attention than Bill Bent. Trust me, KBUD doesn't pay him a big salary because they think he's a swell guy. In fact, he's far from it."

"Tough guy to work with?"

"I'm not looking to cry you a river, but Bill's not the guy you want to show up if you're drowning."

"He can't swim?" Eddie asked with a half-smile.

"Oh, he can swim, I just don't think he'd want to get himself soaking wet."

"How long have you guys worked together?"

"Seven years, although working with Bill makes that seem a lot longer."

"I'm getting the feeling he's less than a joy to work with."

"You've got that right, pal," Barney said with a short laugh. "But Get Bent has been a good steady paycheck for me. Anyone who has been in radio for five years or more knows if you're making good money, and management likes what you're doing, just keep giving more of the same. It's like any other job in show business: If the customers keep filling the seats, or in radio parlance, tuning in, you're golden. When they stop listening, it's just a matter of time before your show gets dumped. A successful show like Get Bent that keeps chugging along year after year, that's a real blessing. The bottom line, management cuts Bill a lot of slack."

"What do you think about Bill and Beverly's on-air feud?"

"Another bump for our ratings. A big bump, in fact. That's really all I need to know. KBUD's owners were very pleased with our numbers before this Battling Bents business got going. Recently, they've been over the moon. Without Bill, those big audience numbers are going to start sliding. Our ratings were strong before Beverly and KLIB. Still, management was very pleased with the additional print and broadcast coverage we were getting. It helped the ratings for all of KBUD's lineup. Right now, Bill can do no wrong. That includes going AWOL."

"What I've been wondering is if one of KLIB's listeners took matters into his or her own hands and decided to take Bill off the air permanently."

"That's always a possibility. An irate listener has been known on rare occasions to silence an on-air personality. You know better than I that men corner the market when it comes to gun violence. On the other hand, it was just two blocks from where we're sitting right now, outside the St. Francis Hotel, where Sara Jane Moore fired a shot at President Ford and missed him by inches. That was back in 1975. Amazingly, a few weeks before Moore, there was an attempt on Ford's life up in Sacramento, by Lynette 'Squeaky' Fromme. I'm still not sure what Ford did to stir up that beehive. Coincidental, I suppose, but amazing nonetheless."

"That was a little before my time," Eddie said.

"Tell me about it, I was in middle school!"

"My parents weren't dating yet!" Eddie said as both men laughed.

"Barney, what do you think about Bill's disappearance? Is he off in the wilderness for whatever reason certain people feel the need to run away, or do you think he's been harmed, or worse?"

"Worse? As in dead?"

"As long as he doesn't reappear, you can't discount that possibility."

"It's hard for me to imagine Bill being gone for good."

"Why is that?"

"Because I've always thought of Bill living a charmed life. I mean, he's always been a bit crazy. Funny as hell, and a real presence on-air, but frankly, I never knew how Beverly put up with him."

"You mean because of the way he talked about women?"

"That's one reason. But I'm sure there were other reasons as well."

"Such as?"

"Hard for me to say. I suppose Bill's sarcasm about relationships was an outlet for a good deal of pent up anger. In other words, he didn't strike me as someone any woman could live with for a long time. I can't imagine too many women who would want to trade places with Beverly Bent. During the time this sniping between our show and Baker and Bent has been going on, there have been moments where I thought the bulging artery in Bill's neck was going to pop."

"So, he got pretty ticked over this whole KLIB thing."

"Absolutely. Anyone who thinks this was just a setup between Bill and Beverly to pump up ratings is off the mark. Bill thought Beverly stabbed him in the back. Joining KLIB and accepting an on-air slot without his knowing anything about it? Wow, you should have seen him the morning we were on the air and I asked him about Beverly doing a morning show of her own."

"Pretty ticked-off?"

"Let's just say I wouldn't want to be Beverly when Bill got home that night. Yikes!"

"I think she assumed as much," Eddie explained as Doris came over and topped off their coffee.

"So, you really think something may have happened to Bill? I mean, like he no longer walks among the living?"

"It's certainly possible. If he had been kidnapped, we likely would have received a ransom demand by now. And if he's alive, he certainly has gone to great lengths to hide the fact. No phone activity on his cell, no use of his bank cards, etcetera. Let's just say all the things that alert us in law enforcement that an individual is alive or that someone else has assumed their identity."

"Really?" Barney said with apparent surprise, leaving Eddie to conclude that this was a possibility Bent's co-host had chosen to ignore.

"Of course, there's a chance he's off playing rebel without a cause."

"I'm assuming you're telling me what you know as of today."

"Correct."

"I mean, if your department has any hard evidence to suspect foul play, you would tell me."

"I'm being straight with you, Barney. The guy has vanished from the radar. The case was just assigned to me Friday morning. There's a chance I'll know more tomorrow, or by the end of this week, than I know today. But so far, we've got zip. No ransom notes, no anonymous threats. He could be fishing in Wyoming or, I hate to say it…"

"Or…?"

"Sleeping near the sea lions by Pier 39 or buried in a thousand places around the Bay Area. As of this moment, I know the singular fact you know, Bill Bent is missing. If you don't want to be tracked in the digital age, using cash and a burner phone is essential, and there's a chance he's doing that."

"I'm not looking to vanish," Barney said with a smile. "But if I was, I understand why that would be essential."

"On the other hand, if someone wanted you to disappear, they're likely going to bury you along with your phone and credit cards. Only a petty thief or a total nut is going to kill someone and then use their credit cards to go on a shopping spree."

"None of this sounds promising for my future at KBUD."

"Is that how it works, the top star vanishes, and you get shown the door?"

"Pretty much. Loyalty means zip in broadcasting. I was the perfect foil for Bent because I could play the avuncular, kooky sidekick. You know, laugh at all the right times, mitigate Bill's occasional over the top statements. But hosting a three-hour morning drive-time show in one of the country's top markets on my own? I'm not that guy. It's like any other showbiz gig that features a lead character, and a co-host. Lose the star, and the sidekick's days are numbered."

"Would you say Bill got along with the station's staff?"

"You mean from the janitor to the general manager?"

"Well, let's just say the people he was in daily contact with."

"I think so. Nick Reade, the station's GM, and Bill knocked heads frequently, but that's not unusual in this business. The general manager runs the ship, and the station's on-air talent never appreciate when any GM has to reel them in for one of a dozen reasons. The clerical, technical, and support staff employees pretty much do as they're told. Managing on-air talent, however, can be like herding cats. They're going to hiss at the boss now and then, but once they've said their peace, they go back to doing the jobs they're paid well to do."

"Who at the station reviews emails and snail mail from listeners? What I'm wondering about is how much fan mail and how much hate mail Bill received?"

"When you've got our ratings, you get lots of mail. I hope, for your sake, Bill turns up before you have to dive into our mailbag. Ever since the Battling Bents caught on with other talk and news outlets, the emails and snail mail have jumped sky-high. You might need a small army to go through all that material."

"I'm guessing with the anti-feminist rhetoric that Bill has become famous for, his detractors can get pretty hot."

"True that," Barney said with a short laugh.

"Any death threats?"

"The last I heard, Bill averages three or more threats per week."

"Do you hand any of those over to the SFPD?"

"You'd have to ask Reade. He might have forwarded some of the more ominous-sounding letters. I don't think the SFPD would do much about it."

"You're right in thinking their reaction, or lack thereof can be inconsistent. Busy and short staffed is not conducive to checking out angry fans and finding out if they actually present a risk, or it's someone just blowing off steam. Threats, however, suggesting bodily harm made by phone or sent in an email under California's penal code can lead to the sender being placed in a county jail for up to one year. There's additional criminal exposure on a federal level when threats are sent through the US postal service."

"I get it, Eddie. But when you're on the air five days a week, and particularly when you do a show like Bill and I have been doing, you get in the habit of pushing nastygrams aside. If one out of ten of those letter writers acted on their threats, bodies would be showing up like this was a war zone."

"Understandable, but just because you, Bill, or the station's management choose to look the other way, has nothing to do with the intention of the writer to cause actual harm. Or, the need for law enforcement, particularly in a case like this, to follow up."

"I appreciate what you're saying, Eddie. But I've been doing radio long enough to see all kinds of screwy listeners. A couple of years ago, one guy threatened to kill our morning weather guy because his clear skies forecast for a Saturday turned into a late afternoon downpour. That passing storm ruined his kid's outdoor birthday party."

"You're joking, right?"

"God's honest truth. When you deal with the public as much as I do, you get a lot of great feedback and support. But a small number of people have a nasty habit of writing to express their hope that you step out in front of a downhill cable car that's lost its brakes. People are generally unaware of this, but most broadcast stations have locked offices and studio doors and one or more security persons, in or out of uniform, on duty twenty-four seven. What we do may sound like fun and games to most listeners. But there is a dark side to broadcasting that people, in and out of the business, don't like to think about."

"A lot more dangerous than the casual, everyday listener would ever imagine."

"Trust me, pal, there are times in broadcasting where it can get downright scary! For us, bag and ID security checks are not a post-9/11 thing; they go back decades."

The early stage of the Bent investigation was as frustrating as Eddie imagined it would be. He placed a call to KBUD's GM, Nick Reade, to ask about any threats received in the last two months.

"You're right in thinking that Bill got more than his share of 'Nastygrams,' as I like to call them," Reade responded.

"When I spoke with Barney Benson, he wasn't certain if you held on to any of the more, let's just say, disturbing letters."

"You mean letters that make a direct threat of harm?"

"Absolutely! Given the fact Bill has been missing for over a week now, we have to consider he may have been abducted, harmed, or both."

"It's a possibility that we've been trying to put out of our minds. You do know Bill has gone AWOL in the past."

"I do. I'm sure for the station and its owners that's a topic of concern. From a law enforcement standpoint, someone like Bill, who is viewed as a mentally competent adult, has every right to go where he wants to and do whatever he pleases. He can take off for a mountaintop in Tibet to meditate with his favorite guru. He needs no one's permission or to share his plans with his employer, family, or friends. That said, it still falls to law enforcement to determine if a crime has been committed in connection with a disappearance. Therefore, an obvious reason to investigate exists. Additionally, all the means we have of tracking an individual's activity, cell phone usage, bank or credit card activity, informs us that Bill is completely off the radar. The explanation for his disappearance is not apparent in any notes or comments he made that we have found."

"I follow," Reade said, realizing that his casual behavior

regarding Bent's vanishing act was no longer a private matter. "Bill has exhibited erratic behavior in the past, so forgive my skepticism."

"I do, sir. And I hope I'm on the wrong track in thinking that he may have been harmed. But the possibility of something nefarious increases every day he is missing. If KBUD has received threats made through the postal service, or captured in emails, or detailed in phone records, it would be helpful if we could review those materials."

"I hear you, detective. When and where can I get back to you?"

"I'll call you back to see what you've located. Please tell your support staff, if they're aware of any threats, I'd like the opportunity to contact these individuals in person or by phone."

"Let me look into it over the next couple of days, and I'll see what I find." With that, Reade clicked off.

That guy's not making my job any easier, Eddie thought. Perhaps he's sitting on something he's not anxious to share. Or maybe he's just accustomed to giving people a hard time.

CHAPTER SEVENTEEN

The next morning, Eddie was at the offices of KLIB for an eleven o'clock meeting with Tom Joseph, followed by a noon lunch with Beverly.

Tom, punctual as always, greeted Eddie in the station's lobby and walked him back to his office. The moment they sat down, Tom asked what had been on his mind for several days: "Any new developments in the search for Bill Bent?"

"Not really, I'm sorry to say. It's still early, but for right now, I have many more questions than answers."

"It seems strange that someone so well-known and with such a large fan base can simply vanish."

"Unfortunately, Bill Bent also had a sizable group of detractors," Eddie said with a half-smile.

"Many of those detractors are likely KLIB listeners."

"You're probably right about that. Yesterday, I interviewed Barney Benson, later I talked by phone with the station's GM, Nick Reade."

"I know Nick. We both started in the business at the same

time as college students majoring in broadcast. We were doing internships at KCBS Radio in San Francisco."

"I'll catch up on the news by tuning into that station when I'm sitting in traffic."

"They run a tight ship. It's where I learned that getting your facts right or wrong can make or break your station's reputation."

"Nick didn't seem too pleased when I asked him to take a look through KBUD's letters over the past month to see how many listeners had strong objections to Bill's on-air work."

"Do you think Bill might have been the victim of a crazed listener?"

"At this point, I'd call it an aspect of the broader investigation. I can't ignore the possibility of a connection. Bent vanished over a week ago, and the case was handed to me last Friday. So far, I've found nothing. On a couple of occasions, Bill went missing for a few days when he was burned out, or on an extended drinking binge, or simply in a foul mood. But a disappearing act of this length, nine days as of today, is something new. At this point, there's a good chance this is not a stunt. One or more individuals may have caused Bent to vanish."

"I imagine it looks more ominous with each passing day."

"Absolutely," Eddie said as he again shared the information that there was no financial, text, or voice communication that evidenced activity by Bent.

"I know Bent was proud of going, as he would say, off the grid. But I can't set aside the possibility that someone, somewhere, wanted Bent to go on a permanent hiatus."

"There's certainly reason to think that's a real possibility, although it would be pretty disappointing to both KBUD and to us. I'm sure that sounds greedy on my part. But I'm certain Nick Reade feels the same. This whole Battling Bents thing has been a ratings bonanza."

"I want to ask you to do the same thing I asked Nick Reade to do. Assign one of your staff to review letters and e-mails starting three weeks ago, which would be a couple of weeks before Bent went missing. I want to see if you come across any threats against him or his sidekick Benson that are of a specific nature. I don't mean a fan of Beverly and Betsy's show complaining that Bent is a terrible person, I'm looking for something a good deal more pointed than that. Someone suggesting our world would be a better place if Bill Bent were not in it. I'm thinking of someone perhaps suggesting that Bent will soon be, or is now, off the air for good."

"There might be several letters of interest, detective. Honestly, I never fully appreciated how unpopular Beverly's husband was with our listeners until this Battling Bents thing got going. There could be a multitude of writers who wanted Bent taken off the air as opposed to being dumped in the bay."

"I'm aware of that. I might follow-up on a dozen letters or more that lead nowhere. On the other hand, if Bent was the victim of a fan who wanted him gone for good, I should follow that now, rather than wait a month and allow the trail to go colder than it might already be."

"I'll put two of my clerical staff on this. In a day or two, we should have some pretty solid idea of what has been said regarding the elusive Mr. Bent."

"Thank you, Mr. Joseph."

"Tom, please."

"Could you give me a little advice about the potential for a crazed fan?"

"Sure, what would you like to know?"

"How common are threatening letters in the broadcast business?"

"That has a lot to do with your format. For example, current events, talk, and opinion formats similar to KBUD and KLIB, are going to get hit a lot harder than classic rock. Although every station, regardless of format, can have its own set of troubled listeners. When you're in front of the public regularly in print, on radio or television, things can get scary at times. Bent stirred up strong emotions, and that amps up the crazies more than a guy playing easy listening and promoting free public dental clinics. When we made the decision to specifically target what Bent was saying, we probably ratcheted up the heat a good deal. I know given the fact that both our fan mail and our hate mail spiked immediately after Betsy and Beverly started their show. But from my earliest work in radio, I learned that hate mail is simply a part of this business. Even at an all-news format, like KCBS, you'll have certain listeners mad as hell about something you said on air."

"Barney Benson told me that KBUD's morning weather guy got a death threat from a listener because he called for sunshine on the day of an outdoor birthday party for his five-year-old. Unfortunately, the party got rained out."

"That doesn't surprise me. Although threatening the weather guy or gal is way up on the crazy listener scale," Tom said with a smile and a shake of his head.

"I suppose it's the broadcast version of good news, bad news," Eddie said, considering the harsh reality of dealing with a vast, mostly unknown universe of listeners. "Stirring things up like Beverly and Bill did makes for great ratings. On the other hand, it can be like poking at a wasp's nest. Lots of excitement, but it can come at a steep price."

"Exactly! In this business, you live and die by your ratings. One of the best ways to boost your ratings is to shake things up with a spat between on-air talent."

"Beverly's and Bill's opposite views on love and marriage and the role of men and women in today's world must have stirred the pot big time."

"Our station's ratings have never been so good," Tom said proudly. "I just hope some listener isn't the reason the Battling Bents might have come to an unexpected end."

Beverly and Eddie sat down at a corner table for lunch at Grazie, a Novato family restaurant on nearby Grant Avenue. One of Beverly's, "happy discoveries," in the neighborhood surrounding her new residence.

Both ordered Portabella Parmesan Paninis and iced teas.

"I assume there's no news regarding Bill."

"None," Eddie said with a grimace. "As I told Sharon this morning, it's like he vanished into thin air."

Eddie caught Beverly up on the last few days of his investigation. He acknowledged that Bill might have established a separate identity and opened new savings and checking accounts using a fake driver's license. "There's also a chance that he made a cash purchase of one or more burner phones, a common practice for people who want to go off the grid."

"Eddie, as we discussed last week, Bill's vanished briefly in the past, but never anything like this." She spoke in a soft voice hoping not to be overheard. Eddie thought that unlikely, given the fact that the restaurant was less than half-filled.

"Plus, Bill seemed to be having the time of his life bickering with Betsy and me over the air five days a week. It seems very out of character for Bill to walk away from a fight. Of course, the longer I knew Bill, the more erratic his behavior became. So, who knows? Perhaps he thinks this vanishing act is a good way to bring even more attention to our very public spat."

Eddie shrugged and decided not to speculate on Bill's motive for vanishing. "When I last asked if you had gone back to your home in Corte Madera, you told me you had not. Is that still the case?"

"Yes, I'm sorry to say. I know it must sound odd my staying away from the place, particularly when there are countless things I'd like to take from the house. Most of my clothing is still there, and a bunch of things that would make my life easier. You know I moved into a new place right near here in Novato. It's a cozy one-bedroom apartment. I already love the place. I suppose the best part is knowing I'm not coming home to Bill."

"Holly told me you found a place when I saw her and Rob last Friday. They've all been blown away, including Sharon, of course, by the great job you've been doing at KLIB."

"It's nice to know that I have a lot of people rooting for me."

"That you do, Beverly," Eddie said with a smile.

"As far as the house is concerned, I was hesitant to go there because, as you can imagine, I didn't want to run into

Bill. Now, with him vanishing, I've been concerned that I'd run into a neighbor who might think my showing up after such a long absence could mean something nefarious. To be honest, Eddie, my life has been going so well since I walked away from Bill and our marriage that I don't want to do anything to screw things up."

"Perfectly understandable! I have a suggestion that could help both of us."

"What's that?"

"Meet me tomorrow down at the Corte Madera house any time after your show. If you can make that work."

"I can, I'll be done with the show by ten and probably need two hours or so to go over program prep with Betsy for the following morning's show. I'll check in with you when we're done. That should be sometime around noon?"

"That would be fine. As your guest, I can come in, take a look around the house, while you collect some of your things."

"It would be such a relief to have you with me. I know there's very little chance I'll run into Bill, but it would be just my luck after all these days if he reappeared on the one day I come to collect my things."

"Besides clothes and other personal items, aren't there some pieces of furniture and such you're going to want to take for your new place?"

"With the success of my show I can afford new pieces; I've already done some of that shopping. Plus, Eddie, the Corte Madera house was of, by, and for Bill. You know the term 'man cave?' Well, that describes the home we shared. From an enormous California king bed, which could comfortably sleep four, to the living room, which Bill turned into his sanctuary for all sports, all the time! I'm embarrassed to say there's very little of me in that home. I suppose that's my fault, but arguing endlessly with Bill is exhausting. If there is one thing he does well, it's wearing people down."

"Wow, Sharon would have tossed me out a long time ago if I wanted to, let's just say 'man-size' our house. I'm not too sure I'd like it either. I don't want to press, but I have to ask: Why did you let him get away with all that? Speaking as just one man, I like what a woman's touch brings to a home. If all you want is a man cave, don't marry, just date!"

Beverly gave a half-smile. "Believe me, I've asked myself that countless times. I think for Bill, it has more to do with domination than anything else. He takes that king of the castle routine to ridiculous extremes. But he's managed to make a living off of it. You have to give him credit for that."

After a few moments of thought, Beverly continued.

"I think most little girls, for good or bad, learn a lot from their moms. My father was a king of the castle type. What-ever he decreed was how it was going to be. My allowing Bill to have his way regarding nearly every aspect of our shared lives came from my not knowing any better. I don't hold it against her. For all I know, my mom's mom was the same way. My maternal grandmother died when I was two, so I have no memories of her at all.

"Well, you've changed your life, and you've done it dramatically."

"Perhaps a little too dramatic, given Bill's vanishing act."

"Is there a chance he vanished to give you a scare? I realize that would be childish, but from what I've learned about Bill, he's not above acting out as Sharon and I some-times see with our little Aaron."

"Agreed!" Beverly replied with a smile that quickly disappeared. "I can't say with any certainty that he's doing this to impress me, scare me, or both."

After a few moments of silence, Beverly asked, "Can a person be in legal jeopardy for vanishing like this?"

"Yes, if they made a false police report, or insurance claim, while living under an alias, or used a co-conspirator to do that. Short of that, no law says you can't go off and live in a cave and cut off communication with the outside world."

"Seems like there should be."

"As much as we talk about crowded prisons, Bev, if we started locking up people for acting irresponsibly, prison populations would triple overnight."

"Gosh, I suppose you're right."

"If you want to vanish, that's your call. But that leads me to a question: Do you think Bill might have hated his life and wanted to go off somewhere to reinvent himself?"

"I really did think that for the first few days he was gone. Now I don't."

"Do you have any theories as to what he might have done, where he could be hiding? Is there a chance, for example, that he went back home to Kingman, Arizona?"

"I doubt that! From what I could tell, he had about as good a relationship with his dad as he had with me. I'm not sure who, if anyone, is actually close to Bill."

"Not even his sidekick, Barney Benson?"

"I never once heard Bill say a kind word about Barney. I think he thought of Barney as a prop. Anytime Barney was too funny or too poignant, Bill was not pleased."

"When I interviewed him, Barney sounded like without Bill he would soon be shown the door by management. A sideshow with no main attraction, was how he explained it."

"Sounds to me like Barney's selling himself short. He's got a lot of fans."

"Well, if your initial thought was right that Bill might be hiding out at some fishing cabin, northeast of Mount Shasta, he's pulled off a fine disappearing act."

"He considers roughing it to be part of his Wild Bill persona. If it causes others to worry, they should get over it and mind their own business."

"Beverly, this really doesn't feel like a stunt to me."

"What's your best guess?"

"I'm sorry to say this, but my guess is that someone wanted Bill permanently off the air."

"I wish that would upset me. But, when I consider the number of times I thought of banging him over the head with one of those baseball bats from his Giants memorabilia collection, it would be dishonest. I suppose that's the bitterness that comes from living ten years under his thumb. Bill made doing a morning radio show sound like a Herculean task. Now that I'm doing one of my own, I would agree it's demanding, but it's also a lot of fun. I get to say what's on my mind, and if you've got a great co-host, like a Barney or a Betsy, three hours can go by faster than you ever imagined."

"Barney gave me the impression that his only true regret if Bill never reappeared would be the loss of a lucrative gig. His boss, Nick Reade, seems concerned only by a potential drop in the station's ratings. I asked if he would get some staff to comb through recent listener letters to see what threats, if any, have been made against Bill. Well, you would think I asked him to go outside and dig a ditch. Let's just say he didn't seem overly anxious to lift a finger to help in my investigation."

"Eddie, I know it can be hard to believe, but Bill was not a guy a lot of people cared about. They loved the fact that his show was so successful and that his ratings made the station a lot of money from advertising. But it was what you'd call a transactional relationship. Give this, in return for that. Nothing more. For all his on-air banter, when it came to Bill as a human being, a responsible member of society, there truly was no there, there."

CHAPTER EIGHTEEN

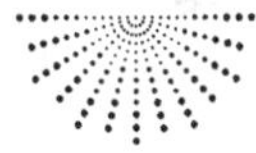

The following afternoon, Eddie was sitting in his car across the street from the house that Beverly and Bill shared for nearly ten years. He was enjoying a few moments of quiet on a sunny, mild day, when he saw Beverly park in her driveway, get out, and start walking toward him.

Eddie stepped out, shook Beverly's hand, and asked, "Are you ready to do this?"

"Ready as I'll ever be," Beverly shrugged as she gave a forced smile, attempting to disguise her discomfort. "I hope Bill didn't change the front door locks."

"If he did, you have every right to call a locksmith and get another lock installed. If your husband ever shows up, one day you might be battling over a hundred and one things in court. Still, for now, in the eyes of the law, you're just a couple who has had something less than a happy union. You are both entitled to unfettered access to your residence until such time as a judge says otherwise."

To her great relief, the deadbolt lock on the front door worked as it always had.

"No change of locks," Beverly said, relieved despite Eddie's assurances that she need not be concerned about entering her own home.

"Maybe Bill had more sense than to change the locks," Eddie said while silently wondering if Bent was alive to do that.

Inside, Eddie thought, what is that awful smell? I hope Holly's suspicion about Bent killing himself wasn't correct, he thought. If she's right, I'll never hear the end of it!

"Wow, let's open some windows and air this place out," Beverly said instantly. "Bill liked to smoke cigars while watching sports. I imagine he really went to town in my absence. They smell the way I imagine a dead body would smell after a week."

"One of my grandfathers was a chain smoker. He died of lung cancer. I've never been a fan of smoking anything other than a turkey at Thanksgiving."

"Lucky Sharon. I'd complain now and then; Bill would tell me that his cigar was going to last an hour. He suggested I go off somewhere and shop until he was finished. I often did just that. I'd drive down to Town Center and eventually wander over to Nordstrom's at The Village. I'd laugh to myself when I thought how much one of those cigars actually cost Bill."

"Did you always leave the house when he smoked?"

"Most times, I would camp out in my bedroom and read, turn up the air conditioner and light a scented candle. Life with Bill was a joy in countless ways."

Eddie smiled and chose to keep his next comment to himself.

Beverly went into the kitchen and reached under the sink to pull out a box of large, heavy-duty, black trash bags. She moved quickly through the bathroom, gathering up hair and makeup products, then onto the bedroom for clothing, shoes, and other items. "I don't know when I'll be back, so I should grab a lot of this stuff now," she called out to Eddie, who had already begun roaming about the house.

Beverly either had no interest in Eddie's snooping or was too busy to pay any attention. Eddie wandered into one of the home's three bedrooms that appeared to serve as Bill's den. He sat down in a large, red leather swivel chair that was placed behind an equally impressive mahogany desk.

"Beverly, do you mind if I poke around inside Bill's desk? I'm hoping to find something that could give us a clue as to where he might have gone."

After a few moments, Beverly stuck her head in and said, "Happy hunting, Eddie. I'm so grateful you suggested this. I guess I didn't want to think about how much stuff I had left here. I'm having a great time collecting it all, so take as much time as you need."

"Will do," Eddie said, happy for the chance to take a dive into Bent's private world.

In the desk's center draw he found a collection of crumpled cocktail napkins. The first one he unfolded read, "Is she really being honest with you?" Another, "Three ways to tell she's playing you for a fool," scribbled on a cocktail napkin from a San Francisco strip club. On a third scrap of paper Bent had written, "The enemy within. Taking back control of your home and your life." Digging a little deeper, pushing scattered items such as Giants and Forty Niners' ticket stubs aside, Eddie found two more crumbled cocktail napkins. One from the Silver Peso read, "When, if ever, are you the king of your castle?" The other from The Two AM Club in Mill Valley read, "Trust a wife or girlfriend at your own peril. Why men so often get burned in relationships."

Wow, Eddie thought, this guy was an endless stream of negative thoughts about marriage and relationships. It's amazing that he and Beverly lasted ten years!

Perhaps Bent needed "the old ball and chain," as he often referred to Beverly on the air, as a prop for his riffs on being a "long-suffering husband." His message lost a great deal of currency if he were single or divorced.

From what Eddie could see looking through a pile of Bent's program notes, he would have been perfectly happy to return to a time when women were denied the right to vote. Better still, only leave home when accompanied by a father, brother, or husband.

Clearly, Bent was born into the wrong century or the wrong part of the world. Eddie dug deeper, hoping to find something that might provide a clue regarding his disappearance.

All four of the drawers of Bent's oversized desk contained scraps of paper many with scribbled notes. This guy wasn't just a little nutty on-air, Eddie thought. He was, "Cuckoo bananas," as Eddie's Uncle Fred was fond of saying.

While interesting, nothing thus far provided a reason for Bent's disappearance. Eddie pulled out the lower left drawer, the only one he had not yet examined.

Blessed with a keen sense of depth perception, he quickly noticed that under loose pages, pay stubs, and restaurant receipts, there was a panel that acted as a false bottom. Clearly, this drawer was less deep than its mirror opposite. Why?

Eddie lifted the loose papers out and stacked them on the

credenza behind him. He then grabbed a silver letter opener and went carefully went around the false bottom until he reached a point where one portion of the wood panel popped loose. A couple more carefully placed pokes, and Eddie lifted the board out.

As opposed to another scattering of loose scraps of paper, he found a collection of four envelopes, apparently personal notes from devoted fans, perhaps lovers, or both. The first card Eddie pulled out was addressed to a PO Box in Corte Madera and had no return address. The envelope was pink with blue and red flowers in the upper left and bottom right corners.

As Eddie suspected, given the fact that it had been hidden, the card was indeed a love note. The letter included a two by three-inch photo of a beautiful brunette, one Eddie guessed to be in her early thirties. Five-plus years younger than Bent.

"Dearest Bill, you are the most wonderful man I have ever met," it began. "Thank you for the beautiful diamond bracelet you gave me last Saturday night. I'm so happy we met. Big hugs and long, slow, sweet kisses! Forever yours, Patricia."

A second card read, "Sweet Bill, our weekend getaway to Post Ranch Inn at Big Sur was the most incredibly romantic experience of my life. The ocean views from our room were unforgettable. Most of all, I loved the view of you waiting for me in that big heart-shaped bathtub. A thousand kisses. Love you more than words can say, Deborah."

From the photo included, Eddie could see that Deborah was a blonde, and like the previous photo, likely five or more years Bent's junior.

There were two more envelopes from different women. They, too, were addressed to the same Corte Madera post office box. Like the first two, they also had no return address.

Eddie didn't take the time to open the others but wrapped each in a blank sheet of paper to protect them from any extraneous fingerprints. After replacing the desk drawer's false bottom panel, Eddie looked for more buried surprises in Bill's man cave. He came up empty. He knew that if the case of the missing radio celebrity continued without resolution or proved to be a criminal act, he would be back in the house for a court-ordered search. For now, however, Eddie was pleased to have uncovered an unknown, and possibly important, aspect of Bent's life.

"Eddie, could you help me carry some bags out to the car?" Beverly called out to him from the master bedroom.

"Of course, whenever you're ready to go, I'm ready as well," he replied.

"I'm ready now."

When they met in the living room, Beverly walked up to him with a smile. "I didn't want to think about how many of my things I had left here. I've been so busy with my show, the new apartment, and most of all trying to put Bill behind me, that I didn't think about how much I had left behind. I can't thank you enough for encouraging me to come here."

"I'm glad you did, and I'm happy I could be of some help."

"Did you find anything that might give you a clue as to where Bill went?"

"Possibly. Like everything else, it will take time to see if it's really of any value. By the way, I assume Bill used a laptop computer."

"Sure. I think mostly to catch up on any games he missed. NBA, NFL, MLB, NHL, the guy was a lot more into sports than he was ever into us as a couple."

"Bill might have used his laptop for more than just sports. Any chance you might know where he kept it?"

"He normally slipped it into his case when heading into work. But I saw where he kept it in his den. Let me take a look, hopefully he left it behind."

Beverly went back into the couple's bedroom and came back a moment later carrying a MacBook covered with decals of local sports teams.

Looks like something a high school kid would have, Eddie thought.

"Take it with you, if you want," Beverly suggested as she thrust it forward.

"I'd like that. Probably little more than a collection of fan and team trivia, but maybe we'll find a clue as to where Bill went."

Eddie's comment passed without notice. In her delight, Beverly appeared to have no interest in any aspect of her husband's disappearance.

After she recruited Eddie's help in moving six black plastic bags out to her car, Beverly pulled him down to kiss him on the check. "Give Sharon my love and tell her I think she married a wonderful guy."

"Will do. Let me know if there's anything else I can do to help."

"Eddie, just tell me one thing."

"Sure."

"Do you think any of us will ever see Bill again?"

"Right now, I'd say your guess is as good as mine."

"How so?"

"Bill, in addition to being what my dad would have called, 'a real piece of work,' is a pretty complicated guy."

"You can say that again. Do you suspect that he was involved with any dangerous people?"

"Honestly, Beverly, I wouldn't venture a guess. But nothing I have come across indicated that he was involved in any such activity. There's still too much I don't know. What I will say is Bill is no ordinary guy."

"You mean because of his celebrity?"

"To an extent, yes, but it goes beyond that. I get the feeling Bill was a risk-taker, in ways most people are not. That can lead to good and bad outcomes. You might say he liked living on the edge. Pushing the limits."

"Have you found examples of that?"

"I'm zeroing in on those facts. Give me a little more time. Maybe I'll have some real answers for you before long."

"Whatever you find, I hope you know how much I appreciate your work. By the way I hope it's not a problem for your boss that you and I know each other?"

"Don't worry about that. In one way or another, everyone knows everyone else in Marin County. This is ground zero for the rule of six degrees of separation."

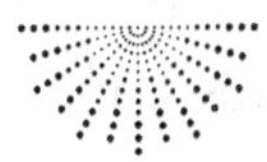

CHAPTER NINETEEN

"What are you up to?" Rob said a moment after seeing Eddie's name pop up on his phone's display.

"What I'm always up to, digging deeper to find the truth."

"That's what I've been doing. Except my digging is to find out if San Anselmo's City Council is playing straight with their voters about the cost overruns on the town's sewer replacement project."

"Wow, well, don't let me keep you from getting to the bottom of that."

"Very funny! So, to what do I owe the pleasure of this call?"

"I need to bounce a few questions off that aging mind of yours, Doctor Watson."

"My noggin is yours for the asking, Sherlock. What's up?"

"The strange world of Bill Bent just got stranger. I want to get your take on what I found and what, if anything, it might mean in connection to his disappearance."

"You're thinking early tomorrow morning, usual time, usual place?"

"Yep. See you at seven at the Bridgeway Café."

After dinner and after Aaron was settled in for the night, Eddie was tempted to share with Sharon the notes he discovered hours earlier in Bent's desk, but he held back. He knew it would be difficult for her not to share such explosive information with Beverly. So, although it was difficult, he kept this new development to himself.

Did this collection of love notes fit into a bigger picture? One that might lead to explaining why Wild Bill disappeared? If he had been engaged in so many affairs, the prospect that Bent was alive likely improved. He and one of his girlfriends could be living nearby or hundreds, if not thousands of miles away.

For all I know, Eddie reasoned, Bent could be on a honeymoon with his second wife somewhere along the French Riviera. It's hard to guess what an eccentric like Bent might be doing or thinking.

Two hours after turning out their bedroom lights, Eddie turned restlessly in bed to the point that Sharon grumbled in a half-sleep state, "Stop tossing and start sleeping."

Early the following morning, Eddie met Rob at the Bridgeway Café. They picked up two sausage and egg sandwiches then crossed over to the opposite side of Princess Street, where they picked up coffees at Starbucks. Crossing back over Princess, they entered Rob's office located on the second floor of an aging Victorian.

After a quick meal and shared thoughts on how Aaron, and Rob's two, Micah and Alice, were all growing like weeds, Eddie said, "I want to share with you four cards I found hidden in Bill Bent's den."

The degree of surprise on Rob's face grew more apparent as he read through each card. Eddie had placed them flat in sealed plastic page protectors in case fingerprints were needed in the future.

Rob repeated a series of "Wows," followed by a shake of his head. He came across references to diamond bracelets, pearl earrings, Big Sur's Post Ranch Inn, and more. The cards, each from a different woman, detailed weekends spent at the Ahwahnee Hotel inside Yosemite National Park; The Hotel Drisco in San Francisco's Pacific Heights neighborhood; and Meadowood Napa Valley, located in the picturesque wine country town of Saint Helena.

"I remember hearing from Sharon that this guy kept Beverly on a relatively tight budget," Eddie said. "Apparently, he was on her case about spending money even though he was well compensated for the success of his radio show."

"Seems like he was a good deal more generous with his girlfriends than his wife," Rob said, bemused equally by Bent's hypocrisy and lavish spending.

"Sharon told me Bent complained about the cost of everything from Beverly getting her hair done to buying new shoes. Of course, if you had seen the bags of clothes, shoes, and God knows what else Beverly carried out of their house yesterday, you'd know that she wasn't deprived."

"Two weeks ago, Sylvia Stokes' column, Tiburon Talk, reported on this wealthy investment banker, who surprised his wife with a weekend getaway to the Post Ranch Inn for their twenty-fifth wedding anniversary. Sylvia made the place sound so wonderful that I was curious about what it cost for a one-night stay."

"High-end stuff, I'm sure," Eddie declared.

"You're right about that. But I thought maybe I could swing it and take Karin down there for our tenth anniversary. Try to guess their average nightly room rate."

"Other than, not cheap, I have no idea. Sharon and I consider a movie at the Sequoia in Mill Valley and having martinis and a plate of pasta at D'Angelo's, to be a mini-vacation."

"Nine-twenty-five per night," Rob said, spitting out each number. "That's just shy of a thousand bucks! And I'm sure with taxes they'd get it over a thousand bucks before you can say flat broke. Most amazing is that's not for the royal suite, that's the going rate. And how about that diamond bracelet? Unless it was fake or stolen, that didn't come cheap."

"Imagine my shock in finding these thank you cards to Bent, aka Don Juan. You have to say one thing, the nickname Wild Bill was well earned."

Rob did a quick online search and scribbled down on a pad the hotels mentioned in the notes. "Get a load of this: the Drisco Hotel, five twenty-five per night; Meadowood, five seventy-five per night; and the Ahwahnee in Yosemite comes in at three-thirty in the offseason to over a thousand in-season. Pretty impressive stuff," Rob said as he handed his quick tabulations to Eddie.

"Geez, Louise! At this point, I don't know if my missing person is buried in an empty lot or relaxing on a yacht off of Catalina Island."

"How do you suppose he's been able to afford all this spending? Some of which had to have happened right under Beverly's nose?" Rob asked as he scratched at the top of his head. A typical reaction Eddie had witnessed whenever his friend was both stunned and amazed.

"One aside, and you're going to love this Robbie boy, each of these cards contained a two by three photo of what I can only assume was the sender. Another equally interesting similarity, each was placed inside an envelope with no return address."

"Were they mailed or hand-delivered?"

"Each was mailed to the same Corte Madera PO Box. Three were postmarked from San Francisco, and one from San Anselmo."

"Dates?"

"Scattered. All within the past eighteen months."

"All relatively close to where Bent lives and works. What did you do with the pictures?"

"I placed a small note on the back of each to connect it to the letter it came with and placed them in an evidence file in my office, which is where I'll put all these cards when I get back to my office."

"What's your next step?"

"I'm going to do a deep dive into Bent's background, finances, etcetera. I'll need to have the department secure the proper court clearances to bring in his bank records, employment records, and so on. That's going to take a while, given that this is only a missing person's investigation.

"I know the guy had a successful show, and he did a lot of advertiser promotional events, so he was earning additional money. This seems, however, to go beyond any of those parameters. If he had unknown sources of income, I certainly want to know more about that. It's especially important to learn if those sources were legit. Potentially, this evidence presents a whole new set of questions."

"I suppose the most important question now, is how do these cards fit into your investigation into Bent's disappearance?"

"At the moment, my theory is pretty simple. It's the same as you would have in a homicide investigation. Think of it in reverse. The less you know, the less chance you have of asking the right questions. Given this collection of love notes, questions are piling up for one simple reason."

"What's that?"

"Bent's world is more complicated than anyone might have first thought. It's hard to say where any of this might lead, but I fully suspect that the deeper I go, the more complex Bent's world will become. Before I stumbled across this collection of cards, I had no idea Bent was competing for a spot in the unfaithful husband's hall of fame."

"That's quite an honor considering the level of competition you have to climb over. Did you think Bent was playing off on Beverly before you found these notes?"

"To some extent, yes."

"Why?"

"If you take what Beverly says at face value, it's not a stretch to envision her husband as unfaithful. If he wasn't, why did he make such an effort to push her away? He's not the first guy to treat his wife poorly. Still, very few guys would host a radio program celebrating their disrespectful treatment of their wife."

"If he was so intent on pushing Beverly away, why not divorce her?"

"I don't think dumping his wife fits in with the character Bent plays on his show."

"And that is?"

"Talented, smart, quick-talking, man's man. A guy who needed a ball and chain as a prop so he could play the role of aggrieved husband. The success of Bent's show depends to a large extent on his marriage. I wouldn't be surprised if it provided a solid reason for him to hold on to Beverly. A divorced Wild Bill doesn't pack the same punch as the doggedly faithful husband."

"So, you're saying in the saga of Bill Bent's life, Beverly's value to her husband was the role she played."

"What was it that Shakespeare wrote?"

"'All the world's a stage, and all the men and women merely players; they have their exits and their entrances, and one man in his time plays many parts.'"

"Wow! You know your classics, Rob. I should have been looking over your shoulder during our English Lit finals."

"I thought you were!"

"Nope. It's the Boy Scout in me. I just couldn't bring myself to cheat. Something that doesn't appear to bother our boy Bent ."

"I'm beginning to think Bent is, or was, one seriously creepy guy."

"I'll not argue the point. Right now, my only focus is on why the guy vanished."

"Maybe one of the gals in his harem learned she was not

his one and only, and 'took the news badly,'" Rob said, using air quotes and flashing a mischievous grin.

"Bent was obviously not shy about making requests of them, starting with the suggestion to send him a two by three photograph. I think you would agree that it is too much of a coincidence to believe he did not request these photos in the first place."

"Agreed. It's not an unreasonable request to send your boyfriend a photo. Anyone who listened to Bent's show knew he was married, even if that marriage was presented as an unhappy one. Posting a picture and a love note to a PO Box is a fairly obvious choice for a man attempting to hide affairs from his wife.

"Therefore, he coaxed them into sending a note, and more specifically, a card with a photo included." Rob said as he rocked back in his desk chair and attempted to imagine that conversation. "Some sweet, seemingly innocent suggestion. 'I want to remember this weekend forever,' he might have told them. 'Send me a small photo of you that I can tuck inside my wallet and have you with me always.'"

After a beat, Rob added: "But why, Eddie? Why do that?"

"Beats me, pal. I imagine it was his form of big game hunting. I suppose these cards and photos were like trophies for Bent. Perhaps it's all a part of his contempt for women."

"How so?"

"Well, if you coax them into sending you a note memorializing your time together, maybe that was his way of keeping score."

"Weird stuff, Eddie."

"Trust me, when it comes to spouses misbehaving, I've seen even stranger."

"I suppose there could be more of these notes squirreled away somewhere."

"I know. Looking for more of these love notes is high on my list, but first I have to wait a week or so and see if our Mr. Bent surfaces. If he does, his extramarital affairs are the concern of a private investigator, likely hired by Beverly in their all-but-inevitable divorce proceedings. It's certainly not a police matter. Of course, if Mr. Popularity shows up on a table in the medical examiner's office, these notes and every other scrap of evidence are highly pertinent in a homicide investigation."

After a few moments of silence in which Rob and Eddie tried to imagine a life that didn't remotely resemble their own, a thought occurred to Rob. "All these high-end places he took women to were either nearby or between a one, to two-hour drive from Marin."

"Yeah, and…"

"Well, it makes me think that all these relationships were with women who probably live locally."

"Seems logical. But that violates one of the basic principles of most philandering spouses."

"Not being one," Rob said with a half-smile, "what would that be?"

"It's the principle every male raven follows when his mate is sitting on her eggs."

"Huh?"

"Don't soil the nest."

"I didn't know that."

"Ravens are clever little creatures, Rob. Bottom line, Bent doesn't seem to be overly concerned about fouling the nest. Perhaps, not the least bit concerned."

"It's pretty strange that so much of this was going on right under Beverly's nose. Don't you think she must have suspected something?"

"That's certainly possible, Rob. There's also a real chance she didn't care. Possibly, that's what Bent was hoping to accomplish by feeding his spouse a steady diet of abuse. Push her far enough away that she had no interest in any aspect of his life. Including the why, where, what, when, and who of his occasional weekend getaways."

"Pretty odd couple."

"Certainly not the relationship that Sharon and I have, or you and Karin. But you know what they say about different folks and different strokes."

"Given the relatively close proximity all these hotels have to the Bay Area, I'm guessing one or more of these women either worked at the station or was connected to one of his program's advertisers. As I understand from Karin, Bent frequently did weekend promotions for his program's sponsors."

"Perhaps that provided the extra cash he needed to dazzle these women the way he did," Eddie suggested. "Without a closer look at his financial records, I have no real idea what money he was making above his regular morning show on KBUD. Certainly, it's time for me to take a closer look at the support staff at his station. If I can add a last name to one or more of these women, I'll hopefully get a lot better picture of what Bent was up to."

"You mean besides being a serial philanderer?"

"Exactly. I don't know if there are prizes for being a horrible husband, but this guy deserves to be in the running for first place."

Friday morning, Eddie called KBUD's station manager, Nick Reade. In their earlier conversation, when Eddie requested a staff person look through the station's mail for the three weeks before Bent vanished, Reade was polite but seemingly disinterested.

"We've uncovered additional information about Bill's disappearance that opens new lines of investigation," Eddie began in the hope of catching Reade's attention. "I'm wondering if you've been able to locate any threatening or hostile letters addressed to the station, to Bent, or both."

"I did pass your request along to my personal assistant after we spoke last week. I've not gotten an update from her, but I'll check in with her, and I should be able to give you an update soon. Call me back in a couple of days, and we'll see if my staff came across any letters that might be of interest to you."

Eddie, fully suspecting that Reade was pushing him off, had to let it slide. He could reason and cajole, but without any specifics as to what happened to Bent, there was little he could do besides appealing for cooperation. Later, if there was evidence that Bent was abducted or killed, he would get a court order demanding that all relevant materials be safeguarded and given to the sheriff's department as part of a broader investigation.

"Okay. This is important, Mr. Reade. I'll call back in two days to see what your staff has found." Eddie said as he clicked off. Eddie's unspoken message to Reade was simple: Help out; it could make a critical difference.

While Eddie sat at his desk wondering if Reade and Bent were somehow connected in having affairs with female staff, advertisers, or others, his cellphone vibrated, alerting him to an incoming call.

One word in caps came up on Eddie's screen, "MAX."

"You know that radio guy you've been looking for?" Max said in his typically casual fashion. "I think he was just delivered to my office."

"What do you mean, 'you think?'"

"Eddie, be honest, if your body had been laying around in a heavily wooded open space, night and day for a good number of days, how great do you think you would look?"

"I'll be right over."

"No rush, Eddie. This guy is not going anywhere."

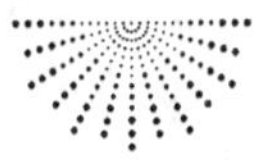

CHAPTER TWENTY

Max Brownstein, the Marin County Medical Examiner, and Eddie were old friends. They both loved the business of crime detection. Both were endlessly curious, and both distrusted politicians, a group that included Marin County's sheriff, Jack Canning.

Eddie was inside the offices of the medical examiner less than fifteen minutes after Max called.

"Have you seen Max?" Eddie asked Doris O'Conner, the operations manager for Max's department.

"Hold on Eddie, he's around here somewhere. I know he was asking if you had arrived just a few minutes ago."

Five minutes later, Max loped casually into the department's reception area and nodded to Eddie to come join him.

"Sorry for the delay in getting to you, call of nature. I had a huge breakfast."

"I didn't know you answered to anyone, no less nature," Eddie responded with a smile.

"The living and the dead are subject to the laws of nature in their own unique ways."

"I won't go there."

"Wise choice, pal," Max responded as he pushed open the swinging door into the examination room.

"Here's your celebrity," Max said matter-of-factly as he walked to the examination table and pulled the sheet down from over the corpse's head to its pelvic bone.

"Yikes! With the possible exception of bodies recovered from the bay, that's as bad a shape as I've seen one."

"Well, speaking of the laws of nature," Max said casually. "I have no idea what Bent looked like before his body spent ten-plus days out in nature, but he's certainly Halloween worthy now."

"I won't argue with you about that. And we're not talking a kid's Halloween party at that. How was he located?"

"He was lying on his back in a wooded area about ten feet below one of the ridge hiking trails up in the Marinwood Lucas Valley Preserve."

"I've been up along there. Some great views, but I haven't been there in years. Who found him?"

"A couple of hikers called him in. It was darn lucky that they spotted him. He was either rolled down into a small gully below the trail, or he was struggling to get up after he was attacked and perhaps fell back. We removed the flannel shirt he was wearing at the time of the attack. With so much flesh already gone, his wounds were not all that obvious at first. But several spots on his blood-soaked shirt provided us with a helpful guide."

"I met this guy a couple of times. He was no movie star, but he looked a damn sight better than this. Any idea what happened?"

"Obviously, the body's in bad shape, but from what I can

tell, he was stabbed once in the gut and then three times in the back."

"How do you suppose that occurred?"

"We know he was on a trail, let's just say, less traveled. It's tranquil up along there. Only locals use them, and only if they're feeling ambitious enough to enjoy a rugged hike."

"I've gone up there a few times," Eddie said. "Great views, but more than a bit out of the way. Any idea at this point as to how the attack unfolded?"

"I can venture a plausible theory. His attacker delivered an initial stab wound to the abdomen. Naturally, the victim clutched the wound and almost certainly dropped to his knees, obviously in pain. It's reasonable to assume that the three stab wounds to the back occurred at that time."

Barney's comment regarding Bill feeling as though Beverly had stabbed him in the back by going on KLIB flashed across Eddie's mind. He could not imagine, however, that Beverly was capable of this level of violence, but professionally he knew this would be the first thought to cross the mind of any other investigator.

"I'm going to try with a couple of instruments to get a closer look and do some radiology on the corpse to see these wounds from every possible angle. With substantial injuries like these, one or more of the wounds to the victim's back almost certainly pieced the heart, lungs, or both. Along with massive blood loss, it would not have taken long before the victim lost consciousness and drifted off on the wings of angels. Blood flow is the magic that keeps us functioning. Lose enough blood, and we simply blink out into the darkness."

"Or in this case, I'm guessing, into Satan's clutches. What

do you suppose happened to the body, Max? It really is in terrible shape."

"From what I can tell, nothing out of the ordinary. We've had some typically warm weather for this time of year. Warm enough to attract a good number of flies, and there's no place they'd rather lay their eggs than on rotting flesh. Eggs to maggots, maggots to flies, that's one part of the circle of life you don't see in any Disney movie."

"Thank you, Mr. Science, for once more giving me a rotten night's sleep."

"Well, you asked, Eddie!"

"Bent was last on the air a week ago this past Monday, so, if he was attacked that afternoon, he was out there for approximately eleven days. His wife didn't live with him at the time he vanished, there's no activity on his cell phone after his final show, so all I know for sure is the time he was last on the air."

"I requested that some of the plants, grasses, etcetera found below and adjacent to the body be brought back to the lab for examination."

"What will that tell you?"

"The death of those plants would likely be caused by butyric acid leaching from the corpse. Most likely, that began three or four days ago, so we can confirm that Bent's body was in the spot where it was left after the stabbing occurred."

"If we have to call the deceased's estranged wife to identify her husband's corpse, the poor thing will probably pass out when she sees the condition of his body. She wasn't fond of the guy, but very few people are ready to see a sight like this."

"Let's spare her that. Dental records will confirm the identity of the corpse. No two sets of adult teeth are the same. By the way, the victim's wallet was found in the back pocket of the denim pants he was wearing and his cell phone in his front pocket."

"Well, that helps explain why bank and phone records show no activity since the time he went missing. It also gives us reason to believe that his slaying had nothing to do with a robbery."

"Agreed. Provided the killer didn't see or hear someone approaching, and high-tailed it out of there," Max suggested.

"That's possible, but it's not a popular trail. One more reason the body wasn't spotted for more than a week. Max, can your office hold off regarding recovery and examination of Bent's remains for a couple of hours? I'd like to tell the widow this news in person."

"Just call my cell and give me the green light. Once you do, we'll announce that we've identified Bill Bent's remains."

Eddie was back in his car, thirty minutes before noon. I can't believe I have an appetite after all that, but I'm starving, he thought. Before considering lunch, he needed to check in with Beverly. Eddie clicked onto her radio program and learned that she and her partner, Betsy, were doing a forum about women in the workplace that would run until one.

Starting work early each day, Rob and Holly always ate lunch by noon. Eddie tapped Rob on his cell's display and connected a moment later. "Hey, what do you two have planned for lunch?"

"We're working on some features for next week's papers.

We're an hour ahead of schedule if you can believe that. What's up?"

"I've got something of interest for your first edition next week."

"Spill."

"Nah, this story is worth a roast beef sandwich with all the fixings from Venice Gourmet."

"I gather by your bribe demand you're joining us for lunch."

"You gather correctly, pal. And since none of us can make our Smitty's meet-up tonight, I think we better talk now!"

"See you in twenty minutes?" Rob asked.

"On my way," Eddie responded as he pressed down on his car's accelerator.

CHAPTER TWENTY-ONE

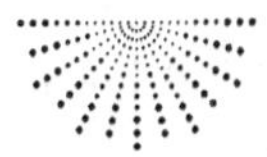

"What's new and exciting in the world of community news?" Eddie asked, having just bounded up the steep steps to *The Standard's* second-floor offices.

Rob and Holly had just finished laying out three deli sandwiches, pickles, bags of chips, and water bottles when Eddie came in with news they were curious to hear.

"Grab a seat, copper," Holly said as she sat down to the lunch she and Rob had arranged on their conference table. During their workweek, it doubled as a layout table for assembling the four times a week puzzle of patching together news, photos, and, most importantly, that edition's advertising.

"I got you a roast beef sandwich on your favorite bread," Holly announced.

"Thank you very much," Eddie said as he pulled off his jacket, loosened his tie, and sat down to join them.

"I can tell you've got something big. I know that cat-that-ate-the canary look you get," Rob suggested with obvious curiosity.

"Oh, it's big news."

"You get a break in the Bent case?" Holly asked.

"Did the jerk finally turn up?" Rob added.

"Bent turned up, but for once he wasn't talking," Eddie responded.

"You don't mean..." Rob said, putting his sandwich down.

Eddie nodded and added, "Just came from Brownstein's. Bent is dead and after eleven days in the great outdoors, he's not a pretty sight."

"I was beginning to doubt he was still alive," Holly added.

"Does Beverly know?"

"I'm planning on driving up to KLIB to tell her in person. I clicked on her show after leaving Brownstein. She's got some special on-air group forum going on. She won't be off for another hour, therefore the pleasure of my company."

"Is she going to be brought in to identify the body?" Holly asked, wincing over the thought.

"Max asked only for her to assist by getting his dentist to provide his most recent set of dental x-rays."

"The body is in that bad a shape?" Rob asked, shaking his head in surprise.

"Well, it's been in the great outdoors for eleven days. There's no way to say with certainty the time of death. Max believes, given the body's poor condition, that it's been where it was found since the day of Bent's last broadcast."

"I didn't know a body could deteriorate so significantly in a relatively short time," Rob said.

"Since we're eating, let's just say that it can, and we'll leave it at that."

"Agreed," Holly added quickly. "I still have half a ham and cheese sandwich to finish. Let's stick to more appropriate topics like, who located the body?"

"Holly, I never knew you to be skittish about gruesome details," Eddie responded with a smile.

"Being in love has brought out her sensitive side," Rob chimed in.

"Knock it off, you two!" Holly fired back.

"That's more like the Holly we know and love," Eddie said with a quick laugh. "As is often the case, the discovery of Bent's body involved a lucky break. An older couple hiking up along one of the trails in Lucas Valley stopped to admire the view. They had their dog with them, a golden retriever that fortunately was off leash. The dog scampered down below the ridgeline onto a second ledge a few feet below. It started barking at something that the dog's owners could not see. They tell him to be quiet and whistle at him to come back up, but he stays there and just keeps barking."

"Sounds like a scene from an old Lassie television episode," Rob said.

"It really does," Holly added.

"Naturally, the couple became curious so they went to take a look, convinced it's a wounded or dead animal, perhaps a coyote. It was an unpleasant discovery for both. You can be sure of that. The wife got very upset, but the husband, a retired fireman, had seen his share of corpses over a thirty-year career. They called the sheriff's office and the search for Bill Bent ended, and the murder investigation began."

"Murder? You didn't say anything about Bent being murdered," Rob said, realizing that the value of this story to his readers just grew considerably. "I thought perhaps he slipped and whacked his head against a rock, which is a blah ending to an exciting life. Does Max have any idea as to how he was killed?"

"That's where I come in. Bent had multiple stab wounds. One to the abdomen, apparently followed by several stab wounds to the back. Max will know more when he does a more detailed examination."

"Well, we've got our lead story for next week. I wonder if we can get Beverly to give us an interview or, better yet, write a piece on the life of her late husband," Rob said, looking at Holly.

"I don't know, Rob. I'm willing to give it a try. It would probably be easier on her if I ask some questions and write the story based on her responses."

"That works! *The Independent*, the San Francisco and Oakland papers will all lead with this tomorrow morning. An in-depth interview with Beverly is something the other news outlets will not be able to get."

"I'll give it a try. We've gotten pretty close over the last few months. Hopefully, she'll be okay talking about this."

Eddie listened to this exchange, knowing that soon he would have to share the news of Bill's death with Beverly. "Canning's office will want to put out an announcement before the end of the workday. If there's one thing that Canning dislikes more than bad press, it's no press at all. Wild Bill was a Bay Area celebrity of note, particularly since the Battling Bents got going."

"You don't think people will point fingers of blame at Beverly?" Holly asked, obviously troubled by the thought.

"Holly," Eddie said with a shake of his head. "Certain

people are likely to believe anything. Blaming Beverly? I wouldn't be the least bit surprised. Working my job, you meet people every day who exceed your expectations and others who fall well short."

"Agreed," Rob added. "Regardless of what all the busybodies are chattering about, my big question is, where do you go from here?"

"For the last several days I've been thinking that Bent was dead. The only thing I felt uncertain about was whether his body would be found. At any given moment there are around 90,000 missing persons in America. Approximately a third of that number are under eighteen and have simply run away from home. The vast majority of cases are resolved, but if Bent had never been located, he'd be far from the first. There was a real possibility he had been harmed because, in over ten days, there wasn't a blip on the radar indicating he was alive. No outbound cell phone activity, no use of any of his three credit cards. Despite his off-the-grid, macho shtick, he appeared to be a pretty conventional guy. At least in all the ways law enforcement views an individual. No criminal record, a steady job, good financial position, and a seemingly stable home and marriage."

"Therefore," Rob said, "the presumption that his vanishing act was made possible by someone who made him disappear. Does Max have any idea other than the apparent stab wounds as to how the actual death occurred?"

"He's using some digital imaging to get a better idea of the nature of the attack. Hopefully, that will give us clues as to the likely height of the attacker, possibly approximate weight, and perhaps, even gender. It's all a bit iffy at this point because the remains are in such poor shape. But, as you both know, Max is likely the most stubborn ME in California. He's persistent when it comes to extracting as much information as possible. Victims do tell tales, including those deceased."

"I don't think there's a better medical examiner in the state. Whatever secrets that body holds, my money is on Max to find them," Rob said.

"I'll drink to that," Holly said, toasting with her can of cream soda.

"Well, that's my scoop for the day," Eddie said as he stood to leave. "I hope you think I earned my deli sandwich," he added with a smile.

"Well earned, pal." Rob said as he patted Eddie on the shoulder. "I'd put you on staff, but Canning would probably disapprove."

"That's fine, Rob. I'll settle for the occasional deli sandwich and bag of chips. I'm the best inside informant food can buy."

Beverly, who shared an office at KLIB with her cohost Betsy Baker, was alone when Eddie knocked lightly on her open door shortly after one o'clock.

"Eddie, what a nice surprise," Beverly said with a warm smile. "Come on in."

"I ran into Tom Joseph on the way into the office, and he pointed me to where you're located."

"It's been great," Beverly said enthusiastically. "Tucked away back here, Betsy and I can have some privacy to work on ideas for upcoming shows without constant distractions.

I've learned that a five day a week, three-hour morning show doesn't just magically come together," Beverly said. "It all seems so casual when you're a listener, but a lot of preparation is needed to put together a show. Now that Bill has been off the air for going on two weeks, it's taken the air out of the Battling Bents routine. Not to mention, nothing is easier to program than bickering back and forth."

"It's about Bill that I came to see you."

"There's been a development?"

All it took was the few seconds that Eddie needed to gather his thoughts, that Beverly instantly sensed what was coming.

"Oh God, don't tell me…" she said breathlessly.

"I'm sorry to tell you that Bill's body was found earlier today."

Beverly began to weep as she stood and embraced Eddie.

On his drive north to Novato, Eddie wondered what Beverly's reaction to his news would be. It was far from the first time he had to break difficult news to a neighbor, a friend, a spouse, or family member, but this was the most unusual of those occasions. A couple, married for ten years, facing the likelihood of a bitter divorce, and engaged in an unprecedented public battle with each other. This was the kind of story he would no doubt share with his grandchildren one day if he was destined to be blessed with a long life.

"How? When? Oh my God, I can't believe this," Beverly said in a breathless moment. Slowly she sat back down, and Eddie grabbed some tissues from a box on a credenza in one corner of the office and handed them to her.

"There's more that I can share with you, but I want to wait until you're ready."

At that moment, Betsy Baker opened the door and quickly assessed the situation. It was immediately apparent that Beverly was distraught. Having met Eddie the previous week when he came to pick Beverly up for lunch, she feared his news was the worst possible.

"Oh my God, is Bill..." Betsy said with a look of astonishment.

"Yes," Beverly said in a choked whisper.

Betsy turned wide-eyed to Eddie for an explanation.

"His body was found early today up on a ridge in the Marinwood open space. Very near one of the hiking trails. It was hidden below a ridge, so it remained undiscovered all this time."

Beverly's radio partner now found herself in the same peculiar situation as Eddie. What to say by way of sympathy to a woman who had publicly expressed, countless times, anger, frustration, and disgust over her husband's behavior?

Beverly gathered herself enough to say, "How did he die?"

"Do you want me to step out?" Betsy asked, uncertain as to whether she wanted to hear a yes or no response.

"No, Betsy. Please stay," Beverly said softly.

Betsy went over and positioned herself on the small settee placed against one wall of the office. Beverly came over and sat next to her. Betsy put her arm around Beverly's shoulder and pulled her in, hoping to give her broadcast partner a sense of love and support.

Eddie, staying perched on the office's credenza, paused for a beat until Beverly indicated she was ready to continue by looking directly toward him after dabbing the corners of her eyes.

"It's a near certainty that all this time, Bill's body was

lying at the very spot where he was found this morning. Nearly a case of hiding in plain sight."

Beverly and Betsy gasped at that revelation as Eddie paused for a moment, grabbed an aging wooden chair, and sat down within inches of the now-famous radio team to share the painful details.

"Bill's body was discovered by a dog belonging to an older couple, whose barking attracted their attention."

Beverly struggled with the thought of how much she wanted to know, wondering if it would take weeks or months before she would again get a good night's sleep. Still, the questions came out of her as if she were doing an on-air interview.

"Why is the medical examiner certain that this was a murder?" she asked.

"Bill's body had multiple stab wounds," Eddie said softly. Beverly winced in obvious discomfort as Betsy squeezed her hand a little tighter.

"I suppose Beverly will be needed to make a formal iden-tification?" Betsy asked.

That was when Eddie shared the horrifying news of why the medical examiner would greatly appreciate Beverly obtaining a recent set of dental x-rays.

"There's no easy way to say this," Eddie explained softly. "Bill's body was in an advanced stage of decomposition. A principle reason the ME believes the body has been where it was found for all the time Bill's been missing."

Beverly's tears stopped and were now replaced by a look of breathless horror. Betsy continued to hold tightly to her. At that moment Tom Joseph tapped on the door, opened it a third of the way and stuck his head in.

"Bad news?" Tom asked, seeing Beverly's stricken expression.

"I'm afraid so," Eddie said softly. "Bill's body was found earlier today."

Tom sat down, feeling as if he had been punched in the chest. He tried to keep from thinking about the impact Bill Bent's death would have on his station's ratings. But he failed. KLIB's future suddenly seemed less promising.

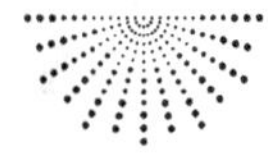

CHAPTER TWENTY-TWO

Saturday morning, the news of Bill Bent's murder was in every Bay Area newspaper, and on radio and television stations from Sonoma to San Jose, from Walnut Creek to Oakland and San Francisco. Most notably, the report of Bent's death lit up the Twitterverse with comments running from, "Rest in peace, my friend," to "Roast in Hell, you chauvinist pig!" From, "A sad day for lovers of free expression," to "He should have been taken off the air years ago!"

Eddie monitored it all from his desk in San Rafael, on one of the two days of the week he regularly anticipated spending with his family at home. That possibility vanished when Jack Canning volunteered Eddie to join him in answering questions at a one o'clock press conference.

Rob called Eddie to say that he and Karin, along with their children, were leaving for a party that night up in St. Helena, a celebration of his father-in-law's seventy-fifth birthday.

"I wish I was spending my Saturday with Sharon and

Aaron instead of sitting up here at HQ preparing for this press conference. I'm meeting with Max in less than an hour to go over our presentation."

"I'm not surprised. Canning roped you in because you're his top investigator."

"Lucky me."

"You know you hate working under someone's thumb, and Canning gives you a lot of space to roam. Ignore the relatively minor aggravations like being called in for one of his dog and pony shows. He couldn't keep every Bay Area journalist cooling their heels until Monday, it's too big a story to hold off until then. Not to mention it will make a great lead for Sunday print editions. With all the noise that was made over the Battling Bents, you know the media was going to want every detail regarding Bill's murder."

"You're right, pal. I've got to take the good with the bad. Does Beverly know about this afternoon's press conference? I never thought to ask Sharon."

"Karin told me that she, Sharon, and Holly all reached out to Beverly late yesterday when the news broke. It seems like she's pretty much staying under the radar, but Holly did speak to her this morning."

"Any word on how she's doing? She looked completely stunned when I met with her yesterday afternoon. I don't think what happened to Bill changed her opinion of him, but the news certainly caught her off guard and was obviously upsetting to her."

"It must be awkward to spend ten years with a guy and end up being not just estranged but combatants in a highly public fashion. And then, something like this happens. Yikes! Regardless of how she felt about Bent, it's got to be an uncomfortable situation."

"Beverly's not the first to lose a husband during a separation battle, but with it being this bitter and this public, it's a situation people will be talking about, at least here in Marin, for a long time. I suspect Sharon will hear from Beverly in a day or two about a place and time for a funeral service."

"I already found that out from my favorite source for information…"

"That would be Holly?" Eddie asked.

"Bingo. Beverly told Holly that the service is set for St. John's Episcopal in Ross at two o'clock on Tuesday. Are you going?"

"Absolutely! Sharon will insist that I go. I'd like to see if one or more of the girls in Bill Bent's photo collection shows up. How about you, Rob?"

"I would say no, but the boss, AKA my bride, told me that I am. And we both know my nosy assistant editor wouldn't miss this funeral for the world. Not to mention, there's no better snoop either of us could have there."

"You'll get no argument from me about that. I'll see you Tuesday, if not sooner, Rob. I assume all of you are staying up in St. Helena at Sharon's parents' place tonight."

"Absolutely. Getting ready for tonight's party, they'll have little if any time with Alice and Micah. You know how grumpy grandparents get when they don't have time with their grandkids."

"Absolutely. Sharon's parents and mine are the same way with Aaron. But we love seeing them together."

"A grandparent's love is a pretty special thing isn't it?"

"I better get ready for that press conference."

"You going to have Max there?"

"Depending on what he tells me when I meet with him in thirty minutes. But the likely answer is yes. He presents difficult details in a detached manner. He's able to make reporters sit up and pay attention without causing them to lose their lunch."

"Details such as what?"

"We'll throw out there something dramatic about the condition of the body, you know how Canning loves to play show and tell. Max was working on a computer animation of the knife assault that killed Bent. It's similar to the animation that held the press spellbound when Max used it to demonstrate the hammer attack on Adams' wife."

"That was gruesome, but certainly some must-see TV. A classic example of you can't look, but you can't look away. So, I'm guessing Canning will be there as well."

"Absolutely, hopefully looking on approvingly. It should be quite a show."

"Any suspects yet?"

"Not specifically. But from what I've learned nosing around Bent's life for the better part of the last two weeks, I should have a list of ten-plus possible suspects by early next week."

"That many?"

"Wild Bill was a real popular guy, if you get my meaning."

"In other words, someone who was likely to get stabbed to death by a long list of suspects."

"Absolutely!"

Moments after getting off his call with Rob, Max rang.

"I was just about to call you!" Eddie said happily. "What have you got for our show and tell session?"

"No, how are you? How is the family? Just straight down to business," Max said in his usual sarcastic manner.

"I'm sorry, Max. Canning's as anxious as a teenage boy about to be grilled by his prom date's parents. You know how jumpy he gets with a high visibility murder case."

"Trust me, I'm familiar with the quirks of our esteemed sheriff. Well, don't worry, I called to tell you that we've prepared a nice show for the ladies and gentlemen of the fourth estate. Ever since that case where I tied in digital x-ray technology with computer sequenced animation, I know what I need to do to hold the attention of a group with limited patience."

"Do you mind giving me a preview? It might give me some ideas for my part of the show."

"No problem. When Bent's body was found, the rate of decomposition had already slowed. In the case of our celebrity decedent, a body that has decayed lying on top of the soil, the area around it invariably will show signs of plant death…."

"Hold it right there, Max! We're trying to give the press corps something they can use at six and eleven on television, radio, and on the front page of local papers tomorrow morning. We're not looking to make them loose their lunch."

"I always forget how sensitive the general public is to the natural process of decay. Shame. I suspect you too could benefit from a post-mortem refresher course."

"You know, Max, it's not because I'm forgetful, or a lousy student, it's because I make an honest effort not to remember."

"And why is that?"

"Because it interferes with my getting a good night's sleep."

"Eddie, I always knew you were a sensitive soul."

Ignoring Max's persistent teasing, Eddie stayed on point. "What's important, Max, as you explained to me yesterday, is that Bent's blood-stained shirt gave us some helpful indications as to the nature of the attack. I assume you're still going with the theory that Bent was fatally stabbed?"

"Beyond a doubt! The digital x-rays prove it, and that's why I prepared a computer animation to show how that occurred."

"Okay, now we're getting to the stuff we can use with the press. They love sanitized violence with a hint of horror."

"You see, Eddie, this is why you didn't stay with science after high school. And to think I was going to explain algor mortis and livor mortis and how they proceed to rigor mortis."

"Max, they're journalists, not pre-med students. And you can at least double their level of comprehension against that of their average viewer, listener, or reader. Now tell me about this knife attack; what did the digital x-rays reveal?"

"Two things principally, one is that the murder weapon was most likely very sharp, in other words, a high-quality hunting knife. The attacker was likely four, perhaps five, inches shorter than their victim."

"How did you learn that?"

"We put the corpse through a cat scan, which helped direct us to specific wound areas that the assault created. With so much soft flesh gone, the exact point of entry is difficult to determine, but the attacker's knife caused damage to ribs three, four, and five. Damage that was easily identified by the scan and a separate set of x-rays. My guess is the attacker was between five eight and five-nine, given the height of the victim, which we have listed as six-two. Of course, those trails slope up and down endlessly, so it's not a certainty that they were on level ground at the moment the attack occurred."

"Any idea as to the make of the weapon?"

"The best we can do is an educated guess."

"And that is?"

"The blade was approximately nine inches in length, and undoubtedly very sharp. The killer was able to do a great deal of damage in what we believe was a very brief time."

"The murder weapon was not recovered at or near the location where the body was found. But do you have an educated guess as to the weapon's style and perhaps, manu-facturer?"

"We're quite confident that the murder weapon was a hunting knife. A company called Spike's Knives makes a knife that's the right length, nine-inch blade, highly durable, lightweight, and razor-sharp. Standardly it's used by hunters. Mostly for gutting and skinning. Not my idea of a fun week-end, but some people enjoy that sort of thing."

"I would have thought you'd love it."

"Not me. The people I cut open have already gone to the great beyond. When it comes to all living creatures, large and small, I can't consider doing harm."

Eddie paused for a moment and then asked, "Was the heart pierced?"

"Yes, but the lungs took the brunt of the attack. It's some-what an educated guess, but we can say with a high level of confidence that this was a savage attack. The assault, most likely, ended quickly. Our theory is the victim was face down near the edge of the ridge. He was pushed with a shoe off that ledge onto a drop approximately three feet below. There's faint evidence remaining of a muddy shoe print on the back of the victim's flannel shirt. Likely, it was put there by the killer when Bent was pushed. I know you would love it if we could pull a print that could give us a shoe size, but it was from the upper portion of the foot. Best guess, if of any value, is that it was a narrow shoe size.

"The body most likely was covered with some dirt, dried weeds, leaves, and so on. It's reasonable to assume that most of that detritus blew away over several nights when winds along those ridges pick up considerable speed. Anyone who hikes along those trails knows that at various points, they can have steep drop-offs or a relatively benign drop to a second ridge below."

While they spoke, Max sent Eddie the forty-five-second computer animation that his team put together to demonstrate the attack.

"Thanks for all this, Max. You've got enough here to catch the attention of the press corps, who in a week or two will no doubt be onto their next big story."

"Good! That's my show and tell, what do you have planned?"

"As best as we know, the murder scene went relatively undisturbed from the time of the victim's death up to the discovery of Bent's body. That's a plus. The obvious downside is the murder occurred in the great outdoors as opposed to say, a home. There we would have had more opportunities for preserved evidence, hairs, prints, and more left behind by our perpetrator. At this point, that type of evidence is scarce, between some rain, wind, and people who hiked over the site of the killing unknowingly carrying off important evidence. Max, I know that the chance of the attacker's skin under Bent's nails could have been a game-changer."

"I checked anyway, Eddie. Even though I would have

been greatly surprised to find a skin sample left by the killer given the time that had lapsed and the poor condition of Bent's body."

"You can't pick your killers or the settings, as you well know, Max. Considering the situation, I'm glad we have already gotten this far. What do you suppose the chances are that Bent's assailant was a woman?"

"Eddie, in the age of equality, as my wife would hasten to remind us both, there's always a chance your killer is a woman."

"From what I can tell, Bent was involved with a number of different women, I mean romantically. Therefore, my question: Could our killer be female?"

"Absolutely, Eddie. The murder weapon, if we're correct in our conclusions, was a lightweight, well-balanced hunter's knife. New, or well cared for, this type of weapon would have dispatched Bent to that great radio station in the sky in remarkably little time."

L ater, after the press conference concluded, Sheriff Canning turned to Eddie and said, "Anytime Max uses a computer-animated simulation of what took place at the murder scene, it goes over well with the press," Jack said happily.

"If one picture is worth a thousand words, these animations are worth ten times that," Eddie said. "I'm certainly going to encourage Max to keep doing them."

"Great," Canning said, flashing a smile infrequently seen other than when he's meeting voters.

Less enjoyable were the questions flying at both Jack and

Eddie after Max had finished. Nearly all of which could be reduced to two frequently repeated lines of inquiry: The first being, "Do you have any suspects at this time?"

Eddie, of course, was non-committal. "Our inquiry has revealed several individuals of interest, but as with any unfolding investigation, I'm not at liberty to disclose specific information."

The second, "Are you looking into the possibility that the perpetrator was a frequent listener to either Bill or Beverly Bent's morning shows?"

"We've begun taking a close look at both letters and e-mails sent to KBUD and KLIB. It's our hope to have that review completed in the days to come."

Eddie took a shot at suggesting the sheriff's department was going to assign additional personnel to review letters passed along by both stations. He had no decision from Canning whether that would happen or not. But Eddie, working every possible angle, had nothing to lose and a great deal to gain by inferring that the department was putting more resources into this investigation than it had until now. "We know both of the Bents received passionate letters expressing support and condemnation. Did a fan act out violently? That's a possibility we'll continue to look into."

Arriving back in Jack Canning's cavernous office, Eddie discussed the possibility of the department expanding the scope of their investigation by actually looking into the hate mail both of the Bents received.

"At this point, there is no way of telling if Bent was ambushed by a deranged fan or killed by someone he knew," Eddie explained. "In looking into Bent over the past couple of weeks, I'd say my list of suspects might exceed a baker's dozen."

"Lucky you," Jack responded with a half-smile. "I'm sure they both had their share of love letters and hate mail. Speaking of fans and detractors, the press corps seemed unusually subdued today."

"I was thinking about that as well. My guess is this whole thing unnerves people in the media."

"How so?"

"I think everyone in the broadcast business sees themselves in the crosshairs at least to some extent," Eddie explained. "Despite their bravado, all of this has to be a little unnerving. I mean the worst of it is obviously being a television reporter, followed by being a radio personality. Before the Internet, on-air television reporters were much more recognizable than radio hosts. But on the web, just about every radio personality now does some online face time by having a minicam in the studio while doing their show. Bottom line, if I was a hater of Bent's gender bias, and there was apparently a small army of people who meet that criteria, finding Bent would not be difficult."

"I suppose I never gave it much thought, but obviously you're right. A lot of these media people are walking a thin line between feeling secure and knowing they're potential targets. So, you think Bill Bent's celebrity led to his murder."

"I can't answer that with any degree of certainty other than to speculate that his fame probably didn't help! Give me another couple of days, Jack. I've been leaning on the management of Bent's radio station to do a careful review of listener mail received over the past month. Hopefully, a few assorted whack-a-doodles will float to the top. And I'll have some fresh leads. I'm also going after KLIB's mailbag. There's a chance Bent's killer was a fan of Beverly Bent and her station. It's not a stretch to imagine one of her listeners thought it was time for Wild Bill to sign-off permanently."

"Okay, Eddie, go do your thing. Just keep me in the loop!"

Eddie smiled, patted Jack on the back, left his office and headed out of the department's headquarters, anxious to salvage the balance of his weekend. He made a conscious decision to keep Bent's collection of love notes, quiet. It might be of potential value, or it might only prove that his wife's childhood friend was spot-on to distrust the man to whom she once entrusted her future.

E ddie was determined to put Bent' s murder aside for the balance of the weekend but, typical of his curious mind, that was impossible to do.

When Sharon took off with Aaron for a Sunday morning playdate at Sausalito's Cloudview Park, Eddie promised her he would use the next few hours to catch up on some much-needed sleep. Instead, he sat down with a pad and pencil and began, as he did with every investigation, by making lists.

First was that collection of thank you notes, with enclosed photos. Every one of those letter writers needed to be interviewed. It was doubtful that any of them were aware that they were part of a group of women that Bent lavished with individual attention. Did one or more of them have the knowledge they were involved in an extra-marital relationship? Before the recent media spotlight placed on Beverly, listeners only knew Bent was married by the frequent complaints he made regarding "the old ball and chain!"

After further reflection, Eddie thought it more likely this group of women were aware of his marriage but simply did not care. More likely was their having no knowledge of each other.

Bent made an obvious effort to keep hidden from Beverly these notes of love and appreciation. If not, why the false bottom to an unlocked lower desk drawer? Eddie suspected there was far more Bent kept hidden from his wife.

Eddie also realized that Bent's collection of girlfriends was likely only one aspect of his deceptive character. How many more lies might be lurking below the public persona of an obviously complicated man?

CHAPTER TWENTY-THREE

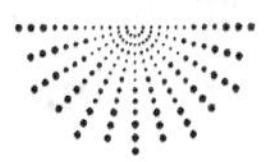

Eddie called Rob early Monday with a request he had made on similar occasions.

"Bent's service is tomorrow at two. I was wondering if you would call Sylvia Stokes and Ted Dondero to see if you can recruit them to join us over at St. John's."

"Sure, I'll give it a try. You're going to need to brief all of us on what you're hoping to find."

"Absolutely, any chance we can do that later this afternoon, say four-thirty?"

"Holly and I can make that work. I'll call Sylvia and Ted to see if they can join us this afternoon, and then tomorrow for Bent's service. What's up?"

"I don't want to ditch on you, but that question will have to wait until later. Canning is as jumpy as a cat on a hot tin roof, and I have to go hold his hand."

"What's he wound up about now? I thought the press conference could not have gone better."

"Canning's like a weathervane, the moment the wind changes direction, his confidence shifts as well. Unfortunately, Jack listened to Barney Benson this morning on KBUD while he was driving into work. Apparently, Benson was suggesting that our department should widen their talent pool on Bent's murder investigation. Bring in some talent from the San Francisco Police Department's homicide division. You know the routine, both of us have heard this our entire lives. They treat Marin County like it was one huge bedroom community inhabited by a bunch of bumpkins."

"I wonder what got Benson going on that? On the radio, he's always so light-hearted."

"I have no idea, Rob. But I'd love to find out."

"Why don't you ask him?"

"I might, but right now I'm leaning on his boss, a guy by the name of Nick Reade, for copies of any threatening emails or letters sent to Bent during the three weeks before his disappearance. One thing at a time, at least as long as I'm running this investigation."

"That could change if Canning starts taking real heat."

"Agreed. I'll give it a few days and see how this shakes out. Right now, I've got to fly, Canning's buzzing for me, again! I'll see you at your place by four-thirty. Send me a text if you can't get the group together or you need to meet at a later time. I'll do whatever works best for all of you."

Fortunately, Sylvia and Ted had no commitments that would prevent them from attending both Bill Bent's funeral and joining Eddie, Rob, and Holly for a meeting that afternoon.

When Eddie arrived five minutes early, he was pleased to

see Rob and his team already in place. All of them had played essential roles in covering the Mill Valley funeral of Michael Marks, the infamous "phantom photographer." Additionally, Tiburon's farewell to the internationally famous fashion model, Willow Adams, who had married Marin's wealthiest resident, and was now remembered as "the wicked wife."

Together the four of them formed a group Eddie named, "The Snoop Squad." As he once explained to Rob, "Funeral services and receptions afterward can be a gold mine of information provided you've got enough people to hear what's being said. Neighbors, friends, frenemies, and admirers all show up. Not to mention the occasional cousin, nephew, niece, widow, stepchild, ex-wife, brother, or sister, all of whom may feel they were cheated regarding how the estate was likely to be divided."

Eddie also realized that while neighbors were open to sharing their thoughts and feelings with other neighbors, they were far less likely to be open and honest if the person they're talking to is an officer of the law.

As Eddie once told Rob, "I'm as welcome at the funeral of a murder victim as an IRS agent at an office Christmas party. Just ask the company owner, 'What did this shindig really cost,' or, 'how much of that booze are you taking home after the party?' And watch people scatter."

Rob knew Eddie's concerns were valid and was only too happy to help. Sylvia, Ted, and Holly were delighted to be called upon. The thought that they could play a small but possibly essential role in a murder investigation was enough to thrill each of them.

"Ted and Sylvia, I'm pleased you were both able to join us," Eddie began. "I'll get right to it because we've got a lot of ground to cover. As you're no doubt aware, I spent most of the last two weeks looking for Bill Bent. Obviously, with the discovery of his remains, the investigation has gone from a curiosity to a top priority. I don't have to tell you how jumpy Sheriff Canning gets when the media is focusing on his department during an investigation, especially when we're dealing with a homicide. And you can double that if the victim was a celebrity."

"I listened to Bent's show a couple of times. The guy was a jerk. I would think there are a lot of people who could be suspects," Ted offered.

"I'll second that motion," Holly added quickly, which brought smiles and a couple of quick laughs.

"I never listened to him," Sylvia said, "but my husband told me he had a large group of listeners. Ninety plus percent men, I suppose, who undoubtedly shared his low opinion of women. I imagine you and everyone else at this table is wondering if this was the work of a crazed hater. From what I gather, Bent was a love-him-or-hate-him kind of guy."

"Obviously, we all want to do whatever we can to help at tomorrow's service," Rob said. "Who are we looking to approach, and what are you hoping to learn?"

"I suspect there's a lot I still don't know about Bent, but it's already apparent that he had a rogue's gallery of admirers and detractors," Eddie began. "Even with four of you there, and I am very grateful for that, you won't have time to chat up all of them, but you can at least make a good start. At this time, it's difficult to say who your top targets are. Let me show you some photos and a few images I printed from online profiles, and then we can talk about dividing up leads."

Eddie began, as Rob suspected he would, with the photos

of the four women who sent thank you notes to Bent for their weekend rendezvous.

"Wow," Holly declared, shaking her head in amazement. "I suspected Bent was cheating on Beverly, but not to this extent. It looks as if he approached having extramarital affairs like it was a part-time job."

"I had much the same reaction when I stumbled upon these love notes Bent had buried in a desk drawer. It's all pretty remarkable. I've made a sheet for each one of you to take. It has a copy of the photo I found in each note and a name to go with the face. Spend some time tonight trying to commit to memory these faces and names. On a separate sheet you'll find images of Barney Benson, Bent's on-air sidekick, the station manager at KBUD, Nick Reade, and Tom Joseph, Beverly's boss at KLIB."

"What's your interest in these three gentlemen?" Ted asked.

"Benson has been agitating on-air for the SF Police join the investigation, and frankly, I'm wondering why."

"How so?" Ted asked.

"I had lunch with the guy a week after Bent vanished. That was before we found Bent's body. Benson was very nonchalant about the whole affair, basically telling me that Bent was very talented, but a real flake. He was pretty much convinced that the whole vanishing act was a tempest in a teapot. He was confident that Bent would reappear. Now he's doing this outraged citizen routine, demanding an expanded investigation. Something about this flip flop seems odd, but perhaps I'm misreading his reaction."

"Maybe he's just incensed that his broadcast partner was murdered. And, perhaps a little embarrassed that he had been so casual about the topic of his disappearance the previous week," Rob suggested.

"Possibly, but what's got him so worked-up?" Eddie asked.

"I don't know, maybe he just wants to see justice done," Rob replied.

"I think it's more than that." Eddie responded.

"Is it possible he's looking for a line into the investigation?" Sylvia suggested.

"You mean Benson's hoping if the SFPD gets in on the case that someone inside the department will backchannel updates on its progress to him?" Ted asked.

"Could be," Eddie said, already impressed with what Sylvia and Ted brought to the conversation. "He's got a lot of listeners in the city, and he's lived there for a long time. If one of you could get him to open up, that might lead somewhere interesting.

"There's someone else at the station I assume will be there tomorrow. Nick Reade, who I mentioned a few moments ago. He's been stalling me and generally uncooperative."

"Uncooperative, how?" Sylvia jumped in.

"I've been on him for over a week to have someone on his staff comb through this past month's listener mail to see if any specific threats were made against his station's number one talent. So far, he's given me zip. When I call him, I get the runaround."

"Perhaps he doesn't like the idea that Bent was slain by a listener, if that is indeed what happened," Sylvia responded. "It doesn't say much for their audience, I suppose. Still you would think, if that's what happened, Reade would want to know about it. After all, he could be next!"

"How common is it for stations like KBUD to get threatening emails, letters, or calls about their on-air talent?" Ted asked.

"Apparently, a lot more common than any of us outside of the broadcast business realize," Eddie responded.

"Kind of makes me glad I work at a community newspaper," Holly said. "The worst I get is a cold shoulder from some local offended by one of our stories."

"I think Sylvia has a good point. Reade might be hesitant to find out that some of his station's listeners are violent nut jobs! Rob said.

"There's something odd about that place where Bent worked, and at this point, I'm not sure what it is. If anyone can chat up either or both of those guys, I'd like to see how they respond to some gentle prodding."

"Such as?" Holly asked.

"No need to be overly aggressive. Just something along the lines of, 'You must have been shocked by this sad news?' See what kind of response you get."

"Sure. I'll give it a try," Holly responded with a casual shrug. "You know I put a lot of stock in the old advice that the answer to every question never asked is NO!"

"Whichever one Holly lands, I'll go after the other," Ted offered. "At seventy plus, I look innocent even if I'm not. I love playing the forgetful, friendly older guy asking a few questions out of idle curiosity. Succeeds nearly every time."

"Go for it," Eddie said. "I'd like to know if Reade is embarrassed by all this, or do his concerns run a good deal deeper than seeing the station's image taking a hit?"

"How about me? I can look pretty innocent," Holly offered.

"You've got to be kidding!" Rob said with a chuckle.

"You just haven't seen my softer side," Holly said innocently.

"Let's keep it that way," Rob quickly replied.

"Anyone else?" Ted asked.

"Yes, one I'd like Rob to corner, if possible. Tom Joseph, Beverly Bent's boss. Here's a photo of him with a little bit about his career and background I pulled off the station's website," Eddie said as he pushed the page forward to Rob.

"What am I looking to get out of him?"

"I think he's romantically interested in Beverly."

"What makes you think that, Sherlock?" Holly asked.

"The way he acts when he's around her. I noticed that particularly on Friday, when I came to tell Beverly that her husband's body had been found. I was in the office Beverly shares with her on-air partner, Betsy Baker. When Tom Joseph came in, he asked if I had any news. Quickly he realized I had delivered what was likely the worst possible news. I got a distinct impression that Joseph wanted to take Beverly in his arms, hold her, and never let her go."

There was an awkward silence in which it was apparent that all four of Eddie's snoops were imagining what that moment in Beverly's office must have been like. Many people go a lifetime never having to tell someone such shocking news. For Eddie, it was part of his job.

"Let's just say you had to be there to fully appreciate why I got that impression," Eddie concluded. "Those two seem more like a couple than many couples I know."

"You don't think he wants to protect Beverly from the awful man she married, and that might have extended to his doing the chivalrous thing and murdering the louse?" Holly asked.

"Not sure if Tom Joseph is capable of such violence, but

there's an outside chance that the guy has a lethal side no one, including me, suspects. I can tell you this, however, both Max and I think the knife attack that killed Bent was probably a crime of passion. There are various ways to kill someone and this was up close, furious, and personal."

"Are you planning on sharing any of what you've told us about Bent's harem with Beverly?" Holly asked.

"I'll have to in the coming days, but not on the day before, day of, or day after her husband's funeral. That feels like piling on. Even though it's more than clear that Beverly was beyond being over him."

"Talk about an awkward situation," Ted said, nodding sympathetically toward Eddie. "I wouldn't want to be the one to share that news with any woman, particularly one who just became a widow. She might have suspected he was a louse, but four different girlfriends. Wow, that's Hugh Hefner worthy."

"Difficult to say, Ted. Beverly stopped caring about her husband long ago. Still, as little as she thought of him in the final months of their marriage, I think what I've uncovered to date might be below her already low estimation of him."

"You couldn't have a lower estimation of Bent than I did," Holly suggested. "And I have to admit, even I'm shocked by this collection of photos and love notes."

"Do you want us to make any of these women a priority? If so, what are we looking to learn from them?" Sylvia asked.

"The thing I'd most appreciate is a reading on whether or not the relationships with any of these women were still ongoing at the time Bent vanished. Or what by now is better described as the time he was killed."

"What dates, if any, were you able to get from the postmarks on these envelopes or dates written by the women who sent them?" Ted asked.

"The most recent was a few months ago, the oldest goes back eighteen months," Eddie responded. "That particular one was mailed from Corte Madera."

"Wow, intimate relationships with four different women in less than two years. I think that qualifies as a serial adulterer. The guy was a scoundrel, plus he had a remarkable amount of stamina," Ted said with a bemused expression. "At my age, it's exhausting to even imagine how much energy he must have put into chasing pursuing and entertaining all these women."

"Agreed," Eddie said with a smile. "Besides his show, according to Beverly, he also did lots of promotional work for the station and advertisers. I guess the guy was one of those people who is on sixteen hours or more each day."

"Do you suspect he had similar liaisons pre-dating this batch of photos and love notes?" Sylvia asked.

"That's certainly a real possibility. Now that this missing person's case is a homicide investigation, I'm on solid ground as far as the scope of my investigative powers. And I'm guessing that unraveling the misadventures of Bill Bent will be no small task.

"I'm going to start leaning on some people in the coming days, beginning with Bent's boss at KBUD. One more reason if someone can buttonhole Nick Reade, I'd like to know how he behaves when he's not talking to a cop. With all the police dramas on TV nowadays, I think a lot of people get more than just a little uneasy when I come up on their radar. His strange behavior around me might be nothing more than I give him a bad case of the jitters."

"I suppose we should start by buttonholing however many of Bent's harem we find?" Sylvia suggested.

"Yes! It would be great if you can talk to all four of them. There's a chance, of course, that none of them will be there. I'd be pleased if you get to talk with just two."

"Eddie," Sylvia began, taken aback by the photo images on a single sheet of Bent's lovers. "I know that Bent was relatively young, upper thirties, but these women look like they're not out of their twenties."

"True. But of course, until you meet one or more of them, none of us knows if several of these photos are five or ten years old," Eddie responded.

"I assume at some point soon you're planning on interviewing each of these women separately?" Ted asked.

"I will. What I'd like each of you to do is when and if you find one or more of these women, see if you can get them comfortable talking about Bent. If they're going to let down their guard, this would be a logical time for them to do it."

"I know Sylvia and I are great at that. We have the advantage of looking like your kind aunt or uncle. We'll see what we come up with," Ted said with a reassuring smile.

"Hopefully, we'll get lucky," Sylvia added, unsure what if anything might come of their outing. Past attempts, however, led to her hoping they would uncover one or more pieces to the puzzle that was now Bent's life and death.

"Catch as catch can," Eddie said with a smile. "Any candid information you get is more than I have now.

"Ted, you might be best with Reade, KBUD's general manager. I don't know what it is, but he gets the hair on the back of my neck to stand up."

"You think he and Bent had some bad blood between them?"

"I'm not sure," Eddie replied quickly. "But I can tell you as active as Bent was with the ladies, he might have gotten himself entangled with some woman Reade is somehow connected with."

"You mean like a sister, wife, etcetera?" Ted asked.

"Any and all of the above. Bent appears to have been an equal opportunity womanizer. And that could be a big thing to learn. It's even possible that Bent was involved with Benson's daughter, who just yesterday I learned is twenty-seven and single," Eddie responded. "I've got a picture of her. She's not one of the women who sent one of these love notes, but that doesn't mean very much. I can't say for sure, but I very much doubt that Bent's womanizing began or ended with the four women I stumbled upon."

"But if Benson is a possible suspect, why is he suggesting expanding the scope of the investigation? Which is what would happen if the SFPD got involved," Rob asked.

"Benson wouldn't be the first perpetrator to send the police off on a wild goose chase," Eddie replied. "Perhaps that's his real desire."

"To throw a wrench into the investigation?" Ted asked.

"Asking another department to get involved is one way to cause needless confusion," Eddie suggested.

"Wow, Benson as Bent's killer! Now that would be one helluva story," Holly said, shaking her head.

"This isn't the first time I've been confronted with a victim that attracted a lot of potential suspects. Warren Bradley, our gossiping gourmet, had half of Sausalito loving him, and a sizable portion of the population wanting to throw him into the bay dressed in a cement overcoat."

"You can add Michael Marks, our beloved phantom photographer, to that list," Ted said.

"And a sizable portion of the socialites of Belvedere and Tiburon would have happily seen the beautiful Willow Adams disappear," Sylvia added.

"Well," Eddie said after a pause, "I'd put our dearly departed, Mr. Bent, right up there with the best of them. I'm glad my Sharon never knew about Bill's two-timing her life-long friend. I'd need to add her to my list of suspects."

CHAPTER TWENTY-FOUR

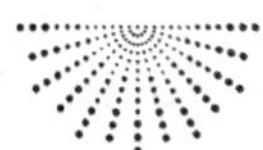

Eddie's Snoop Squad agreed to rendezvous twenty minutes before the scheduled start of Bill Bent's funeral service. The four of them met in the parking area that once was adjacent to the Northwestern depot for the Town of Ross. In recent decades, well after Marin County's electric train service passed into history, the quaint building has served the small picturesque town as its post office.

Rob, Holly, Sylvia, and Ted walked across the road to the large green space known as Ross Common, which borders the town's elementary school.

"Seems awfully quiet today. The kids must all be inside doing their schoolwork," Ted said.

"You don't see as much of that as we did," Sylvia said. "Kids inside doing schoolwork, I mean. Sometimes it seems like recess has become the biggest part of the day. But what would I know, it's been a long time since my children were school-age."

The group walked up to the three-way stop at the corner

of Lagunitas Road and Shady Lane, directly across from the main entrance to St. John's Episcopal Church.

"Okay, group, are we ready to do this?" Rob asked, hoping they would return to this same spot in less than two hours, each by then having each gained at least one valuable piece to the puzzle Eddie was attempting to assemble.

"We've got a lot of players to deal with," Holly said. "I'm uncertain as to the outcome of this little fishing trip, but let's cast a wide net and hope we catch some interesting information."

"Well, as my dad was find of saying," Ted offered, "nothing ventured, nothing gained."

"I'm going to do my level best to corner one of Bill Bent's ladies," Sylvia expressed confidently. "I'm still in shock by what Eddie showed us. Particularly Bent's lavish spending."

"I'm determined to corner one or both of these station managers, Tom Joseph from KLIB, or Nick Reade of KBUD," Rob added. "I think they're sitting on information that could help Eddie in the Bent investigation. Maybe I can encourage them to let one or more gems slip out."

"I want to corner Bent's sidekick, Barney Benson," Holly offered. "From the way Eddie has described him, I think he's susceptible to a little bit of flirting. I'm happy to flirt if it gets me some information."

"Okay, let's do this," Rob said, anxious to get started. "And this time, let's all sit separately. Who knows, one of us might be lucky enough to sit down next to one of Eddie's targets."

Although it was ten minutes before the start of the service, the one hundred plus year-old church was close to capacity by the time Eddie's team stepped inside.

"With this crowd," Rob said softly to Holly, "the four of us couldn't have found enough space to sit together even if we wanted to."

"Pretty big turnout for a guy as widely disliked as Bent," Holly said just above a whisper.

"I'm guessing a third or even half of this crowd is made up of fans of his show," Rob replied. "I can see Eddie sitting next to Sharon, who is sitting next to Beverly in the front row. Who do you think is the woman on the other side of Beverly?"

"I've seen her picture on KLIB's website. That's her broadcast partner, Betsy Baker."

By now, Ted and Sylvia had slipped into separate pews on opposite sides halfway down St. John's long aisle. A few steps below, to the side of the altar, the mahogany casket, polished to perfection, had been placed. Next to it stood a horseshoe-shaped wreath of red and white roses with a sash around it that read, "KBUD STRONG."

"Looks like his station is making a show of it," Holly said in a whisper.

"I suspect the show is more for Bent's fans and the media than for KBUD's staff."

"You go down the left side of the church, I'll go down the right. We better get some seats before we have to stand through the entire service."

"Agreed. Maybe you should have thought twice before wearing those heels. You're not trolling for Mr. Right."

"I found my Mr. Right in Scott! Remember? But when I'm around these many people, I dress to impress. I'm shallow, what can I say?"

None of Eddie's snoops anticipated that the service would stretch to nearly a full hour. Rob was glad that he covered his bet and transmitted to the printer tomorrow's completed edition before leaving for the service. While Rob didn't know how the afternoon would unfold, he knew that Bent was a local celebrity whose murder was widely reported. Of the funerals they had attended as a group, this one had drawn the largest gathering. Nice for Bill's admirers to see, but a bigger challenge to Rob and the rest of the group to locate their targets.

The reception, as is most often the case, began soon after the service's conclusion. It was held in St. John's Parish Hall, adjacent to the chapel. KBUD, apparently, chose to send off the man that kept them at the top of the ratings in style, Rob thought.

Only Willow Adams, the wife of Tiburon billionaire William Adams, had a more lavish post-service reception. Unfortunately for Sylvia, Rob, Ted, and Holly, all of whom had early light lunches, there was little time to enjoy food or casual conversation.

Holly, having seen several headshots online of Barney Benson's round face, assumed he was a man of generous proportions. He was busy, as many other mourners were, circling the buffet table. Holly came alongside him just as he reached for two pieces of the ham and cheese quiche.

"Wonderful spread, isn't it?" Holly asked with a smile.

"It is indeed!" Barney replied. "Do I know you?" He asked in the carefree manner that had made him so popular on the radio over the past twenty-five years.

"Beverly and I have been friends for many years. I've been to a couple of summer cookouts the Bents held at their place in Corte Madera, but I don't recall meeting you there."

"You're right, it couldn't have been there that we met. I rarely come out to Marin on summer weekends. Too many tourists jamming up traffic on the Golden Gate Bridge heading north to Sausalito, Vista Point, and Muir Woods in the early part of the day, and too many folks from the city heading home from Marin County beaches in the late afternoon. I suppose I just hate sitting in traffic, particularly on a Saturday or Sunday." Barney said with a smile. "Ironic, when you consider I've made a living helping to entertain people who are sitting in traffic."

"I'm lucky when it comes to traffic. I live and work in Sausalito. My commute is a ten-minute walk every morning."

"Where do you work?"

"At a community newspaper," Holly said, but quickly realized she didn't want to go there. Luckily, Barney was more into the quiche than the conversation, so she smiled and continued. "I feel bad for Beverly that something so awful happened at a time when she and Bill were arguing so publicly. Most couples can resolve their differences without having to fight it out every weekday morning on the radio."

"I've meant to reach out to Beverly, but my plate's been pretty darn full lately. Going solo on KBUD's morning show has been a big change."

"It must be a difficult time for you, between the demands of doing the show every morning while also dealing with Bill's disappearance and then his death."

"Not the best of times for any of us at KBUD."

"That's certainly true for Beverly as well. I'm sure she'd appreciate hearing from you."

"Well, no time like the present. If you haven't offered her your condolences yet, why don't you come with me?"

"Sure," Holly said nonchalantly, wondering if Benson was trying to put her on the spot to learn if she was indeed close to Beverly. Or, perhaps, just a local fan with an overactive imagination.

The two of them weaved through the crowd, a few recognizing Benson and calling out, "Barney." But mostly, they proceeded unimpeded until they found themselves standing next to Beverly, who was surrounded by Sharon and Karin. When all three of the women said, "Holly!" in unison, and gave her a kiss on the cheek, Benson knew that this short, attractive woman, was indeed part of Beverly's circle of friends.

After a momentary pause, Beverly said, "Barney, it's been ages since I've seen you!" Barney gave Beverly a kiss on the cheek and expressed his deepest condolences.

"Everyone at the station is trying to wrap their minds around this. Bill was a part of the KBUD family for so many years that I can't imagine the place without him."

"This is just nuts, who could possibly want to harm Bill?" Beverly said, while thinking there were likely several good suspects among Bill's rabid fans and detractors. But how could she give voice to such a thought without sounding cynical, given her new life as a radio celebrity on a station with a radically different agenda?

Both Sharon and Karin, well aware of the role Holly was playing, discreetly drifted into the crowd to let the three of them talk. At the same time, Holly, as they expected, held her ground, waiting to see if Benson would come forth with actionable information.

"It certainly is bizarre. I can't imagine anyone wanting to hurt Bill," Barney exclaimed in a tone that Holly found less than credible. "As best as I know, everyone liked him. I know he got his share of hate mail, but even I get one or more nasty-grams a week, and I'm just the jovial sidekick," he explained with a look of bemused amazement.

"I'm dumbfounded as well," Beverly responded. "And now with Bill's body being found, I've already gotten a few, 'You'll burn in hell for doing this!' letters from insane people over the last few days."

"I hope you mean letters to the station and not your home?" Holly asked.

"Yes, letters sent to the station. Still, it's uncomfortable to realize how many mentally unstable individuals are out there," Beverly responded.

"Boy, the whack-a-doodles don't waste time jumping on anything, without any regard for the truth," Barney said, shaking his head. "Of course, Bill always got his fair share of hate mail."

This caused Holly's curiosity to perk up, knowing Eddie's frustration with Nick Reade not identifying threats sent in letters, emails, or by phone to KBUD.

"We're out of a job in the broadcast business without loyal listeners," Barney said. "But it would be nice if there were fewer oddballs mixed in with our loyal listeners and fans."

"How are your two girls?" Beverly asked.

"They're certainly not kids anymore," Barney said with a shrug and a half-laugh. "Charlotte's engaged, she's now twenty-nine, but her kid sister, Janice, is still playing the field."

"She's two years younger than Charlotte, correct?"

"You have a good memory, my dear. Janice is as boy crazy today as she was in high school. She's a handful. I can promise you that," Barney said, flashing a smile, followed by a grimace.

Is it possible that Janice was one of Bill's conquests? Holly made a mental note to remember Benson's youngest daughter's name.

Ted was doing what he did best: playing the affable senior. He put his hand out to everyone he made eye contact with while flashing a kind smile. He was particularly pleased when one of those mourners responded to his greeting by saying, "Hi. I'm Nick Reade, do you live here in Marin?"

Eddie had shown all of them a picture of Reade from KBUD's website, but it was not close enough to Reade to be easily recognizable. My lucky day, Ted thought in an instant he smiled and said, "Yes, I live here in Marin. In fact, I have my entire life."

"Hard place to leave, I suppose," Reade responded.

"Well, for me, it certainly has been! Good weather most of the year, a little too much rain some winters, but you have to pay the price in rain days to live in a place this green for most of the year. You live in Marin?"

"In the city, although I think I'd be happier out here."

"Well, it's a great place to raise a family, but nowadays with all the young professionals living here, there are a lot more choices for singles to have a social life than twenty years ago. You hitched, or still enjoying the single life?"

"Single and planning to keep it that way," Reade said with a short laugh.

"I think that's the way most men feel until the right gal comes along, and suddenly that resolve to live the bachelor's life doesn't seem to make much sense anymore. "

"I suppose I've not met that lady yet."

"You will! Do you work in the city?" Ted asked innocently, already knowing the answer.

"I'm the general manager at the radio station Bill Bent worked for. How did you know Bill?"

"Marin is a lot smaller than a lot of people think. I tell folks that all the time. I'm friends with people who know the Bents, and I had a couple of occasions to meet them as well. Seemed like a happy couple, although that dust-up between them on their radio shows would have you thinking otherwise."

"You ever listen to either of them?"

"Some. Their shows were hard to avoid with all that chatter about the Battling Bents. But I'm not much of a radio listener or a TV watcher. I'm more the newspaper and magazine type. That way I follow what I'm interested in instead of being spoon fed my daily dose of what's happening in the world. How long have you been in the broadcast business?"

"Went into it straight out of college. I majored in broadcast journalism and landed a job and kept at it. I did it the old-fashioned way, working my way up the ladder one step at a time."

"You must have worked fast; you look pretty young to me. Of course, seeing the world through my eyes anyone under sixty looks young!"

"I was in the right place at the right time when I landed

the job as GM at KBUD. Some things you accomplish by design, some by luck, but mostly a combination of both."

"Are you happy doing what you do?"

"There are days I am, and days I'm not."

"Embracing the good while trying to avoid the bad, I suppose."

"You have to do that in the broadcast business. No one is going to run a radio station, regardless of the format, and be pleased with what they're putting out twenty-four seven. That's a lot of programming. You have to learn how to value the exceptional and tolerate the mundane. And believe me, in my business, you see a lot of the mundane."

"What did you think of Bill Bent's show? I mean, just between you, me, and the lamp post."

"Honestly, not my thing. And I'll tell you privately, he was not the easiest guy to deal with, but that's showbiz: sweet and sour, sunny and stormy, easy and difficult. If you want to meet a wide variety of personalities, go into broadcasting. I imagine you could say that about other businesses. But it seems on-air people, 'talent,' as we call them, are a breed apart."

"I've always wondered how radio stations handle angry listeners. I mean, people who get all fired up about someone like Bent because they don't like his point of view."

"That's one of the most unpleasant aspects of my job."

"How so?"

"Most people write to radio stations for one of three reasons. They want an autographed photo of an on-air personality. They're responding to a promotion, like an advertiser-sponsored contest. Or, they're writing to tell you how much they love or despise one of your on-air talents."

"I'm guessing Bill Bent had the biggest mailbag of all," Ted said with a knowing smile.

"By far. In fact, you see that guy over there standing next to the woman who is standing near Bill's widow, Beverly?"

"Yeah," Ted responded casually, while amused that the couple Reade was pointing to was Eddie and Sharon.

"He's been bugging me to have my staff plow through Bent's mail to see if any of his letters contained death threats."

"Is he a cop?" Ted asked casually.

"He's a detective with the Marin County Sheriff's Department."

"You going to follow-up?"

"I suppose I'll have to, now that we know Bill's disappearance was anything but innocent. Still, it's a colossal waste of time."

"Why is that?"

"If I had ten bucks for every piece of hate mail someone like Bent received over all the years he's been on the air, I could afford to buy a condo apartment in Marin, probably in San Francisco even. And let me tell you, places in the city don't come cheap. I've checked out several."

"I've heard! So, what do you do with those letters?"

"We hold onto letters for about ten weeks and dump them after that. A couple of times, we have flagged a writer because they're sending hate mail on a repeat basis. Our security people, we hire out for that, will send the writer a response. They're warned that we'll have to forward their letters to local law enforcement if they persist in making threats."

"You ever have to do that?"

"Twice, and believe it or not, neither of those were threats against Bent," Reade explained, flashing a bemused smile. "One was sent to Barney Benson for disagreeing with Bent regarding women receiving equal pay for equal work. Bill opposed the idea, big surprise there. The other was made against a financial investment guy we have on regularly. That particular writer insisted he lost thousands of dollars following our guy's advice. That might or might not be true. Trust me, there's no shortage of oddballs out there!"

"Does this stuff ever rattle you or others at the station?"

"It's one of the unhappy realities of the business you learn to live with. It's why we keep the doors to the station locked, and there is always a security person on duty twenty-four seven. Coming up in the business, I can tell you it's just something you learn to live with. That may not be the case in Scottsbluff, Nebraska, or Pismo Beach, California. But if you break into any of the bigger broadcast markets, having security in place has been part of the business for as long as I can remember. In fact, I'm certain, for a lot longer than that."

"So why not just hand the letters you have over to that cop you were pointing out? Or any cop for that matter?"

"It's not something people in my business like to do. Ninety-nine-point nine percent of these writers are simply blowing off steam. We don't want a listener getting a knock on the door from the police with the letter they wrote to KBUD being stuck in their face. Remember, today's angry letter writer is tomorrow's biggest fan."

"I never thought about it that way, but it does make sense. It sounds like you've got a lot on your plate. I don't suppose Bill Bent will be an easy person to replace."

"No, he won't," Reade said looking frustrated by the new reality he was facing. "Believe me, the ratings he generated made me look good, and more importantly, made the station's owners happy. Strong ratings are great to have, but just like good times, they don't last."

"You're wise beyond your years," Ted said while giving Reade a pat on the shoulder. "I suppose you could say if you could work with a talent like Bent, you likely could work with anyone."

"Managing Bent was like moving pots around on a hot stove. You always needed to handle with care."

"How so?"

"There were days I was thankful to have Bent as one of the station's keys to success. Other days I would have been happy if he walked in and told me he was quitting. Let's just say, he wasn't one of the world's best team player."

Sylvia devoted an hour the previous night, as did Holly, to looking over Eddie's printed sheet with the names and faces of women who had written thank you notes for romantic weekends with Bent. From their cards, mailed in envelopes that had no first or last name, or home address, Eddie only had a first name at the end of each note. That was all Sylvia had to go on.

She needed, however, only a moment to realize that standing three feet from her was one of those women. Sylvia watched as she dipped a jumbo shrimp into a bowl of cocktail sauce and then placed it in her mouth minus the last inch of tail and shell, which she deposited back onto a coated paper plate that contained two other oversized shrimp.

"Those look delicious," Sylvia said in a voice just above a whisper as she slipped alongside. "I should grab a few of these shrimps; I never had the chance to eat lunch."

"Neither did I, and they are delicious. I was starving during the last part of the service," the young woman responded. She quickly dapped her lips, somewhat embarrassed, having been found enjoying her food on such a sad occasion. Relieved to know that she was not alone in feeling desperately hungry, she thrust her hand forward.

"Meredith Newell, but my friends call me Meri."

"My name is Sylvia, Sylvia Stokes."

The two smiled and nodded before Sylvia quickly added, "Well, since we're both here for the departed and we both missed lunch to make it here on time, I'll consider myself a friend and call you Meri as well."

"Yes, please do. In fact, now that I no longer feel guilty about eating, I'll walk over with you and get some of those little ham and cheese appetizers. I should never skip lunch. I probably have that blood sugar thing I always hear people talking about."

"I'm exactly the same way!" Sylvia explained. "A few bites of something delicious was just what the doctor ordered."

Having quickly gained a degree of fellowship, Sylvia began with the most logical of questions: "How long did you know Bill?"

"I didn't know him all that long, or all that well. But we did have some fun together. He was a fascinating guy. I think a little crazy as well." Meri added in a soft voice, apparently concerned about being overheard.

"How did you meet?"

"I worked at a bar near Bill's radio station."

"I thought he did an early morning show. Was he around late in the afternoon and into the evening?"

"I have no idea when Bill got any sleep. Sometimes he would

show up at three in the afternoon, but other times, when I was working a late shift, he'd walk in after midnight. I think Bill was the original hard-partying guy. Several times, near closing, which was around one in the morning, I'd see Bill leaving with a few of the regulars claiming they were going off to a party."

"That's amazing when you consider he did an early morning show," Sylvia said.

"Every now and then, he must have done his show after getting little if any sleep. I'd be putting on my sleep mask to block out the daylight around seven in the morning, and I'd hear his opening on KBUD. He sounded raring to go. It was a mystery to me how he did that unless he was taking something to get amped up if you know what I mean?" Meredith asked, wondering if a woman Sylvia's age had any idea what she was talking about.

"I do know what you mean! I didn't listen often, but when I did, he sounded like he was well-rested and ready to do a great show."

"My theory, he either was blessed with a great deal more energy than the average person, or he got an assist from Big Pharma. Perhaps a bit of both."

"Really?"

"Those drug companies are a lot more dangerous than people know. If they had their way, everyone would be taking one drug or more every day. Say, you don't suppose that Bill knew something about how Big Pharma operates, and they needed to keep him quiet?" Meredith asked with the wide-eyed look of an individual well-schooled in conspiracy theories.

Interesting thought, but this wasn't the information Eddie was seeking. Sylvia knew she needed to get the conversation back on track. She quickly decided to be far more direct.

"I wonder if Bill had one or more extramarital affairs?"

Meredith shrugged and then asked, "What makes you think that?"

"Bill seems to have been one of those people who lived more than one life during a relatively short lifespan. He was still in his thirties at the time of his death. Perhaps he had an insatiable appetite for doing a great many things over a relatively brief time."

"I see what you mean, and having known him, I think you might be right. Bill did act like someone who was always in a hurry to go and do everything he possibly could. I think that pertained to his love life as well. He might have liked the idea of having a harem for all I know. I'm glad I kept him at a distance."

"How so?" Sylvia asked innocently.

"Well, just between us," she said softly, "Bill asked me if I wanted to go off and spend a weekend with him."

"He did?" Sylvia said, wondering if she had overplayed her reaction.

"Oh, I would never do such a thing, but it didn't surprise me that he asked. He suggested the Hotel Drisco, a real high-end place in San Francisco's Pacific Heights neighborhood."

"Was it because he was a married man that you said no?"

"I wish I could tell you that was my reason, but I'm not going to lie to you, Sylvia. I knew Bill was married, and I had long assumed it was not a happy marriage. As I said, he never seemed to be in a hurry to get home. Plus, I did not want to be in the middle of what looked to me like a messy divorce in the not too distant future."

"What made you think it would be messy?"

"Well, I don't know if you ever listened to Bill's show, but I heard him consoling guys who were going through a divorce. He got so angry about women taking guys to the cleaners because, as he put it, their husbands foolishly wanted to do the right thing.

"Bill reminded me of the guy on the highway who goes flying past you driving like a nut, a drunk, perhaps both. Whenever I see that I slow down, fall back, and try to avoid trouble. Having an intimate relationship with Bill would involve taking the kind of risk I'm not comfortable taking. Bill Bent was an accident waiting to happen."

"My dear, you're wise beyond your years," Sylvia said as she gave Meredith a pat on the arm.

With the post service gathering inside St. John's Parish Hall already beginning to thin, both Rob and Holly were feeling disappointed. Holly's intercept of Barney Benson was the only item that felt like an accomplishment.

"Not one of the more promising of these gambits," Rob said as Holly and he stood near one corner of the reception hall and commiserated over relatively thin results.

"Rob, look over there."

"Where?"

"The guy in the dark suit, white shirt, gray tie, with a coffee cup in his hand. Isn't that Tom Joseph?" Holly asked.

"I think you're right. Here, hold this," Rob said as he handed Holly a plate with half-eaten portions of three-bean salad, potato salad, and egg salad. "I'll be back."

Rob snaked his way through three groups of remaining mourners until he was at Joseph's side.

"Tom? Right?" Rob said with a warm smile and an open hand thrust forward.

"That's right, Tom Joseph. Do I know you?"

"One of my wife's closest friends works at your station, Beverly Bent. I'm Rob Timmons, my wife is Karin."

"Oh, Beverly just introduced me to your wife. It's nice to meet you as well."

"I haven't had a chance to speak to Beverly yet. I got here a little late, but I was glad to see such a big turnout."

"Yes, the turnout was good to see. I'm sure Beverly was pleased. A lot of people in broadcasting knew Bill."

"He was an interesting character, wasn't he?" Rob asked with an arched eyebrow.

"If nothing else, Bill Bent was that."

"Odd situation, though."

"You mean the way Beverly and Bill bickered back and forth in the weeks before his death?"

"Exactly, there are a lot of unhappy couples that don't get to slug it out on competing radio stations. Not that it didn't make for interesting listening," Rob added quickly.

"I know it might sound ridiculous, but it's kept me awake recent nights trying to convince myself that Bill's death, his murder I should say, had nothing to do with the Battling Bents. But my mind keeps going back to that thought."

For a brief moment, Rob wondered why Joseph would make such a comment; then, he decided to ask.

Tom thought about Rob's question for a few moments. He looked down at his shoes while his hands stayed shoved deep inside his pants' pockets. "I thought that Beverly going on air would be a ratings bonanza."

"Was it?" Rob asked quickly in the hope that all Joseph was looking for was someone to talk with.

"It's no secret to people in the broadcast business that KLIB was not on the radar before the Battling Bents. Now it's one of the Bay Area's top-rated stations, so yeah, having them face off every morning helped my station immeasurably."

"But..."

"It's just a lousy feeling to think that some KLIB listener might have taken Bent out."

"But you don't have any reason to think that other than a general suspicion, correct?"

"Yes, that's true. But the possibility has been keeping me awake at night."

"I assume you have nothing concrete like a letter from a listener or a threat that was called in within days of Bill's murder?"

"That's true, I don't. But not everyone who wants to kill somebody goes running to the media, or their shrink, for that matter."

"Agreed. All I can say is there's an excellent chance Bill's murder is completely unrelated to his on-air antics."

"I just hope Beverly doesn't hate me for what's happened."

"Well, Beverly's very close to her friend Sharon, and Sharon is very close to my wife, Karin, and I've heard nothing like that."

"Beverly is one of the best people I've ever met. The way she was treated by Bill was disgraceful. I just can't figure out what it is with some guys. You would think he'd have the good sense to know how lucky he was to have someone like Beverly for a life partner. I suppose some guys are just too blind or too dumb to know what a good woman they have until they lose her."

Earlier, Holly had seen Sylvia talking with Meredith, which made her even more determined to find one of Bill Bent's other girlfriends. For a third time, Holly's eyes scanned the remaining attendees. She felt a rush of excitement when her eyes fell upon the woman who thanked Bent for a lavish weekend at Big Sur's Post Ranch Inn.

What was her name again? Holly thought as she moved closer, hoping to catch the attractive young woman who had long, flowing, auburn colored hair.

It was Deborah! That's undoubtedly her!

"Haven't we met before?" An innocent-sounding question Holly used previously on unsuspecting individuals.

"I'm Deborah Schiff," the young woman responded with a smile, wondering if she had previously met this short woman with dark curly hair, bright eyes, and a warm smile.

"I'm Holly Cross. I've known Beverly and Bill for many years."

"I just met Beverly for the first time today, but I worked with Bill for a few years when I was a producer at KBUD."

"Are you still working at the station?"

"No. I left a couple of years ago."

"Did you and Bill stay in touch?"

"Not really. Beverly was my real reason for being here today."

"Did you get to say hello to her?"

"Not yet, but I want to go over and do that before I leave.

I'm delighted with what she's accomplished at KLIB. I think Beverly and Betsy Baker are the best new broadcast team in the Bay Area. I hope the loss of Bill doesn't do anything to change that, we need more people like those two hosting Bay Area radio programs."

Weird, Holly thought, she's not saying what I'd expect to hear from someone who had an affair with Beverly's husband. The post-service reception was winding down. Now was the time she needed to press for relevant answers.

"Beverly has had a tough time these past few days. I feel almost guilty about going out of town, but my boyfriend invited me to go down to Big Sur this weekend. He made reservations at Post Ranch Inn," Holly announced with an innocent smile.

"Lucky you. I've never stayed there, but I know a few people who have. They all tell me it's fabulous. You should tell Beverly. I'm sure she wouldn't want you to give up something like that. Particularly if it means your boyfriend will lose a room deposit. From what I hear, that place is three times as expensive as other lodgings near Big Sur."

Wait, Holly thought. What's going on! I'm sure this is the woman I saw in the photo enclosed in that thank you note to Bent describing their weekend at Post Ranch Inn.

Deborah's response clearly threw Holly for a loop. Now what? She wondered, knowing time was running out.

She took Deborah's hand as if they were old friends, looked her in the eye and said, "Thank you for those wise words. You're right. Opportunities like this for us working class gals don't come along very often. I think I will go."

"Smart choice," Deborah said with an approving smile. "I'm going to go over and give Beverly the big hug I've meant to give her since Bill's service ended. If you'll excuse me."

Holly watched Deborah walk off. She was dazed by the woman's reaction. What was that all about? Holly thought as she looked around at the scattering of people left in Parish Hall.

The four members of Eddie's snoop squad walked back to their cars in silence. Whatever happened it would all have to be sorted out the following morning when Eddie was scheduled to debrief them. Holly hated waiting for answers. But with another two hours of work waiting for her and Rob back at their office, waiting was her only option.

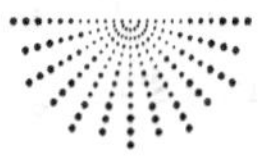

CHAPTER TWENTY-FIVE

"How did your snooping go?" Scott asked Holly as she stood over a hot stove, preparing one of their favorite home-cooked meals, salmon with penne pasta in a white cream sauce.

"I'm glad you asked! Odd is the only word that comes to mind."

"What makes you say that?" Scott said as he worked on opening a chilled bottle of chardonnay.

"We all went back to work after the reception. Rob and I had several things we needed to do to prepare for tomorrow's deadlines, so we had agreed in advance not to have any conversations about our snooping after we left the service. Taking nearly three hours out of the middle of a workday is never easy for us. Anyway, Eddie is meeting with all four of us tomorrow morning, so I'll get an idea then what Rob, Sylvia, and Ted learned. All I can tell you is what I learned wasn't a heck of a lot."

"Did you come across anything that struck you as odd?"

"Usually, I'll pick up a trail of breadcrumbs that helps to

advance Eddie's investigation. In the two targets I talked with, I came away with more questions than when I began."

"Sounds like a frustrating afternoon."

"It was! And no one else seemed excited on the way back to where we parked. I would describe the four of us as pretty well stymied. Well, maybe not Ted. But he's an optimist by nature so you can't tell much by that. Anyway, it didn't feel like a banner day for Eddie's snoop squad."

"Sorry to hear that, sweetie."

"Something strange is going on, Scott. Maybe when we put all of our information together, this will make more sense. But if everyone came away with as little as I did, we didn't make any real progress. Perhaps we were just fishing in the wrong spot."

"Keeping with that thought," Scott said, "open the oven and check the salmon. I think it might be close to done."

Rob, Holly, Ted, and Sylvia came into their morning meeting with Eddie hoping one or more of them had collected some valuable information. It didn't take long before they were disabused of that assumption.

Eddie went around the room and took a reading from each member of his team.

Ted reported, "Nick Reade, the KBUD GM, is a nice enough guy. Perhaps a little burned out with his job, which seems understandable after all the time I spent talking to him."

"Any idea why he would be sitting on threatening letters that Bent might have received from listeners?"

Ted provided a detailed synopsis of his conversation with Reade. "Eddie, I think he's tired of jerking your chain regarding listeners writing in about Bent. I'd give him another try. He seems reluctant because, as he explained, no one who runs a radio station is anxious to have a longtime fan, who blew his top over a particular show and sent a letter to the station, getting a knock on the door from the police. In the era of social media, you can bet that experience will be all over the Internet before you can say 'listener boycott.' The next time you call Reade, make it crystal clear that you're looking only for letters, if indeed there are any, that make specific threats to Bent's wellbeing."

"Good advice, Ted. I'll do that. Any feeling about Reade and his relationship with Bent?"

"I think the only thing that Bent represented to Reade was a highly rated morning show. He more or less suggested that Bent was a pain in the neck, but if disliking high strung on-air talent like Bent makes you a suspect, I think most station managers would be possible suspects."

"As long as we're talking about radio station general managers," Rob offered, "I had a pleasant conversation with Tom Joseph, Beverly's boss."

"What was your take?" Eddie asked.

"In a word, lovesick."

"Really," Eddie and Holly said at the same moment.

"Yeah, really!" Rob responded with a smile. "Like a schoolboy with a crush."

"What makes you say that?" Holly asked.

"Comments like..." Rob paused to look at notes he had written down after dinner last night. "Okay, here's a perfect example, 'Beverly is one of the best people I've ever met and the way her late husband treated her was unforgivable.'"

"I think we can all agree with that," Sylvia said.

"Okay, how about this one: 'You would think Bent would have the good sense to know how lucky he was to have someone like Beverly. I guess a lot of guys are too foolish to know what a good woman they have until they lose her.'"

"Sounds like he has a pretty big crush on Beverly," Ted said.

"Either a crush or he's simply a big fan," Eddie offered.

"I might be wrong," Rob said, "but I've seen my share of guys who have it bad starting from high school on. I'd say Tom Joseph was a pretty good example of one of those lovesick puppies."

"Do you think his feelings for Beverly were strong enough that he might want to see her free of her husband?" Eddie asked with an arched brow.

"I'm uncertain about that. For one thing, I don't know if Beverly's boss is capable of harming any creature bigger than a housefly. But I think you need to put this guy on your radar. I walked away from our conversation with two strong impressions: One, Tom Joseph would happily run away with Beverly if she felt the same way about him and two, Joseph has a real disdain for the way Bent treated her.

"But I also realize that in most situations like this, despising someone and/or wishing them dead is a far cry from acting on those feelings. That said, Eddie, you need to be aware that there's an outside chance that Joseph is your guy."

"Noted, Rob," Eddie said with a smile. "I'll plan on interviewing him further and dig around regarding his background before he arrived at KLIB.

"Holly, I heard you buttonholed Barney Benson. As you know, I interviewed him about Bent when he was still a missing person. I'm interested to know what you thought of him?"

"Comes off as a bit of a slick character. Let's say he doesn't seem like the most honest individual I've ever met."

"I had the same feeling when I interviewed him. Of course, being a glad-hander and a fast talker doesn't make him a suspect. Not to mention, his professional life is all about chatting people up, so it's a part of his persona."

"While I wish there was more to report regarding Benson," Holly said, "the one comment he made that stuck out, and it could be a groundless suspicion on my part, is Benson noted his daughter Janice, age twenty-seven, is apparently boy crazy, which Benson seems to find quite troubling."

"I'd be nervous if I had a boy crazy daughter, I suppose I should say, granddaughter," Ted suggested with a chuckle.

"Sounds to me like an overprotective dad. Janice did not send any of the letters you uncovered," Rob said, turning to Eddie. "But if Bent was the playboy we all suspect him to have been, then you might want to dig a little deeper into Benson and his daughter."

"That, of course, assumes there was a connection between the two when none may have existed. But I can't rule it out, so you're right, Rob, it's worth taking a closer look."

"Speaking of Bill Bent's adulterous behavior," Sylvia interjected, "I had a very odd conversation with Meredith Newell. She was supposedly one of the women that wrote to Bent. This was the one we believed spent a weekend with Bent at the Hotel Drisco in San Francisco."

"She didn't open up about her weekend rendezvous with Bent?" Eddie asked.

"Not only did she not share the details of her weekend with Bent, as best as I can tell she was never there."

"Never where?" Rob asked.

"At the Drisco Hotel in Pacific Heights."

"I assume you think she's lying?" Rob asked.

"No, I don't think she's lying, and here's why. She came out and told me that Bill had invited her to spend a weekend with him in San Francisco, and she mentioned that particular hotel. But she told me he was too odd in his behavior to be trusted. By way of example, she cited his advice to husbands in separation battles with their wives. The last thing she wanted was to find herself in the middle of a messy divorce."

"Sounds like she thought Bent was an accident waiting to happen," Ted offered.

"Exactly," Sylvia said nodding approvingly at Ted's assessment.

"I think Meredith Newell was being honest about not taking Bill up on his offer for a weekend at the Drisco," Holly announced.

"Why is that?" Eddie asked, growing more amazed by the moment. "Did you speak to her as well?"

"I didn't speak to Newell, but I spoke to another one of Bent's letter writers, Deborah Schiff. I buddied up to her, probably in much the same way Sylvia struck up a conversation with Meredith. It was getting late, and the gathering in Parish Hall had thinned to a third of what it had been forty-five minutes earlier. Probably like Sylvia, I kept looking for one of the women who wrote to Bent. Deborah and I talked long enough for me to learn that she had been a producer at KBUD and had worked with Bent at one point. She didn't strike me as being one of Bent's biggest admirers. In fact, she was quite complimentary of Beverly's on-air work at KLIB, saying it was in support of her that she chose to attend the service."

"Did she say anything about Bill Bent?" Eddie asked.

"Nope, just a passing reference."

"So, you don't think she had an affair with Bent?"

"Honestly, she's a pretty good poker bluff if she did. But you know me, I had to prod her with an invented story that introduced the topic of the Post Ranch Inn…"

"What did you say?" Rob asked, always in awe of Holly's ability to invent a fabrication on the spur of the moment.

"It was easy, I told her that I wanted to stay in town over the weekend to be close by in case Beverly needed me. But I felt bad about my boyfriend paying a deposit on a room down at the Post Ranch Inn. Then I added how I had never been there, but I'd been told it's a must-not-miss experience."

"What did she say to that?" Sylvia asked anxiously.

"She claimed never to have been to Post Ranch, but she had been told it was an extraordinary place and suggested I explain my situation to Beverly, who she thought would more than understand."

"She said she'd never stayed at Post Ranch?" Eddie said, clearly astonished.

"Yep."

"Do you think she's lying to cover up a weekend she spent with the husband of a woman she claims to admire?" Rob asked.

"Sure, that's a possibility, but I have to say, she's one heck of a good liar if she was making all that up."

"After speaking to Meredith Newell, I don't think either of these women are covering up about supposed affairs with Bent," Sylvia said confidently.

"To borrow one of my grandpa's favorite expressions, this is a fine kettle of fish," Ted said, looking bemused by the mystery.

"If Meredith did not send that note, and this woman Deborah did not write a note of thanks for a weekend visit to a place she's apparently never been," Rob said, "then who in God's name did send those notes? Not to mention the enclosed photos!"

"At this point, pal, I have no idea," Eddie said with a shrug. "I've had curveballs thrown at me before, but this one is up there near the top of the list."

For a brief time, all five of them sat in silence, considering how this collection of notes came into existence.

"Neither you nor Sylvia discussed any of this after the service?" Eddie asked with apparent surprise.

"I can't speak for Ted or Sylvia, but Rob and I rode up together, and as soon as I finished with Deborah, we both said a few quick goodbyes and hurried back to the office. You know what our weekly deadlines are like, Eddie."

"As for me, I went back to my car in a daze," Sylvia added. "After my conversation with Meredith, I kept thinking maybe she was misleading me, even though that didn't make sense. Now, after hearing Holly's conversation with Deborah Schiff, I don't have any doubt about what she told me. I'm kind of glad Holly and I didn't have the chance to talk about this until now. I'm relieved that Meredith, as was my impression after I talked with her, was not dishonest. It's certainly possible that one of them invented a story to hide an affair, but not both."

"Agreed," Rob and Eddie said simultaneously.

"There is, however, one important difference in what we heard from both women," Sylvia said. "Meredith told me that

Bent had invited her to spend the weekend with him at the Drisco. When I pressed her about that, telling her I heard it's supposed to be a wonderful place, she just shrugged. She said she didn't want to get involved with a married man, and that applied particularly in the case of Bill Bent."

"Why do you think it was particularly true regarding Bent?" Eddie asked.

"Meredith detailed how she frequently saw Bent at all hours while she was a waitress at a bar in San Francisco near Union Square. As I think all of you know, KBUD is in a building at Post and Mason very close to where Meredith worked. She seemed convinced that Bent was addicted to amphetamines or some other drug. She explained that something had to be keeping him going day and night."

"Tell me more about that," Eddie said.

"According to Meredith, Bill was in her bar until final call, which is around one in the morning. Considering he was on the air by seven, and you would have to assume preparing his show at least thirty to sixty minutes before that, it's not surprising she was astounded by how he could keep those hours."

"Wow," Eddie said with a look of amazement. "Bent gets more interesting with each passing day."

"Based on what Holly and Sylvia just shared," Rob said, "I'm guessing that Bent was an even worse husband than we imagined."

"How in the world did Beverly put up with that guy for so many years?" Holly asked.

"Some people have a high tolerance for pain. Physical, emotional, or both," Ted offered.

"I imagine Beverly was well practiced at the art of looking the other way," Sylvia suggested. "I pressed Meredith to explain why she turned down Bent's invitation to spend a weekend with him. She said that she had a strict rule not to get involved with married men."

"I suspect that rule," Holly added, "applied especially to men she thought were unstable as well. She was in a position to know just how peculiar the hours were that Bill kept. It's not a stretch to imagine she found many other aspects of his personality to be troubling as well."

"For my two cents," Ted said, "I'd guess that Bent made up the letters you found from these two women and, obviously, if that's the case, then probably the other two letters as well."

"That's some seriously weird stuff," Rob said, shaking his head.

"I can see at this point why you would say that, Ted. But that doesn't begin to explain why he would do such a thing," Eddie added.

"Perhaps Bent was stranger than we previously thought," Holly offered.

"Yeah," Rob said with a short laugh. "And that was already pretty strange."

"The first thing I need to do when I get back to HQ is have all of these thank you notes gone over by one of our staff who does FDE and compare that with Bent's handwriting."

"FDE?" Ted said with a quizzical look.

"Forensic document examination. In law enforcement, you often encounter forged documents. It won't take our person very long to tell us two important things: First, if all the notes were written by the same person and second, if the handwriting matches Bill Bent's."

"You think this guy wrote these gushing thank you notes

to himself?" Ted asked, amazed by the thought of such a deception.

"I have no idea who wrote those notes," Eddie responded. "I can't even say with certainty that he was the individual who placed those envelopes under a false bottom in the lower drawer of the desk in his den. But a determination that these notes came from the same hand would tell us something we don't know for certain at this point. I'll happily admit it would be a head-scratcher as to the who and why of it, but that aside, whatever we learn will hopefully point us toward other answers."

"I've always been fascinated by the study of handwriting and what it tells us about an individual," Ted said, wondering how this collection of notes came about.

"I think you might have graphology and forensic writing analysis confused," Eddie replied.

"I'm not sure what either of those is?" Sylvia said.

"Graphology is a form of handwriting analysis, considered by many to be a pseudoscience," Rob said. "It's things like if you place the bar in crossing your 't' high, you're an optimist, if low, you're a pessimist."

"You mean it's a lot like astrology, only instead of looking at the planets and stars for answers, you're studying someone's penmanship," Ted said with a grin.

"Exactly, Ted. Forensic writing analysts are trained in picking up similarities in an individual's writing style, even when they are consciously trying to make it look like the handwriting of another person. The question now is whether these letters are similar to Beverly's or Bill's writing," Rob suggested.

"Why in the world would Beverly write those notes?" Holly asked, certain the very possibility was ridiculous.

"I have no idea, Holly," Rob responded.

"Neither do I, and I'm the lead investigator on the case," Eddie said as he sat back in his seat. He tried to imagine a scenario under which Beverly Bent may have planted those letters inside her late husband's desk.

"Gosh, Eddie, I hope you're not feeling like you're running in circles," Sylvia said in her usual caring manner.

"It's all pretty nutty, but after further investigation, there might be some logic to all this. When a case twists in one direction and then appears to go in another, you can't allow yourself to get frustrated. At this moment, I have no idea whether these notes are breadcrumbs on the trail to unraveling Bent's homicide or a meaningless detour. But how a set of love notes from different women expressing gratitude for lavish weekends wound up in Bent's desk is an aspect of this investigation I can't ignore."

"If nothing else, just learning from the analyst that these notes were all written by the same person will tell you a lot," Holly offered.

"Absolutely," Eddie said as he stood to leave.

"Well, good luck," Sylvia declared with an encouraging smile. "I suppose none of us were as helpful this time as we have been in the past."

"I've never known two homicide investigations to follow the exact same path," Eddie assured her. "I think this kind of background gathering is invaluable in opening up lines of inquiry that I may have never known to follow. What I learned about these two station general managers, Reade and Joseph, will help me understand their motives and allow me to move forward more productively. In fact, Reade at KBUD is my next stop of the day. And Benson's daughter, Janice, might turn out to be more important than any of us imagine.

Most importantly, Sylvia, the fact that we've learned these two women, Meredith and Deborah, may not have been involved in the letters I found in Bent's home likely saved me from running down a series of blind alleys."

"Well, thank you for saying that, Eddie," Sylvia said. "All of us are aware of how hard you work and it's nice to know that we weren't out there spinning our wheels just to bring you little information of value."

"If the notes I found were forgeries then you and Holly helped get me off the wrong path and perhaps onto the right one."

"I just can't imagine how these notes of love and appreciation came into existence?" Holly said with a discouraged shrug.

"I think we all feel like that," Rob said. "Perhaps it's like the old saying, 'God closes a window and opens a door.'"

"Could be. After I see Reade at KBUD, I'll find out about getting an analyst to start working on Bent's collection of love notes. I'll stay in touch through Rob and keep all of you updated."

"Eddie, time for one more quick question?" Ted asked.

"Sure."

"The photos of those women enclosed with the notes you found. If they were fabricated, how did Bent get hold of their pictures?"

"That's easy," Rob jumped in. "All the time, I take candid photos with my phone without the kids realizing what I'm doing. They think I'm reading something on the phone's display, but I'm actually watching them do something adorable. If the phone is on silent, they won't even hear a click."

"I do the same thing with my grandson," Sylvia said.

"Edit the image afterward to anything you like, and now your subject has posed for a headshot they never knew was taken," Rob added.

"Then send off the edited image to one of several online photo print companies or walk into a Walgreen's or CVS, or other places that have photo printers and get a two by three or any other size picture you want," Eddie concluded with a shrug and a smile. "Pretty simple stuff in the age of digital everything."

"I could write a book called *All The Things I Don't Know*," Ted said with a smile.

"I'll be happy to be your co-author!" Sylvia added with a laugh.

"By the way, Eddie," Holly said quickly, "What did Sharon think about how Beverly is holding up?"

"After we got Aaron to bed last night and had a little time to ourselves, Sharon told me that Beverly seemed like a woman with a great weight lifted off her shoulders."

"Do you think she meant having gotten through the service or knowing she never had to worry about dealing with Bill again?" Rob asked.

"I'd say a little bit of both."

CHAPTER TWENTY-SIX

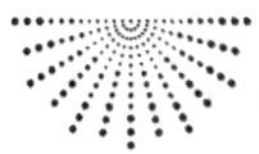

Eddie started his car and realized he had a full hour before his 11:30 meeting with Nick Reade at KBUD. Even though he had eaten breakfast a few hours earlier, he was starving. The easiest thing to do was to drive a couple of minutes north, out of Sausalito's small downtown, over to his home on Litho Street. There, he could grab a quick bite and pick up the thank you card Beverly had sent after Eddie met her at the Bent's Corte Madera home. That would provide a sample of Beverly's handwriting as well.

Given where they were found, hidden under a panel in Bill's desk, it was likely the notes, if indeed forgeries, were created by Bent's hand. On the off chance that the notes were a deception created by Beverly, that would be even more puzzling. Beverly had obviously grown to despise Bent over the ten years of their marriage. Perhaps, she simply didn't care what Eddie found.

He quickly sliced a bagel, toasted it, and then slathered it with butter and jam. It took him just a few minutes to locate the card Beverly had sent.

"Yes," Eddie said softly to himself as he pulled the card out from under a pile on his nightstand. Eddie, a persistent but impatient reader, always had at least two books and several magazines on his nightstand. If his days were less trying, he might have had better luck reading more before he drifted off to sleep. Given what they were he was lucky if he made it more than ten or fifteen minutes before falling into a deep sleep.

"No true crime stories?" Sharon had asked one evening a week earlier as she looked at the books stacked by his bed.

"I get enough true crime at work."

Eddie sat on the edge of his bed and looked admiringly at Beverly's penmanship. I wish I could write this legibly, he thought. He placed the card in his jacket's inside pocket, grabbed his car keys, and headed out the door.

Traffic crossing the Golden Gate was moving nicely, giving Eddie added confidence that he would make his meeting with time to spare.

Twenty minutes later, he was in Nick Reade's office. To Eddie's relief, he found Reade to be a changed man. He began by apologizing for his behavior over the past week.

"I don't have any excuse for giving you a hard time other than this whole thing with Bill hit me pretty hard. It's a gut punch, to be honest. Upsetting on a personal and professional level. On top of my own feelings, there's the hole Bill's death blew in our morning lineup. No matter what I or any staff member thought of Bill personally, he won't be an easy talent to replace."

"I'm sure he won't," Eddie said empathetically, following Ted's advice to play nice with KBUD's overworked and over stressed station manager.

"I appreciate your pulling these letters together for me. Likely, none of Bill's listeners would actually act on any threats, but now that we have a murder investigation, we have to look at this case from every conceivable angle."

"Until your request, I hadn't looked at any of Bill's letters from listeners in over a year. Actually, I was even more reluctant to do that after Bill's body was found. That might sound counter-intuitive, but it's the dark side of talk radio. Stirring the pot, you might say. Unfortunately, there are listeners, who cannot distinguish between provocative conversation and a call to arms."

"That's totally understandable," Eddie said. He had little doubt that Reade, and others in his position, blurred the line between responsible and irresponsible programming in favor of improved advertising revenues.

"The two I found particularly troubling I put on top of the pile. One is a letter from a listener down in Brisbane who tells Bent that guys like him make things much worse for men everywhere. Here's an excerpt:

"I can't imagine how many relationships you have ruined with your big mouth. I had been dating the same woman for nearly a year until one night when the topic of your show came up. She said you were a jerk, and she didn't want me listening to any more of your 'garbage!' One thing led to another, and before I knew it, she told me we were finished. I was pretty mad at her that night and for the next few days. Then on Friday, I had my boss get on my case about some product that went out late. I blew my top and told her all you women are the same. Three days later, I was called in to see the company's personnel director. I was given a two-week severance and told not to come back. What started all this was the stupid ideas you put in my head. I hope something equally awful happens to you. Or worse!"

Wow, Eddie thought wondering if the size of Bent's fan club was exceeded by the number of detractors he had accumulated over the years.

"This second letter," Reade continued, "details the story of a man who, thanks to Bill's insistence that men learn to lay down the law, told his intended bride that she was far too controlling and a few other things I won't repeat! This letter ended similarly.

"There are several others like this, all of them taken from the past couple of months, so they're relatively recent. I never did a deep dive into Bent's mailbag. I suppose I'm guilty of focusing on the audience numbers his show generated and not at the damage he caused in the lives of some of his listeners."

"From the package you're giving me," Eddie said, "It looks like there are another twenty-five letters in here."

"I'm sorry I didn't alert you to these letters earlier. I suspected it wouldn't be good news, which is the real reason I was reluctant to look."

"What's past is past. I very much appreciate the time this must have taken for both you and your staff."

"Are you going to follow up with any of these letter writers?"

"I'm not certain at this stage. We're developing a few promising leads, which have nothing to do with Bill's fans or detractors. I'll get back to you before we move ahead by calling or paying a visit to one or more of your listeners, if it indeed that's needed. Hopefully none of these individuals acted on their anger, but in my line of work you have to expect the unexpected."

Both stood and shook hands. Eddie reached the door of Reade's office when he turned and asked, "Any chance Barney Benson is still around, or has he left for the day?"

"He might still be here, let me check for you."

A moment later, Reade put down his office phone and said, "His producer said he just left."

Eddie placed his card down on the center of Reade's desk. "Ask him to give me a call when he finishes his show tomorrow. I have a few more questions for him regarding Bill. There's a chance Barney might be able to help."

"Sure," Reade said, sitting back in his desk chair wondering what new leads Eddie might be following.

"Darn, I almost forgot, would one of your support staff, or one of your producers have a few samples of Bill's handwriting? We need to check it against something we came across at his home that might be a forgery."

"If you've got five minutes, take a seat out in the reception area, and I'll see if I can locate something for you right now."

In less time than Eddie anticipated, Reade returned with program log notes from a show done the day before Bent went missing. "I've made a few photocopies of handwritten notes Bill did while he was on the air. I hope this will do the job. Let me know if there is anything else we can do to help. Finding Bill's killer would be a great relief to everyone who works here."

After a second handshake, Eddie was on his way to the building's elevator bank, delighted by the change that had come over Reade. I should have more of my targets talk to

Ted, Eddie thought, having discovered one more way his group of snoops helped in an investigation.

Earlier, Eddie had spoken with Melissa Jacobs, the document examiner, and confirmed their mid-afternoon meeting. He had two hours and decided it would be a good idea to grab some lunch before leaving the city. On his way out of KBUD's studios, he ran into Barney Benson, who greeted him like he was an old friend.

"I was wondering if you were around. I thought I had just missed you."

"I was on my way out when one of the staff pulled me into their office for a question about an advertising promotion. Have you got a couple of minutes? There's something I'd like to discuss with you."

"Yeah, I've got more than a couple of minutes, I'm actually ahead of schedule. I've got a meeting at two o'clock up at the sheriff's office in San Rafael. I was going to grab a burger. Want to go back to that place you took me to, what was it called?"

"Honey, Honey."

"That's the place. Have you eaten?"

"Yep, about an hour ago. But I didn't have dessert."

"Good, let's go."

In the few minutes it took to walk to the corner of Post and Taylor, the two of them discussed the disappointing season the Giants were having.

"Three World Series championships in five years, I don't suppose we'll see that again," Barney said.

"Probably not, but anything is possible, particularly with more reliable pitching and hitting," Eddie suggested. "There's a lot of competition out there. It wasn't all that long ago there were half the teams we have today. The era of dynasties might be at an end, considering how thin top talent is spread."

When they walked into Honey, Honey, they grabbed a table. Eddie quickly ordered that burger and fries he had been thinking about for most of the past hour, and Barney happily asked for a slice of apple pie and a cup of coffee.

"Are you making any progress?"

"Are you thinking about making any more suggestions to your listeners about SFPD getting involved in my investigation?" Eddie asked, putting him on notice that he was not pleased with the recent vote of no confidence in the Marin County Sheriff's Department.

"Sorry, pal. Nothing personal. I have to throw some chum at that angry mob of listeners we get every morning. I suppose I should say, I get, since the days of Wild Bill and Barney Benson have come to an end."

"I'm sure it's not easy carrying the entire morning program on your own."

"Let's just say calling it an adjustment is a huge understatement."

"You still of the opinion that KBUD is looking to replace you with a new morning team?"

"Probably. But management might be quietly looking around for a new lead guy to take Bill's slot and keep me around as the show's co-host for the sake of continuity."

"It's got to be tough, wondering what they're going to decide and when that move will come."

"Not as tough as people outside of broadcasting might think. If you want job security in this business, work for your family's radio station. If not, do your best work, stay positive, and keep a bag packed at all times. Oh yeah, and don't forget to save some money. You never know when that next job may appear."

"Spoken like a man who has seen good times and bad times."

"That I have, my friend."

"I saw you at Bill's service yesterday afternoon. I had to leave before the reception got going. What did you think?"

"Nice turnout. Bill was never Mister Popularity around the station, but people tend to put the bad aside and focus on the good at times like these."

"That's certainly true."

"Glad I had the chance to meet your lovely wife. Sharon, right?"

"That's my sweetheart."

"She told me about how close she and Beverly were growing up in Tiburon, going to the same elementary school and all. Girls bond in ways boys rarely do."

"Agreed. I'm glad that Beverly has a group of friends to help support her through this. I'm sure it's been a tough couple of weeks for her. Obviously, she and Bill had what they call irreconcilable differences, but this was not how she imagined their marriage ending."

"Do you really feel sure about that?"

"You're not suggesting that Beverly Bent had anything to do with her husband's death?"

"I'm not sure if I think that or not, but I feel there's a good chance her boss at KLIB might have."

"I'm all ears, Barney. Tell me what you're thinking."

"I overheard Tom Joseph, you know him, I assume, the station manager at KLIB?"

"Yeah, I know the guy."

"He sounded pleased that, as he put it, 'Bent is out of Beverly's life for good.'"

"That's interesting. Whom was he sharing that opinion with?"

"Betsy Baker, Beverly's broadcast partner."

"Barney, were you eavesdropping?"

"In broadcasting we call it keeping your ear to the ground. In an industry where talent often has a limited life-span, you need to pay attention to details."

"So, you think Beverly's boss might have been involved in Bent's death?"

"I don't know. I saw Joseph and Beverly talking. They seemed, I don't know how to put this, a little too close?"

"Well, it's certainly worth my taking a closer look. I agree with you that Tom Joseph is clearly pleased and proud of Beverly's work at KLIB. If that extended to his wanting to free her from what you, I, and just about everyone else within a hundred-mile radius of where we're sitting, considered a wreck of a marriage, that's another matter entirely."

"I thought it was interesting that I overheard him calling Bill a sorry excuse for a man and his adding that KBUD should have shown him the door long ago. That's why I'm passing it along."

"Well, it's not hard to see why he might consider their marriage to be less than ideal."

"True. Marriages hit the rocks every day of the year, but few as publicly as Bill and Beverly's."

"From what I know, Bill and Beverly's feud sent the ratings of KLIB through the roof. It would be hard to imagine a station manager wanting to put an end to a run like that."

"You would think. But two things can change that.

Station managers, particularly ones who are relatively young and single, change jobs frequently, and secondly, everyone in the broadcast game knows that the new hot thing is quickly replaced by the next new hot thing."

"So, you're suggesting that for Beverly's boss, love trumped ratings," Eddie said with a smile.

"Could be," Barney added with a smile of his own. "Tom wouldn't be the first person to act against the interests of his station's owners. Particularly if he's thinking about jumping to another broadcaster. He could write his own ticket at this point. Taking a station near the bottom of the ratings and moving it to number one. If that doesn't push your resume up to the top of the pile, and increase your market value, I don't know what would."

"Okay, Barney, I'll give Joseph a closer look."

"Good! I realize it might be nothing, but I wanted to be sure this guy was on your radar."

"Noted."

CHAPTER TWENTY-SEVEN

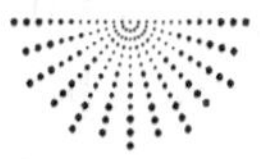

Melissa Jacobs took her work seriously. As most individuals involved in document examination can tell you, attention to the smallest detail can make a big difference.

She worked independently for various law firms and government agencies, one of which was the Marin County Sheriff's Department. Like her work, she was a no-nonsense individual who, in her twenty-plus years as a document examiner, exposed dozens of forgeries and verified countless documents as genuine.

"What have you got for me, Eddie?" Melissa asked as she sat down at an available workstation and took out the tools of her trade, which began with her putting on a pair of surgical gloves.

"I've got a series of four notes sent, supposedly, from four different women. Without going into needless particulars regarding this case, I've been able to track down two of the supposed writers. Separately interviewed, both have provided good reason for us to believe one or both of their notes are forgeries, since neither woman appears to have any knowledge of the claims made in the notes they supposedly wrote.

"Further, I have samples of writing by two other individuals I consider most likely to have created these forgeries, if indeed either of these two notes were faked."

Eddie then placed samples from the programing log sheet that Bill had completed during his final week at KBUD, and the note of thanks Beverly had written him.

"I have just two questions. First, do you believe the same person wrote these two different thank you notes? Second, if these thank you notes were created by the same individual, were they written by either the person who created these office worksheet notes or the person who wrote this thank you note?"

"Okay, let's get some added light on these documents," Melissa said as she opened a portable lit magnifying device and slid the samples into view for a much closer look.

Both of the thank you notes were written in cursive, as one would expect. For a few minutes, Jacobs patiently went back and forth, making several observations from the shape of capital T's to the Y's in "Thank you," and the uppercase L in the word "Love."

Finally, Melissa pulled back, stood up straight, and said, "Both of these notes were created by the same person."

"Wow, so these notes were forged. Take a look at these two writing samples and see if you can match either of these samples to the forgeries."

"Sure. Let's see if they do."

Eddie watched in silence as Melissa studied Beverly's note and Bent's on-air program log. Back and forth between samples she went, noting consistent characteristics. When she was confident of her conclusion, she turned to Eddie and said, "The person who forged these thank you notes also wrote these two samples you provided," Melissa said as she pointed to Bill Bent's program notes.

"Damn. That's remarkable."

"To be honest, Eddie, this was no master class in forgery. Let me show you just a few of the telltale signs that make it clear which one of these two writers created these forged notes."

Melissa walked Eddie through lines that crossed t's and letters that slanted in a particular fashion to explain her conclusion. "None of us give it considerable thought, but over the years, we all develop unique styles of writing. It can be an individual's habit of where they place the dot over the letter 'i' or dozens of other small strokes and punctuation marks. I would think that if the forger, in this case, gave any serious thought to these two notes being analyzed by a forensic document examiner, he or she would have made a far greater effort to disguise this deception, but that's not the case here. Frankly, I think a relatively new student of the dark art of forgery would have picked up the distinct similarities in these two writing styles."

"You're pretty certain of your conclusion?" Eddie asked with a smile and a raised eyebrow.

"Only about 99.9 percent," Melissa replied with a smile.

After Melissa departed, Eddie returned to paperwork that had been awaiting his attention for the past several days. Whether dealing with petty theft or grand larceny, a barroom assault or a ballpark brawl, a domestic dispute or the rare instance of homicide; at some point in the process, every action can be subject to review by administrative staff. Or, the courts. That means memorializing the who, what, where, when, and how of every incident.

Nearly three hours later, when Eddie had cleared this work off his desk, he called Rob's cell.

"What's up, Sherlock?" Rob answered cheerfully.

"Some news that set me back on my heels. Can you spare thirty minutes, I've got some strangeness I have to talk over with you."

"Sure. Karin called a few minutes ago to say that she was taking our two darlings up to Cloudview Park to meet Sharon and Aaron for a little late afternoon playtime."

"Good, I hope your kids wear my little guy out!"

"I hope they all wear each other out. Karin and I would love a quiet night. Meanwhile, I'm here doing my usual thing."

"Great. I'll see you in twenty minutes."

Eddie walked into Rob's office, carrying two cold bottles of beer and still shaking his head over Melissa Jacobs's document analysis.

"Beer! Just what the doctor ordered," Rob announced happily.

"I thought you might be needing some liquid refreshment by now."

"What's up?"

"Something doesn't add up," Eddie said, sitting down on a

fading blue couch, the one comfortable piece of furniture in either of *The Standard*'s two offices.

After a long pull on a cold Heineken, Rob perched on his desk, impatiently he said, "Out with it, Eddie. You've got that frustrated look you get when someone tells you two plus two is five."

"You'll think the same when I tell you what the forensic document examiner told me about two of those love notes I found in Bent's desk."

"Don't tell me…"

"They were written by Bill Bent."

"Damn. That is some seriously whacky stuff! I'd laugh out loud if it wasn't so bewildering."

"My thought exactly."

"Why in the world would Bent do something like that?"

"That's what this meeting is about. I'm not a late afternoon beer delivery service."

"Too bad, I could use a service like that."

"I'm hoping you've got some idea as to why anyone would do something like this! Writing thank you notes to yourself; that's pretty loony stuff, even for Bill Bent!"

"We both knew something was screwy after Holly and Sylvia told us about their conversations with those two women."

"The day after Bent's body was found, the Saturday you went up to Napa with Karin and the kids, and Max and I did our dog and pony show for the press, I came back home, sat down, and started writing out random thoughts about the murder and about Bent. My first thought regarded the deceptive nature of the guy. Sending love letters to yourself with photos enclosed, however, that's beyond your everyday garden variety strange. But bizarre behavior, good or bad, generally grows out of some form of motivation. What was driving Bent?"

"I agree, Eddie. Do you have any thoughts on what his motive might have been?"

"Believe it or not, I do. I'm not saying this would make much sense to a normal person, but few would argue that Bill Bent was a poster boy for normal. But why the notes to himself?"

"It's possible that Bent wanted Beverly to find those notes and begin divorce proceedings. They were hidden when you found them, but if he had lived longer, it's probable he had planned on moving the notes to a place where Beverly would stumble upon them. Or, decide the whole idea was impractical, and destroy his handiwork."

"Huh?" Eddie said, nearly choking on his beer. "That doesn't make any sense."

"It does make sense if you consider the world-class ego of Bill Bent."

"I'm not sure I'm following, Rob."

"Bent's Superman, at least in his twisted view of the world. He wanted out of his marriage, but Beverly, apparently, kept hanging in there."

"I'm with you on that. A lot of women would have said, 'I'm out of here,' a long time ago. But you've got to admit, Rob, when she did leave, it was a parting for the ages!"

"Amen, pal! But before that, Beverly hung in while Bent piled on the abuse."

"I think her mom conditioned her to behave that way."

"No doubt! But then my wonderful, trouble-making co-worker talks Beverly into approaching KLIB for a job, and the Bay Area starts listening."

"True, Rob. But why did Bill create these phony love notes in the first place?"

"Because he wanted Beverly to ask him for a divorce. As we know, all his previous disrespectful and abusive behavior did not accomplish that."

"But he could have just asked Beverly for a divorce."

"Absolutely, but that doesn't square with the personality he played every morning on KBUD. Remember, Bent is the long-suffering husband. He wanted her to do the asking when it came time for them to separate."

"But if it got messy and went public, her charging him with adultery and/or his having a string of women he treated lavishly—that doesn't sound too admirable."

"Eddie, you're not considering the individuals who formed his core audience. From their perspective, he was bound to cheat on that shrew of a wife, who for so long 'ignored all his needs,'" Rob explained, using air quotes. "But, despite all his suffering, he continued to provide her with a good home and a generous allowance. To his fellow suffering men, he's a stand-up guy."

"You know that's a load of crap, right Rob?"

"Absolutely, but it's not a pile of horse poop to his fan base. To those guys, Bent's a hero because he suffered in silence. It's only natural that he needed the loving arms of another woman. Or, in this case, women."

"Sounds pretty nutty, but you've got a point. Her tossing him out gets Bent out of the bind of leaving Beverly. Plus, to his audience, he's a good provider to a woman who did not deserve such a terrific guy."

"Exactly, Eddie!"

"There really are some dumb people out there. You would

think in my line of work I would have accepted that a long time ago."

"You'll never go broke underestimating the intelligence of a mob."

"That's some screwy stuff, Rob. I suppose what we suggested to Ted about Bent creating pocket-sized portrait photos is exactly what happened."

"Sure. Why not?"

"As long as your brain is up and running, any thoughts about who might want to kill Bent? Barney Benson thinks it might be Beverly's boss, Tom Joseph."

"I could see Joseph as a suspect. I think he likes Beverly in more ways than just her being a moneymaker for KLIB. Plus, she's attractive and bright. After Bent, Beverly certainly needed a knight in shining armor. But I can't see him as a guy capable of that level of violence, do you?"

Eddie finished the last of his beer while he thought about Rob's question. "No, I don't see him stabbing someone to death. Talk him to death, well that I could believe."

"Then, who?"

"Well, wait a minute, Rob. It's a long shot. But suppose one of those four notes I found was the real deal?"

"Not following you, bro. How could that be?"

"Maybe Bent got one thank you note from a woman for a romantic weekend they spent together, and that note formed a template for other notes he conjured up. Obviously, I'd have to go back to our document examiner to verify that theory. But there's a chance one of the notes she hasn't seen is the real deal"

"Why the hell would he do that?"

"Pride, possibly. Remember, we're talking about a guy who isn't the world's most rational individual. But if one of those two remaining notes is real, there's a chance I might have something of real value."

"Possible, or you might simply have found one more woman happy to be rid of Bill Bent."

"True that! But if one or both of those cards was not forged, that leaves us with one or more suspects, not currently on my radar. If I come up empty, I'll have to keep looking in other places. But just maybe, please God, I'll catch a break."

The following morning, Melissa Jacobs gave Eddie the news he spent part of a restless night thinking about.

The third of the four cards Eddie found turned out to also be forged by Bill Bent. But, when Jacobs held up the last card, she smiled and said, "This one is different! I have no way of knowing who wrote it, but I have a high degree of confidence that this card was not written by the same individual who created the other three."

Eddie thanked Melissa and went to work on locating the writer of that fourth card.

CHAPTER TWENTY-EIGHT

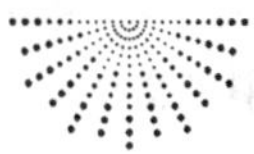

By lunch on Friday, Rob and Holly had completed the busiest part of the workweek. Near the end of their meal, Rob broke the news that two, and possibly all four of the love notes addressed to Wild Bill were forgeries created by Bent.

"That's incredible," Holly said, nearly choking on the last few potato chips she had gotten to go along with a roast beef sandwich and a large coffee. "Why did you keep a gem like this to yourself?"

"I was so astounded when Eddie told me about the forgeries, that I kept my yap shut for fear both of us would spend too much time scratching our heads, and too little time focusing on our work."

"I can't say that I blame you for not telling me. I can't even imagine how you reacted when Eddie told you!"

"I reacted like someone waking up in the middle of the night, hearing an air horn going off in their bedroom. I was speechless! In our work, we've covered some whacky stories. After all, this is Marin County!"

"Forged love notes being written by the supposed recipient? That's a level of whacky even I can't imagine."

"I know, Holly. It's not been easy to keep my yap shut. There's a part of me that still can't believe Bent wrote those notes to himself."

"We knew he was a whack-a-doodle. That, plus his abusive behavior, was why I thought Beverly needed to move her life forward without the guy. I have to admit, this is irrational behavior beyond what I thought Bent capable of."

After a few moments of silence, Holly asked, "No word from Sherlock since he told you about Bent's forged love notes?"

"Nope, he went out of here late Tuesday with that wild look in his eyes, you know what that's like."

"I do! I call it Eddie's 'I can't stop until I solve this' look."

"Exactly! I haven't heard from him about happy hour at Smitty's tonight. I'm assuming we're on for our usual end of week cocktails, but when Eddie goes into full bloodhound mode, I don't know if he thinks about anything other than the next clue he's trying to track down."

"Well, let's go over at our usual time, and maybe Sherlock will show. If not, most likely, we'll hear from him unless he's out on the scent. Either way, I'll be ready for my usual martini, and we'll have fun trying to figure out what in the world Bent was up to, forging love notes to himself."

Four hours later, seated at Smitty's, Holly and Rob ordered their usual drinks. As time slipped to a quarter past five, they both felt an increasing sense of disappointment. Whatever was keeping Eddie was apparently so demanding of his attention, he perhaps forgot their weekly get together.

"The old boy must be hard on the trail. Usually, when he's hung up, he'll call and let us know he's late," Holly suggested with a martini in hand helping her celebrate the end of another long work week.

"Agreed," Rob said, hoping to see Eddie walking through Smitty's swinging door at any moment.

By the time it was five-thirty, both Rob and Holly stopped looking up in anticipation of Eddie's arrival.

"Should we order a second round?" Rob asked.

"Go ahead, it's on me," they heard Eddie say.

"Gosh, we had given up hope of you making it here tonight," Holly said, happy to see Eddie's smiling face.

"Hopefully, that smile means good news," Rob said.

Gail, their longtime cocktail waitress, greeted Eddie with a peck on the cheek and her usual question, "Guinness?"

"Two, one for me, one for Rob, and get this lovely lady a second martini."

"You're happy it's Friday," Gail said, pleased as well to see Eddie.

"I am! And for more reasons than just it being the weekend."

As Gail went off to get their drinks, Eddie sat down.

"Something tells me our favorite bloodhound found what he was looking for," Rob offered, hoping he was right.

"Hold onto your seats boys and girls, Bill Bent's confessed killer is at this very moment is in lock-up."

"Wow, you got your man already?" Rob said, extending his hand to Eddie.

"I didn't get my man. I got my woman," Eddie said as he

flashed a satisfied smile and thanked Gail for a much-antici-pated beer.

"Woman? My God! Not Beverly," Holly said anxiously.

"Holly, what in God's name gave you that idea?" Eddie asked.

"If I was married to Bent, I would have killed him ages ago. Perhaps with an ax!" Holly explained with a satisfied smile.

"Well, you're wrong, Lizzie Borden! Beverly only figura-tively cut Bent down to size every afternoon on her show. The woman we arrested today, Patricia Shaw, did that literally."

"A KLIB listener?" Rob asked.

"Nope. A KBUD listener, in fact. She was the chair of 'Women for Bill Bent!'"

"Oh, my God!" Holly said, chocking on the first sip of her second martini. "I never knew there were women goofy enough to listen to Bent, no less organize a fan club. Gosh, my mom was right, it really does take all types. So, I guess she figured out Bent wasn't the great guy she thought he was."

"Well…"

"Okay, Sherlock, enough with the suspense. Details!" Rob insisted, on the edge of his seat. "How did you pull it all together. And so quickly? With someone as irksome as Bent I thought you'd be in for a long slog."

"Rob, I thought the exact same thing. I somehow manage to land homicides with a dozen likely suspects. I thought that's what I was facing. Thankfully I stumbled across those love notes."

"Love notes? I thought the notes you found were all

bogus?" Holly asked as her brow wrinkled and her eyes narrowed.

"Three of them were fakes, but obviously they all needed to be checked by the document examiner. Turns out, lucky number four, the last of those notes, was the real deal. After that, as they say at the pool hall, 'I ran the table.'"

"How so?" Rob asked, hanging on Eddie's every word.

"I got several lucky breaks. All of which began after learning that one of those love notes was the real deal. For all we know, that real note might have given Wild Bill the idea to create those bogus love notes."

"What in the world was Bent thinking when he created phony love notes that he sent to himself?" Holly asked, still dumbfounded by what she had learned hours earlier.

"Hold that thought, Holly. First, let me tell you about Bent's actual lover. Obviously, I needed to begin by locating this woman and finding out if indeed she was real. Remember all The document examiner could tell me was that the card was not created by Bent's hand. Still, the very first question that needed to be answered was: Did this woman exist?

"On a hope and a prayer, I called Barney Benson and asked him if he had met or knew of a Patricia Shaw? Without a moment's hesitation, he says, 'Sure, I know Patricia, she's the marketing director for one of our sponsors, Spike's Knives.' That's when I almost dropped the phone."

"What the heck is Spike's Knives?" Holly asked breathlessly. "And why did you nearly drop the phone?"

"Because, a few days earlier, Max Brownstein took an educated guess and told me that the knife used to kill Bent was likely, and I quote, 'A high-quality hunting knife used for skinning and gutting animals, like the ones made by Spike's Knives.'"

"Yikes!" Holly said nearly choking on a sip of her martini.

"So how did Ms. Shaw come to use her company's product to ventilate the body of our least favorite radio personality?" Rob asked.

"Let me guess," Holly said rushing to beat Eddie to the answer. "He promised he would leave his wife and they would live happily ever after, but he failed to keep his promise."

"Wow, Holly, it's almost like you knew the guy," Eddie said with a laugh.

"When you came knocking at Ms. Shaw's door, did she fold right away?" Rob asked.

"Trust me pal, I didn't come alone. I went with a small show of force. Three deputies and I were all wearing vests just in case our suspect had traded in her knife for a gun. After I learned that she knew Bent and had stayed away from his memorial service, having not been sighted by my snoop squad, or for that matter by Barney, I was pretty sure I had a probable suspect. It could have all been coincidental, but in my line of work taking unnecessary risks can be a fatal mistake. So, we came prepared for trouble hoping there would be none."

"Kind of ironic that the guy who disrespected women in countless ways is killed by a woman he had taken as a lover," Holly observed.

"I imagine they went for a hike together and their conversation did not go well. Did you get any idea if she planned on killing him when they went out for their hike?" Rob asked.

"I don't think she had planned on killing him. She opened up about that when we talked on our way up to the county prison. She claims the killing was not premeditated, but the result of an argument Bill instigated. I never pressed her for any details. She wanted to talk, so I simply listened."

"From what I knew of Bill, that sounds highly credible," Holly said.

"If I were her, I'd hope for a jury that has as low an opinion of Bent as the three of us have," Rob added.

"But if his death was the result of an argument, why was she carrying such a deadly weapon?" Holly asked.

"Two points of note. First, Shaw worked for Spike's Knives for over ten years. If anyone is going to carry their product she would. Second, do either or both of you remember a few years back when a bicyclist was killed by an overly protective mama mountain lion up on Mt Tam?"

"Sure," Rob and Holly said in unison.

"Poor guy was an example of wrong place at the wrong time. It was a sad story, which scared our readers into a letter-writing frenzy!" Rob added.

"The bicyclist and Shaw were in the same graduating class at Tam High. She claims that after that attack, she never went hiking without her trusty knife. She was ready to take on a lion, bear, or..."

"A lousy boyfriend!" Holly added in a rush.

"Did she share with you what their argument was about?" Rob asked.

"Probably Bill reneging on his commitment to leave Beverly," Holly said with a shrug.

"Give that lady a prize," Eddie responded. "You have to admit, when it comes to enraging someone, few ever did it better than Bill Bent."

"No argument there," Holly said. "Just ask any of Beverly and Betsy's loyal listeners."

"Sounds like, in this case, the best the DA will get is a manslaughter conviction," Rob suggested.

"That would be my guess," Eddie said. "Unless the defense is inept enough to seat a jury of KBUD listeners," Eddie said with a short laugh. "I think murder one is out of reach. Unless evidence is found of premeditation. And, I don't think that's going to happen."

"Wow, I can't imagine Bill Bent getting a woman so enraged that she'd stab him multiple times. Not!" Holly said with a roll of her eyes. "Bent must have said something that put her over the top. Did Shaw say what that was?"

"She did. And considering she was hoping for the past two years that Bent was going to leave Beverly and marry her, you can imagine that did not go well."

"Gosh, ya think?" Rob said, shaking his head.

"File that under what happens when you play with fire," Holly added. "So how did Bent provoke her?"

"Shaw claims he was cheating on her. She confronted him about it, and when he concocted a patently false story, she pressed harder. Finally, he caved and let Shaw know that her worst fears were valid. He was seeing someone else, and he thought it wise if they quote, 'went their separate ways.'"

"I'm guessing Shaw didn't warm to that suggestion," Rob said.

"Apparently not. Add to that, lover boy started detailing the many ways she had quote, 'Disappointed him!'"

"I'll wager he was well-practiced at that routine," Holly said. "The 'all the ways you've disappointed me' speech is one he gave Beverly many times."

"He did have a gift for gab," Rob said with a smile.

"Yada, yada, yada," Eddie added. "The next thing you

know, Wild Bill is on the receiving end of a knife meant only to protect Shaw from a dangerous animal."

"Well if the shoe fits…" Rob offered.

"I suppose there's some poetic justice in Bent being killed by a woman he drove over the edge," Holly said confidently.

"I'm just glad that woman wasn't Beverly. It would have broken Sharon's heart to see Bev's life ruined over someone as worthless as Bent," Eddie said.

"I could have been that woman, Shaw!"

"Kill him, yes," Rob said. "But, Holly, you would never have dated Bent in the first place. You deserve a great guy like Scott, and I think I speak for Eddie as well when I say we're happy he came into your life."

"Amen, brother," Eddie said, tipping his glass.

"I'm thankful too, boys. And I feel sorry for Patricia Shaw. What she did was over the top crazy, but Bent had a talent for bringing out the very worst in people. I wonder if Beverly ever considered killing Bill? I know I would have!"

"If Beverly had any such thoughts, it would only prove she was human," Eddie offered.

"Well, on the upside, you caught a big break for a change," Rob said.

"And very thankful I did! I wish you had both been there when Barney told me that Patricia Shaw was the marketing director for Spike's Knives, I'm pretty sure all the blood rushed out of my head. I really did go numb for a moment. She might just as well have pinned a note to Bent's body with her name and phone number. Believe me, I was dreading this investigation. The line of people who were only too happy to see Bill Bent go off the air permanently was pretty darn long."

"Three fake love notes and the last one hits the jackpot.

That's a rare break indeed?" Rob said, finishing the last of his beer.

"Amen, brother!"

"When Shaw lost it with Bent, I'll bet she never thought about the love note she sent reappearing?" Holly said with a slow shake of her head.

"She might have thought about it later," Eddie replied.

"If she did, it's a certainty she said a prayer that Bent had tossed it in the round file," Rob suggested.

"The only silver lining for Shaw is the note strengthens her case that the killing of Bent was not premeditated," Eddie explained. "She really loved the guy and the note lends credibility to that claim."

"Eddie, what in the world was Bent thinking with sending those love notes to himself?" Holly asked, still puzzled by this bizarre aspect of Bent's behavior.

"It's a safe bet that none of us will ever know for certain, so we're only left with theories."

"So, what's your theory, Sherlock?" Rob asked.

"I think in time, Bent was going to let Beverly stumble upon these notes he created in the hope that she would leave him, and he'd be left telling his audience that he was guilty of being popular with the ladies. None of us can say for certain what Bent was thinking, but that's a plausible theory."

"It's also possible that if Beverly ever stumbled upon Shaw's note, he wanted to create the subterfuge that he was involved with more than just one woman," Rob suggested.

"Such a whacky guy," Holly said, shaking her head. "When and if he ever left those notes for Beverly to find, do you think he would have included the only one that was real?"

"My guess is the note from Patricia Shaw would not have been included. But like the two of you, I'm not interested in doing a deep dive into the mind of Bill Bent. My job was to find his killer. I'll leave the rest of Bent's story to journalists, criminologists, psychologists, and other mental health experts."

"Well, I'm just glad you caught a big break for a change," Rob said as he patted his friend on the back.

"Rob, it's like being a door-to-door salesman. You spend the entire week trying to sell your wares and keep coming up empty. You get back to your office feeling totally discouraged, the phone rings and it's someone asking if you have a dozen widgets for sale? Hard work is always important, but equally important is the occasional lucky break. For once, I got a really big break."

"Speaking of lucky breaks," Holly said as she paused for a moment to finish the last of her second martini. "Beverly was fortunate to get out of that marriage when she did."

"Do you think she would have lost it with Bill one day and grabbed a carving knife from the kitchen drawer and do to her beloved what Miss Shaw did?" Rob asked.

"You never know when someone is going to reach the point of no return. Totally lose it and do something they'll regret the rest of their life," Holly responded.

"I'm glad that someone was not Beverly. I would have hated coming home to tell Sharon that Beverly was going away for what might be a very long time," Eddie said.

"She's made a life of her own," Holly declared with a smile.

"The best thing she could have done," Rob said as he gave Holly a pat on the hand and a warm smile.

"Really," Eddie added. "Sharing your life with a horrible husband, or a wicked wife, is no way to live happily ever after."

EPILOGUE

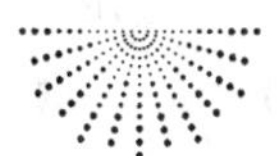

The shock waves from Bill Bent's death, and Patricia Shaw's trial for manslaughter, took the better part of a year to diminish. Shaw benefited greatly from troubling stories, widely circulated, regarding Bent's private life.

Rob, Holly, Sylvia, and Ted discussed sharing what they learned about Bent's predilection for creating forged love notes. They concluded his odd behavior would reflect poorly on Beverly and chose to let that aspect of the story vanish.

Fears that the audience for Bent and Baker in The Morning would diminish with the loss of their on-air nemesis faded as the program continued to grow in audience share.

KBUD's general manager, Nick Reade, anxious for what he called "a change of scenery," accepted an offer to manage a classic rock station in Los Angeles. "I need to go to a new market, a bigger one, where I can forget I ever knew Bill Bent," Reade explained to his few close friends, days before his departure.

Barney Benson, who had surprising success going solo mornings on KBUD, stopped talking of his days with Wild Bill. He brought a more mature, thoughtful tone to his show. Or, as Barney explained to his loyal fans, "We could all benefit, men and women, from talking less and listening more."

Tom Joseph left KLIB to take Nick's position at KBUD. After making the switch to his new job, Tom and Beverly felt more comfortable throwing a party for their mutual friends, in and out of broadcasting, to announce their engagement.

The night of their big party, Sharon, Karin, and Beverly cornered Holly and asked, "When are you and Scott going to have an announcement of your own?"

"Soon," Holly replied with her best Cheshire Cat grin. "We've all had enough excitement to last for a while. Besides, when Scott's on summer break, we may go off to somewhere exotic and tie the knot."

"Oh no, you don't," Sharon said. "Karin, Beverly, and I have waited too long to see you become a bride. If you want to marry in Tahiti, we'll have to come join you there."

"Agreed! There's no way we're going to miss that ceremony," Karin said. "Not to mention, I want to see Rob pass out when he sees how much a roundtrip ticket to Tahiti costs."

"Well, maybe you can have two ceremonies," Beverly offered. "One barefoot on a white sandy beach, surrounded by endless ocean and one here in Marin, surrounded by countless friends."

"That would be nice," Karin added as Sharon quickly agreed.

"The best part is not the ceremony, but what comes after. Hopefully, years of love and devotion," Holly added.

"Agreed!" Beverly said with an approving smile. "I married Bill when I was far too young to know the pitfalls of making a bad choice. I don't think I understood that life partner meant a lifetime commitment."

"Lifetime commitment means different things to people at different ages and stages of life," Karin suggested.

"Exactly," Holly added quickly. "With every passing year I'm learning that life is a long journey, and with the right partner, it can be the happy journey you hoped it would be."

At that moment, Eddie, Rob, Scott, and Tom walked up and joined their partners.

"What are you ladies talking about?" Eddie asked.

"The art of finding a loving mate," Holly said as she gave Scott a kiss on the cheek.

"Easier said than done," Tom said quickly as he put his arm around Beverly and gave her a kiss.

"Amen to that," Beverly added.

All in a circle, Scott raised his glass and proposed a toast. "Here's to all the loving couples lucky enough to find lasting happiness."

Rob followed with a second toast, "And for all of us who chose badly once with a wicked wife, or a horrible husband, here's to having the courage to give lasting love a second chance. Or a third, fourth, or fifth chance. It's more about the journey than the destination."

"To Tom and Beverly," Eddie said as he raised his glass. "May you both know the joy of a long and loving marriage. And one day, look back with satisfaction, having shared in a happy life!"

NEXT UP!

THE MALICIOUS MAYOR

(Book 6)

When the home of Mary Anderson, Sausalito's longtime mayor, is destroyed in a landslide, her admirers and detractors hold their collective breaths as teams of emergency workers remain hopeful that she'll be brought out alive.

The news that she did not survive is greeted with stunned silence by many who cannot imagine their small city without Anderson. In less than a day, a second shockwave rocks Sausalito when the county medical examiner issues the result of her autopsy. Hours before the slide occurred, the longtime politician was murdered in her home.

Suddenly a story that was of passing interest to Marin County Sheriff's Department lead investigator Eddie Austin has become a top priority. As always, Eddie calls on the help of his childhood friend, newspaper publisher, Rob Timmons, and his assistant editor, Holly Cross. Together they must untangle the history of a politician, who, in a twenty-five year career, was happy to reward her friends and even happier to punish her enemies.

HOW TO REACH MARTIN

Martin Brown is an author and journalist whose articles on health and relationships have appeared in *Redbook, Playboy,* and *Complete Woman* magazines.

He and his wife, novelist Josie Brown, live in the city of San Francisco, where their grown children and granddog also reside.

For more Murder in Marin mysteries visit:
murderinmarin.com

Or go here to quickly sign up for Martin's newsletter:
subscribepage.com/MartinBrownEletterSignUp

You can also find Martin at:

facebook.com/MartinBrownCA

twitter.com/MurderInMarin

9 781970 093131